NEVER DID I EVER

The Quest for Magic

NEVER DID I EVER

THE QUEST FOR MAGIC

Never Did I Ever 1

Cassidy Jones

Elizabeth Erselius

gatekeeper press™

Tampa, FL

NEVER DID I EVER
The Quest for Magic

Published by Gatekeeper Press
7853 Gunn Hwy, Suite 209
Tampa, FL 33626
www.GatekeeperPress.com

Library of Congress Control Number: 2022949997

ISBN (paperback): 9781662932748

*A special thanks to Chase Jones, our awesome
and talented creature designer!*
-Cassidy

*Nathan, Noah, and Abigail Erselius
A feedback team for the history books.*
-Elizabeth

Contents

NEVER DID I EVER: Frozen Waves

SO THIS IS EARTH

"Don't," the fifteen-year-old duchess pleaded. "You—are you really going to leave?"

"Yes!" eighteen-year-old Laura snapped. Then her expression softened when her sister's face fell. "I'm sorry. But I *need* to go."

"No you don't!" her younger sister argued.

"Jennifer!" Laura yelled. "This is important. I'll visit."

"No, you won't," Jennifer whispered, as she collapsed to the ground. "I know you won't."

Laura sank to her knees next to her sister. "I promise I will."

"I'm coming with you," Jennifer said, her expression suddenly determined.

Laura rolled her eyes. "No, you aren't. We've been through this. I go, you stay."

"I'm not a dog!" Jennifer argued as she bounded to her feet "We're *both* going to Earth, and you can't stop me!"

This is ridiculous, Laura thought, as she got up off the floor and faced her sister.

"I can so!" she retorted. "You are going to stay here. You're the heir to the throne anyway."

"No, *you* are," Jennifer told her sister. "I'm the youngest, you're the oldest, so if anyone goes, it's me."

Laura sighed. Telling her sister what to do was about as pointless as a figure of speech.

"Y'know what?" Laura sighed again. "Fine. You can come. Now let's go, before the portal moves!"

Jenny nodded. They jogged into the deep, dense candy cane forest and stopped once they reached a coconut snow clearing. A giant sparkly, violet portal was glittering fiercely, and gusts of salty, sandy wind blew from it.

"I-is this a good i-idea?" Jennifer stammered.

"I don't know," Laura said sarcastically. "Is it?"

Jenny crossed her arms. "Stop being mean!"

"Uggh," Laura groaned. She grabbed her sister's hand. "Uh, no *way* are you going to Earth in a dress. That's going to be *really* weird."

"Fine!" Jenny whined. "I'll be back in a few minutes."

Jennifer pointed to the ground, closed her eyes, and a glowing, vibrant purple light enveloped her as she transpor- ted herself back to the palace.

She took in every last detail, wondering if she would ever see it again. Pointing to the ground again, she teleported back to the portal where Laura was waiting, and together, the sisters stepped out of Candyopolis and into their future.

"So, what exactly are we doing here?" Jenny thought to ask *after* she had jumped through a magic swirly-portal.

"I don't know why *you* came, but I want to live a normal life. I don't want to be a duchess!" She surveyed their surroundings. They were standing in the middle of a bustling park, but nobody seemed to notice as the portal closed behind them. "I can't sit back and watch Mom and Dad allow Malcora the Ice Dragon to overthrow Queen Viola of the Dragon Kingdom!"

"They're not willing to listen," she continued. "They only care about Candyopolis' future, not any other kingdom! It's just *wrong*, and they won't pay attention unless it threatens their precious throne!"

"Yeesh, no need to get angry," Jennifer said. "So, we gonna buy a house, or what?"

"Um . . ." Laura hadn't thought about that at all. "Yes?"

"Great, where's the money?"

Laura pulled a stack of green paper from her pocket. "I have about two thousand," she told her sister. "That's more than enough." She tapped the shoulder of a man who was passing by. "Excuse me, how much does a house cost?"

"About five hundred thousand dollars on average," he said simply.

"No!" Jenny wailed. "We can't pay that much! We don't have parents anymore, or jobs, or even a place to stay!"

"Well," the man said, a look of sympathy sneaking its way onto his face, "I happen to own a nice beach house that I rent out, but recently, no one is wanting to stay here. A coincidence, I guess."

"How much will it cost?" Laura asked, wringing her hands. "Maybe we can get some job or something, and . . . rent an apartment?" She was in full big-sister panic mode.

Well, although I don't know you two . . . you ARE orphaned and homeless," he said thoughtfully. "I guess I can rent it to you . . . for a thousand dollars."

He mumbled under his breath, "Margie's going to kill me."

"Are you serious?" Jenny yelled. Then she lowered her voice and said, "Thank you so much."

"Yes," Laura said. "Um, would you—"

"Get you a ride?" he finished, smiling.

"No," Laura informed him sharply. "We'll walk. I just wanted the address."

"Certainly." He wrote it on a piece of paper, and Laura thanked him and handed him the money.

They waved down a taxi, not actually wanting to walk. Even though Laura was upset with her parents for making her be royal, she knew enough from books not to get into a car with a stranger.

"To . . . this address," Jenny said, passing him the slip of paper. He drove for about ten minutes, huffing and puffing like the big, bad wolf for no apparent reason.

"All right," the driver huffed as he pulled up in front of an enormous house. "Here you go."

Laura handed him a five-dollar bill.

"What about a tip?" he asked.

"Sure," Jennifer said. "Call your mother. I bet she misses you."

"That's not what I—" he began. "Oh! That *is* a good tip. Thanks!"

"Come on, let's go." They exited the car, and entered the house.

The sisters toured the small bedrooms first. Both of them were decorated with similar colored beds, one had a black desk in it, the other white. The kitchen was next. It had lots of counter space, beautiful cabinets, an oven, a microwave, and a fridge. The dining room was all similar in color to the kitchen and the living room.

"Hey, what's this?" Laura asked as she felt a knob on the wall. She turned it and opened the door to an attic.

Chapter One

AGAIN

"*WHAT?*" the twins, Chidi and Alexis, exclaimed in perfect unison.

"You have *got* to be kidding me," Alexis exclaimed, throwing her reddish-brown hair over her shoulder. "We're moving *again?* We move *all the time.*"

"Yeah," Chidi added. "Why can't we pick a place and stick with it?"

"Girls, your father's job is important," their mother reminded them, giving a stern look with her sparkling green eyes. "And we don't move *all* the time."

"Yes, we do!" Alexis complained, but her mother silenced her with another stern look. "Now, girls, calm down. Let me show you a picture of our new house!"

Chidi looked in horror down at the picture of the slightly rundown house. It was painted a nice green color, with wood accents of brown and a little bit of black lining the roof. There were many, many trees lining the perimeter of the house, and some trees looked like they got struck by lightning.

"Isn't it . . . nice? It even has a little treehouse in the backyard!" Mrs. Parris exclaimed. Chidi sighed and rubbed her temples.

"And," Mr. Parris added, as he walked into the den. "It has a bedroom that you girls can share! But we need to get packing for our *new* house!" He and Mrs. Parris strode off to their bedroom to get packing.

"I. Hate. Moving," Alexis said, dribbling her basketball down the hall.

"I know," Chidi agreed. "But we can't *not* go. We can't stay by ourselves."

"Can't or won't?" Alexis asked. When Chidi looked at her strangely, she added, "I'm kidding."

"I don't think we're supposed to play with balls in the house," Chidi said, ever the stickler for rules.

"Who cares?" Alexis asked, tightening her reddish-brown ponytail. "In a few days, we'll be living in that barn Mom showed us. Someone *else* will live here."

Chidi braided her thin black hair, which showed she was thinking.

Chidi was of average height with black hair and her mother's emerald green eyes. Alexis was tall and strong with azure blue eyes. Both girls were somewhat thin and, at this moment, very annoyed with their parents.

"Maybe we could keep ourselves from moving," Chidi said thoughtfully.

"What?" Alexis asked. The twins had moved around about twice a year, and at age eleven, almost twelve, they were sick of it. But, they had never thought about *not* moving. "How do we do that?"

"Maybe we could . . . not pack?"

"Really?" Alexis asked, stepping into their room. There were a few boxes labeled <u>CLOTHES</u> and <u>ART SUPPLIES</u> that weren't unpacked from their last move, about seven months ago. "That would never work."

"I can't believe we have to move a week before our birthday!" Alexis said, climbing the ladder to her bunk.

"I know," Chidi said, staring at the faded blue walls that she had finally gotten used to. She glared angrily at a photo of her parents, each holding a girl in their arms. She was in her father's, and Alexis her mother's. How could they be so happy just to move around all the time? And didn't they know that their daughters couldn't stand it?

Why can't I have magic powers that people have in books? Why do we have to move around all the time just for Dad's job? And Mom has trouble finding work since we move all the time! It only benefits him, right? I think they should think about us before making a big decision like this. And why can't we pick a place and stick with it? I haven't even had time to find a volleyball team! Why us? Chidi wondered.

She flung herself on her bed and let the angry tears roll down her face.

....

5:35 P.M.

"Kids! I'm home! I brought your favorite!" Mrs. Parris said as she walked through the front door.

"Really? Chinese food?" the twins said, giving her skeptical looks from the overhang.

"Yes! Chinese food! And I baked cookie dough brownies for dessert!" Mrs. Parris said happily. "I know it's your favorite, Alexis."

"*How in the world* is she happy right now?" Alexis whispered while shaking her head. They both came downstairs and sat down at the dinner table.

"Alright kiddos, we have made an executive decision, since you two seem very much *against* moving *again,* we have decided to get you girls your very own pets!" Mr. Parris declared.

"*WHAT?*" the girls said in perfect unison again. "Awesome!"

"What *kind* of pets?" Alexis asked suspiciously.

"Yeah," Chidi added. She was expecting it to be some kind of little fish, but her father opened a small box with a tiny, orange kitten in it.

"This is for you, Chidi," he said. "She's all yours."

Chidi caressed the soft, snuggly kitty head and squealed, "Thank you so much!"

Alexis began to protest, but her mother handed *her* a slightly larger box. Alexis sat on the floor and gently opened the folded flaps. Inside was a brown puppy. Her eyes widened.

"C'mon, boy," she said. "C'mon!"

....

7:00 P.M.

"What're you gonna name that dog?" Chidi asked her sister that night.

"I don't know yet. What about that cat?" The little orange kitten had gotten on Alexis' nerves, since she had been batting at her ponytail like it was a toy, even after she threatened to drown it in chow mein.

"I think I'll name the sweet little thing *Ginger,*" Chidi said, rubbing the ball of fuzz that was currently napping on her lap.

"Ginger? That is the most hilarious name ever!" Alexis teased.

"Just kidding!" she said when Chidi gave her a wounded look.

"Let's see, what would be a good name for this sweet pup?" Alexis muttered, almost to herself. She began to make a list. "Spot, Brownie, Mask, Bagel, Loaf, Tumbles . . ."

"*Bagel? Loaf? What kind of names are those?*" Chidi said, bursting into laughter because Alexis had been thinking aloud.

"Mew!" the little orange kitten complained as she was launched off Chidi's lap when she fell backward laughing.

"Hey! Stop teasing me! *Ginger* is a ridiculous name too!" Alexis countered.

"Girls! Stop fighting this instant! *Why on earth* have you not started packing? Chidi Ann Parris, and Alexis Blaze Parris, I am *awfully, awfully disappointed in you both,*" Mrs. Parris said as she walked into the twins' room.

"Uh-oh," Chidi said. She knew a lecture was coming their way and a harsh one at that.

"Listen, both of you. Look, I love you both so very much, and I know it is hard for you guys to move again, but *please, please* be cooperative. Now, turn off the lights and go to sleep. Goodnight, my little chipmunks," Mrs. Parris said calmly, weirdly going from her mad stage to a cool and collected mom in seconds.

"Sorry," Alexis whispered to Chidi.

"It's okay," Chidi said softly as she picked up Ginger and slipped back into the bottom bunk.

"Mew, mew mrow!" Ginger meowed excitedly as she climbed over to her food dish that was stuck to the post of the bottom bunk.

"Oh, calm down, you silly kitty! Don't choke!"

"Tumbles! Let me pick you up! Stop it! Ha ha!" Alexis said, wrestling the young, playful puppy into submission.

"Tumbles, huh? That's a cute name!" Chidi commented below.

"I know! Anyway, goodnight!" Alexis said happily from her bunk.

This human is cute when she is sleeping, Ginger thought happily. *Oh, why did she call me Ginger? I guess that is my name now . . . maybe I should curl up next to her*—Ginger's thoughts were cut off by sleep when she rested her head on Chidi's arm.

. . . .

The next morning

After breakfast, the twins had started packing, only because their dad told them to.

"Alexis, did you take my hairbrush? I've been looking for it all morning, and I still can't find it!" Chidi called from the bathroom closet.

"Why would I steal your hairbrush? That's a silly thing to assume," Alexis yelled back. "And why would I want your pink one anyway?"

"Girls," Mrs. Parris warned, "Why would anyone *steal* anyone's *hairbrush?*"

"Okay! Sorry! It was just an assumption . . . ," Chidi mumbled.

"Ruff!" Tumbles barked, to get the twin's attention.

"What *is it*, Tumbles?" Alexis said, trying to take Chidi's volleyball trophies off the shelf.

"Ruff!" Tumbles barked again, starting to chase his tail around and around.

"Oh, my word! Look at you!" Chidi said, clapping her hands.

"Huh? What's going—oh you silly dog!" Alexis exclaimed. Ginger started to chase her tail too.

"Oh, my word! You two are so silly!" Chidi said.

"I love you both!" the twins exclaimed.

....

2:00 P.M.

"Ugh, I. Hate. Packing," Alexis said.

"I know, you've told me a million times already—oh wait, make that a million and *one* times." Chidi ran her fingers over Ginger, who was busy swiping at her new toy.

"Girls, keep up the good work! Remember, we're moving next week! I have a dispatch for my Police Unit tonight!" their dad called from downstairs.

"*Wait, next week?*" the twins exclaimed.

"Yes, girls, the moving truck comes on Wednesday, so keep working hard!"

After he had left, Chidi yelled, "*Wednesday? That's in three days!*"

"I know! How can they tell us that we have to pack everything in three days without any type of warning!"

"This is so, so, so, unfair!"

"Ruff," Tumbles complained, wanting to play.

"Not right now, boy," Alexis said. "I want to play too, but I gotta pack."

....

5:00 P.M.

"Chidi, want to come help me with these cookies?" Mrs. Parris called from the kitchen.

"Sure! I'll be down in a minute!" Chidi replied.

"Mom, can I go out to the shed to pack my tools? And the extra seeds?" Alexis asked.

"Yes, and pick the watermelon, strawberries, and other fruits. And dig up the carrots and potatoes too." While Chidi was baking and Alexis was gardening, the cat and dog started to get into mischief. Ginger started to push Tumbles down the stairs.

"Ruff! Ruff!" Tumbles barked frantically.

Chidi ran to the room as soon as she heard Tumbles' pleading barks.

"Ginger! Stop that right now!" Chidi yelled at Ginger, and scooped her and Tumbles off the stairs and onto the couch downstairs.

"Chidi, come take the cookies out of the oven!"

"Mom, one second! I'll be right down! I have to get Alexis first!" Chidi called, running outside.

"Whoa!" Alexis yelled, almost dropping a watermelon. "What's going on?"

"Ginger pushed Tumbles down the stairs, and he might be hurt, so I thought I should tell you. I need to get back to the kitchen, okay?"

"That evil cat! How could you let her do that? I thought you were going to keep her under control! That's awful!"

"I didn't do it!"

"Well, you let it happen! And she's *your* cat!" Alexis said, running inside. "Tumbles! Here, boy!" Tumbles ran to his owner, barking something.

To Alexis, it sounded like he was asking for a steak. "Please, please, please!" he seemed to say. Then she realized that he actually *had* said it.

"Wait, Chidi, did you hear that?"

"Uh *yes, that was too creepy!*"

"Um, you know I can hear you, right?" Tumbles said.

The twins stared at each other, the fight about Ginger completely forgotten.

"Well, at least I trapped Ginger in the pet crate," Tumbles continued, "so she won't be giving me any more trouble. That cat! She's *ridiculous.*"

"You trapped Ginger in the pet crate?" Chidi said, looking ready to start shaking Tumbles upside-down or hang him by his ears.

"Yeah. There a problem with that?"

"Chidi! The cookies! I'm waiting!" Mrs. Parris called again.

"Keep that crazy manic dog under control, and *get my cat out of that crate!*" Chidi shouted at Alexis.

Alexis pulled Ginger out of the pet crate, then climbed the stairs, holding one pet in each arm.

"Okay," she said. First, she placed the kitten on Chidi's bed. "I'm going to teach you both some basic commands. First is—"

"Yawn," Ginger said. "I know *sit, stay, heel, roll over.*"

"Stop complaining!" Tumbles ordered, tackling Ginger.

"Stop it, you crazy pets!" Alexis pulled the fight apart.

"But—" Ginger protested.

"No, stop. I know that you both know how to *sit* and *stay* apparently, so practice those while I get Chidi. If either of you do something you shouldn't, I'll punish you *both*. Got it?"

The pets grumbled but agreed. Alexis left for the kitchen.

"Alexis, can you try these cookies?" Chidi asked Alexis. "They're chocolate with chocolate chips, chocolate chunks, dipped in chocolate and drizzled with chocolate. With chocolate!"

"Mmm. These are good," Alexis replied, munching into one.

"Chidi, Alexis, get packing! The moving truck comes in two days," Mrs. Parris said, poking her head into the kitchen.

After the two girls were locked in their room, Chidi said, "How is Ginger?"

"Good. Uh, Chidi? She's the same—SHE CAN TALK. Like a person!"

"L-let me try. Ginger?"

The little cat crawled out from under the bed.

"It's Chidi, right?"

Chidi stared at Alexis. "Our pets can talk." Then she realized what she said. "Our pets can talk!"

"Um, all animals talk," Tumbles said slowly like he wanted to make sure the twins understood. "It's just that no humans on Earth can understand us. Well, until now."

"Um, yeah," Chidi said.

"I *think*," Alexis said, rubbing her temples.

"Let's keep packing." Alexis began to take down Chidi's watercolor paintings from the walls and empty Chidi's trophies and awards.

"Okay," Chidi agreed.

"I'll help," Ginger said to the twins sweetly. So Alexis, the height-loving twin, slid the moving ladder and untapped all the things hanging from the ceiling and passed them down to Chidi, who placed them in a small box. Next, they worked on the desks. Alexis pulled her small gadgets out of a beautiful, hand-carved box that she had bought at a yard sale. She counted them quickly but carefully, placed them back in the box, and then began to clean the drawers out.

Chidi gently laid her watercolor pictures and volleyball trophies in another wood container, along with an embroidered pillow that Alexis had made her. Then she took another box, this one the size of two decks of cards side-by-side, and slid all of her award-winning photographs inside.

"Have you finished in the garden?" Chidi asked Alexis.

"Oh, no. Can you help me?"

"Sure." So the girls, the pets at their heels, went outside to pack up their garden.

As the girls picked blackberries off of vines, Chidi said, "I wish we had a say in moving. I mean, we move like twice a year! And we're almost twelve, so we'll have moved *twenty-four* times in our *lives*! And we've never been able to adjust before we move again. And the only person that it benefits is Dad. And they never ask *us* what we think. It just goes, 'We're moving again! We're moving again! Aren't you excited? Yay!' Aren't you tired of it? And I haven't taken dance classes for at least a year. We move too much. And here we go again! Moving all over again!"

"I know," Alexis said. "And our birthday is on Friday!"

"At least Mom half-homeschools us. Imagine trying to find a different school every six months."

"And my basketball team has the championship tournament tonight! Hopefully, they'll let us go. I'm the team captain!"

"Yeah," Chidi agreed. "I was just getting used to this house, and now I have to get adjusted all over again!"

"And we made a friend, my coach's daughter. It seems like the only thing that matters in our family is Dad's job!"

"It's *so* annoying."

After the girls were inside, their mother said, "Chidi, can you cook up some canned soup? Your father has a meeting tonight. About—"

"The move?" Alexis asked crossly.

"Yes. And Alexis, you're going to have to miss your practice or whatever tonight."

"NO!" Chidi wailed.

"Chidi, what has gotten into you? You're not usually this angry."

"I'll tell you what's wrong," Alexis said while Chidi collected her breath.

"We move twice a year, this time it's the *week of our birthday*, I have to miss my *tournament* for the *championship*, Chidi doesn't get to play volleyball, and we don't get *any* say in moving! That's what's wrong!"

"That's because your father—"

"Our father cares about his job?" Chidi said. "We just want a choice."

"Girls," Mrs. Parris said wearily, "I'm sorry. Alexis, I'll try to take you and Chidi to the game. Okay? Now eat some soup."

Chidi warmed the canned soup, and the family sat at the table, silently sipping tomato soup from plastic spoons.

· ·

7:30 P.M.

"Warm-ups, team!" Coach Wheeler shouted. "Captain? Start with twenty laps, half the court!"

There were groans from most of the nine-person team. Only Alexis and Keesha Wheeler weren't complaining.

"C'mon, team!" Alexis called. "Twenty laps! Now!" Alexis began to sprint around the court, Keesha at her side.

"So, Alexis, race ya to twenty laps!"

"You're on," Alexis said, taking off. Alexis won, then began to take charge. "Pick a partner and practice passing. Then we'll do fifteen laps while dribbling a ball. Got it?"

Alexis passed the ball lightly to Keesha, and Keesha neatly dribbled forward five feet, then bounced it back.

"Grab a ball and start running!" Alexis coached her team. "No, Allison, don't just carry the ball, dribble it. Otherwise, you'll get a foul. Carla, don't run to the sides. The other team could trap you. C'mon, guys, we gotta win this! Remember what we've learned!"

The coach blew his whistle. "Round up!" he called. "The first game is starting!"

They won their first two matches and came to the last one.

From the start, Alexis had the ball. She passed to a girl named Natalie, who scored. The entire team worked together, and, at the final second, Alexis shot a three-pointer.

"We won!" the team cheered.

Alexis was still catching her breath when her mother and Chidi ran up to her.

"Wow, Alexis! That was amazing! You won the championship with *one* shot!"

"Yes," Mrs. Parris agreed. "That *was* quite impressive. I'm glad we could come. Now, let's get home so that we can pack up. The van will be at our house tomorrow."

"What? You said it would come Wednesday! Tomorrow is Tuesday!" Chidi exclaimed.

"Well, your father decided that sooner was better. It will be there at eleven." The drive home was silent, with the girls slipping quiet glances at each other.

"That stinks," Chidi said, once they were back in their bedroom.

"Yeah," Alexis said.

"We should finish packing," Chidi said from the floor where she was pulling the twins' chocolate and candy stash out from under her bed.

"Pass me a piece of gum, will ya?" Alexis asked, picking Tumbles up and rubbing his stomach.

"That feels *good*," Tumbles said.

"What about me?" whined Ginger. "What about *me*?"

"Okay, Ginger. Come here." The orange ball of fuzz crawled into Chidi's lap.

"Here." Chidi tossed a pack of strawberry gum to Alexis. Alexis popped a piece in her mouth, then passed it back.

"Well, this is just *great*," Alexis said. "We're moving *tomorrow*. I'm just *so* excited! Aren't you?"

"I know," Chidi said, joining Alexis' pathetic game. "Aren't you just dying to move into a barn and live in a closet? And to move away from *there*, too? Right? It'll be so amazing!"

Alexis sighed. "Why us?"

"Uh-huh," Ginger said, upset that Chidi had stopped brushing her fur.

"At least we have Ginger and Tumbles," Chidi said.

"Speaking of the best animals in the world," Alexis said. "How can we understand them? I mean, like talking to them. We *know* what they're saying. Who else can do that? We can *communicate* with our pets. That's unbelievable. Why could we do that?" she rambled. "It's just really weird. And can other people do it? Or are we the only ones?"

"I bet I know what it is," Chidi said with a sly grin. "It's magic."

Chapter Two

MOVING DAY

"Girls!" Mrs. Parris sang as she opened the door. "Time to get ready to go!"

Chidi pulled the green-and-white blanket over her head. *Let this be a dream*, she thought.

"Chidi! Alexis! Wake up!"

"I'm not awake," Alexis mumbled from her bunk. "I'm sleeping."

"Well, it's time to wake up," Mrs. Parris told her, closing the door as she left.

Chidi hopped out of bed, almost stepping on Ginger.

"Oh, Ginger, I'm so sorry." Chidi bent to pick up the little kitten. "Come here."

"Hmmph," Ginger purred, wriggling out of her grip. "Okay, okay, we're good! I smell tuna."

Alexis sat up, her blue-and-green comforter half falling off of the bed.

"Let's get dressed and brush our hair, then get some breakfast," she told her twin, climbing down the ladder with Tumbles in her arms. The girls got ready for the day, then went down the hall and into the kitchen where their parents sat at the table.

"Tumbles, you silly pup, stop squirming!"

"I want to eat!" Tumbles said.

Chidi and Alexis looked at their parents to see if they had heard it, but Mrs. Parris only looked away.

"That ridiculous dog," Mr. Parris said, sipping his coffee.

"Hmmph." Tumbles turned his nose up at the twin's dad.

"Tumbles, Ginger, sit," Chidi commanded. The two pets sat obediently, staring at the girls, hoping for a snack.

"Wow, girls, you really have trained those pets well. I'm very impressed! The pet treats are in that box. And I have a baggie of pre-cooked bacon. Those can be training treats," Mrs. Parris said.

"Why again did we get these animals?" Mr. Parris grumbled.

Alexis literally bit her tongue to keep from informing him that they could talk. Chidi opened and closed her hand to remind Alexis not to say a word.

"Something wrong, Dad?" Chidi asked.

"Sorry, just a tough case involving a whole crime scene. I have no idea where to start."

The girls poured bowls of cereal. While they sat down to eat, the moving van arrived, and the workers started gathering up boxes.

"Smoothies?" Mrs. Parris asked. "I picked them up this morning from the restaurant down the street." Chidi got a pineapple raspberry, and Alexis got a banana strawberry.

"Okay, can we have our treats now? I'm hungry!" Ginger complained.

"Yes, yes, one second—Oof!" Alexis grunted, her sentence cut off as she ran into one of the moving guys, who were making trips up and down the stairs.

"Oh! So sorry, ma'am!" he said.

"It's fine," Alexis replied sharply. "Thanks for the bruise!"

"Alright! We're leaving! Get your pets in those crates, and we're out of here!" Mr. Parris called to the twins.

"Okay! Be down in a minute!" Chidi called from upstairs, where she was shoving last-minute items into her backpack.

"Can I just be held instead?" Ginger whined.

"No, you have to go in the crate. Now. Please?" Alexis asked.

"Fine, fine, fine. Whatever," Ginger muttered, climbing in the cage.

"Okay, let's go," Alexis sighed.

....

3:00 P.M.

"Care for some music, girls? It's a long drive to Northern California!" Mrs. Parris sang to the girls in a too-sweet voice.

"No, thanks, I'm sketching," Chidi said. The girls sat in silence for many long hours as they drove, occasionally switching freeways or stopping for gas. Finally, they came to a hotel.

"How far away is California?" Chidi asked.

"About a three-day's drive," Mr. Parris said. Tumbles yelped in surprise. "Alexis, please keep that dog from barking the entire trip."

"Sorry, Dad."

....

5:30 P.M

The Parris family went into the hotel and booked two rooms.

"You girls will have room 233, and your father and I will be in room 232. You'll have the extra keycard to our room in case anything happens. Okay? And—"

"Laura," Mr. Parris said. "They're big girls. They'll be fine. Nothing's going to happen."

Mrs. Parris nodded.

"We'll go into our room," Alexis said. Chidi rolled two suitcases while Alexis carried the pet carriers.

Once they were in their room, they began to look around. There were two beds, a TV, a microwave, popcorn bags, and a coffee maker.

"Yum!" Ginger yelled.

"What is it, Ginger?" Chidi asked, as she and Alexis walked towards her. At the entryway, there was a bowl of assorted candies and snacks.

"Nice," Chidi said. "I'll have some corn chips."

Chidi was just swallowing a chip when she heard a pounding on the door. She looked at Alexis. Alexis peered through a hole in the door.

"It's a man and a woman, both in business suits. Should we open it?"

"I don't know," Chidi said, a shiver going down her spine. "Are the windows closed?"

"Yes," Alexis said. "And the door is locked."

"Text Mom and Dad," Chidi whimpered. The twins had an emergency cell phone, and they had never had to use it before. Just thinking about it made Alexis nervous.

"Okay." Shakily, Alexis texted their mother and explained the situation.

>Alexis

Laura<

Hey, Mom. There are these weird people outside our door.
Why are they there?
We're kinda scared

I see them. Did you lock the door?

"I got a reply," Alexis said a few seconds later. "I said we locked the door, and then she said just to wait and see if they leave, they probably got the wrong hotel room."

"Oh no." Chidi looked around nervously. "Where's Ginger and Tumbles?"

"I'll find them," Alexis promised. "You watch the phone."

"Actually, could I go with you ? We can take the phone with us."

So the sisters walked through their room until they found the pets hidden under a bed.

"We were so worried about you two!" Alexis cried.

"Speaking of worry," Chidi said. "Are they gone yet?"

They looked out of the peephole, only to see the man talking to Mr. Parris.

"Oh, no," Alexis said. "Dad has the badge out."

"Yeah," Chidi added. "He never gets the badge out unless it's really dangerous."

Ring-ring-ring!

Alexis checked the phone. "It's Mom calling."

"Hey, Mom," Chidi said.

"Are you girls okay? I knew we should have gotten only one room. I'm so sorry. You must be so scared. Are you alright?"

"Yes, Mom," Alexis said. "We're alright. You don't have to worry."

"I was so nervous. I didn't know what to do! You girls were in a hotel room with two complete strangers knocking on the door!"

"Who are they, Mom?"

"We don't know, sweetheart. Your father and I will come over in a few minutes. Hang in there."

"Well, that settles it, I officially do not like this hotel. It gives me the creeps," Ginger said, pouncing on the doorknob.

"Okay, while we're stuck in here, Tumbles, care to explain how we can understand you?" Alexis asked.

"It is a sad and dreadful backstory, so I'm not sure if you would like to hear it," Tumbles said dramatically, flopping on his back. "I actually don't know," he muttered under his breath.

"Oh, stop being so dramatic and—"

The knock on the door came again, and again, then, they heard a voice outside the room.

"Hey, I don't think they're gonna open up, we should go before that officer makes us leave again . . . we were lucky he had to take a call," said the man outside the door.

"We need to get a hold of those kids and their mother. They're valuable resources," the woman said. "I kinda feel bad for those kids, they don't know they're being hunted . . ."

"Maybe you do, but I don't. So, if you don't want a raise, feel free to abort the mission." The voices grew smaller as the people walked away once more.

The twins felt safer, now that they were gone.

"Did you hear that?" Alexis whispered once the mysterious strangers were gone.

"Yeah, I did! It sounds like they are trying to capture someone!" Chidi replied, leaning down to brush orange cat hair off her designer jeans.

"Wait, they said something about *those kids and their mother*, do you think that means . . . us?"

....

6:45 P.M.

The twins were getting ready for bed when Alexis peeked out the peephole in their door. "Hey, I think I see something on the floor outside the door."

"Really? You're not just trying to scare me?" Chidi replied, a hint of suspicion in her voice.

"No, I'm telling the truth! I'm gonna go out and get it real quick, okay?"

"Okay, just be careful, I don't know if those weirdos will be coming back."

"I will, 'kay?"

Chidi nodded. Alexis gently opened the door and grabbed the envelope.

"Maybe it's some kind of 'Thanks for staying here,' gift," Chidi guessed.

"Maybe," Alexis sighed. "Should we open it?"

"Let's go over to Mom and Dad's room. After hearing those people talk, I'm kinda *freaked out!*" Chidi replied, and the tone in her voice sounded like she was *very* anxious.

The twins walked over with the pets.

"Can you recall if they mentioned the package?" Mr. Parris asked, observing the envelope from all angles.

"No, they said nothing about it, but—"

Riiiiiiip!

"Tumbles? What are you doing?" Chidi yelled.

"Fixing your problem!"

"Okay, did anyone else hear that?" Alexis said, sounding very flustered.

"Hear what?" the parents said, though the girls thought Mrs. Parris had a guilty expression on her face.

"Oh, never mind that, but—but—Tumbles! Why did you open the package?" Alexis said.

"Ruff!" he barked.

"It's fine, let's just look inside," Chidi said, trying to loosen the tension. She picked up the contents of the package. "It's a . . . card? It has a person in a black suit on it."

Dexter Graham.
Age: 42 years old.
Class: Technic Spy
Agents: Layla M., Jonathan N.
Only Classified Personnel May Read Further
Target: a woman and her two daughters.
Staying in rooms 233 and 232 at the
Lavender Hotel. Capture and Containment
until further notice.

Capturing this asset will result in a
25,000 dollar raise. Call (632)-687-0946.

When Chidi finished, all the faces in the room went pale.

"Um, they could be like super police or something, right? And they could be looking for . . . bad people in another Lavender Hotel?" Alexis whispered hopefully.

"Do you *really think that?* Or are you trying to make yourself feel better?" Chidi asked.

"No and yes," Alexis replied in a barely audible squeak.

"That's odd. I saw him drop the package, but it didn't look like it was on purpose . . . ," Mrs. Parris informed her husband.

"Freaky," Ginger purred, barely listening as she concentrated on kneading a blanket. "Okay, forget it, probably just some weird people trying to scare us. Let's go to bed."

Chapter Three

NOT SO NICE TO MEET YOU

"I am *so* freaked out!" Chidi said once the girls were locked in their bedroom.

"I know!" Alexis said.

"I'm just glad you have to talk about it, *cause it's sooo interesting,*" Ginger said sarcastically. "Let's just go to bed, it's, like, 9:00."

. . . .

8:45, the next morning

"Hey, kids! Wake up! I am talking to you! Yeah, you!" chirped a robin, sitting on the windowsill.

"Wha . . . ? Oh, I'm up! I'm up!" Chidi sat up in bed, staring at the robin in the window.

"Huh?" Alexis mumbled, rubbing sleep from her eyes.

"Wake up, Lexi!" Chidi said, getting out of bed. "There's a talking robin on our—"

"Wait," Alexis said. "I think we can understand—all animals. Doesn't that make sense, Chidi?"

"I think you're right." She yawned sleepily.

"Yeah, so, uh, my name's Redd, and I think you're . . . Luxa?" he said, pointing his wing at Alexis, then he said, "And you're . . . uh, Choodi, am I right?" He motioned to Chidi.

"Whoa, whoa, I'm Chidi," Chidi said, throwing off her blanket.

"And I am Alex-is, not Luxa, or whatever you called me," Alexis said, frowning at the strange robin. "I'm guessing your name is Wedd?"

"Who are you?" Tumbles said, coming from his dog bed on the carpet. He sniffed. "I'm guessing robin, and—oh!"

"I'm Redd. Are you . . . Tuber?"

"I'm Tumbles."

"I'm *hungry!*" Ginger's awaited whine came.

"Coming!" Chidi called. "Come in, uh, Redd."

"The crazy cat's name is Hungry?" Redd asked politely, looking like he had never seen a cat before.

"No, it's Ginger," Alexis said. "But if Chidi had named her Hungry, that wouldn't be a mistake."

"Lexi!" Chidi called, dumping food in Ginger's bowl.

"What?"

"Mom is calling. She wants us to come over right away."

"Okay. I'll leave the pets to play with Redd."

The sisters walked across the hall and slid the keycard into the lock.

"Mom?"

"Close the door," Mrs. Parris said.

"Did you find anything new? About those people?"

"Yes. Your father contacted the people that were on that business card. They're after us."

"What do you mean, us?" Alexis asked worriedly.

"Me, you, and Chidi," Mrs. Parris said.

Chidi sank onto the stiff couch. "Why?"

"I . . . don't know."

Mrs. Parris wrung her hands, as though she had an idea she wasn't willing to share.

"We're going to have to leave soon. We're going to get in the car, then drive as far as we can. We'll go to a hotel farther than we were going to. We'll try to get to California today and get to our house tomorrow."

Mr. Parris hugged his daughters. "I'm sorry, girls. It's not fair for you to go through this."

"Through what?" Chidi asked, obviously concerned.

"Somebody trying to track you down. Sometimes it happens to me. Being a police officer or a relative of one isn't the best. Since I have to lay down the law, I can't bend it or give someone that I like too many chances. So people don't like me too much, those people that break the law. But I'm so sorry. This isn't the kind of thing I want my kids to go through. Not my sweet, sweet girls." Mr. Parris shook his head. "They're obviously after you for some reason, and I guarantee it's because of me."

"Um . . . yeah . . . ," Laura said weakly. "I'm sure that's the cause."

"I'll pack up our stuff," Chidi offered.

"I'll help," Alexis added. *I'll take the credit while Chidi packs. Pure hilariousness,* Alexis thought as they exited the room. *Classic 'I win you lose' situation.*

....

9:00 A.M.

"Ugh," Ginger complained. "I'm so *hungry!*" She paced around, looking for something to eat.

"There's *chips!*" Tumbles exclaimed.

"Do *not* eat corn chips, Tumbles!" Alexis ordered. "You will get so sick!"

"Fine, fine," Tumbles grumbled. "But most dogs are actually *allergic* to things like that, and I'm not."

"I wanna try!" Ginger whined.

"No! You will get sick too!" Alexis scolded.

"Stop it, both of you," Chidi said, picking both pets up. "We have to start packing before those weirdos start pounding on our door."

"Hello?"

"Oh, no," Alexis said. "It's that woman. She's wearing a suit, I think."

"Is anybody there?" the woman said in a sickly sweet voice.

"This is so freaky," Chidi whispered. "Should we get Dad?"

"I'm so nervous. And why do they want to get us?"

"I really don't know, but just be quiet!" Ginger whisper-yelled.

"Maybe . . . ," the lady said. The door flew open.

"Oh, hi," Chidi said. "Um, are you part of the housekeeping staff? I know my father arranged for you to clean our rooms today, for the new arrival. Right?"

"Um . . . sure. Of course. What's your name?"

"Oh, if you're on the staff," Alexis said, popping up by her sister. "You *should* know our names. The housekeeping staff promised that they had spoken with you. Layla, right?"

"Yes," she said, glancing around nervously. "I wasn't alerted."

"Well, I would *hate* to call your company workers *liars,* but that's the way it looks, huh?"

Chidi nodded.

"Then I guess I'll be talking with the manager. Hey, you should come. Help us with it. They might even send the police down. The chief is staying here at the hotel, in room 232. *Right* across the hall from us! Isn't that so funny! I suppose we should head over and have a little chat, now, shouldn't we? Am I correct?"

"Well . . . I suppose you are."

"Sorry, Layla, but we have some serious work to do. I don't want something like this to happen again, okay? Lying like that . . . it makes my blood boil! Just to see the things people nowadays get away with. Things like stealing a two-cent toy are on the news, but lying hotel workers are never mentioned! They should lay down the law—"

"Layla!" somebody said.

"Um, sir," Layla said. "I just . . ."

"I did not tell you to do this!"

"But, Mr. Dexter, sir, you told me there was a twenty-five thousand dollar raise for whoever captures the k—"

"Layla, you are going back to work NOW!" the man thundered.

"That's Dexter, I'd guess," Chidi whispered.

"But, sir, what about Project Zuincchils-3pic?" Layla cried.

"I'm sorry, kiddos," Dexter said. "We didn't mean to disturb you. Bye-bye, now." He shut the door in their faces.

"Call Mom," Chidi said, pushing a chair by the door. "That was so scary."

"Yeah, but it was kind of fun," Alexis said, pulling the cell phone out of her pocket.

"Fun? How was it *fun*?"

"Okay, it was scary too."

Ring! Ring!

"Mom?" Chidi asked. "That lady, Layla, was here. And that man, Dexter. But Alexis held the lady off until Dexter came and basically forced her out. And they *do* mean us. They're trying to capture us. We don't know why they want us, though."

"Alexis is there with you, right?" Mrs. Parris's voice came through the speaker.

"Yeah, she is. And we're all ready to go. The pets are even ready to get in their crates."

"Okay. Your father and I will bring our stuff over and then we'll go to our new house. We're going to go as far as we can. We'll buy something to eat soon."

"Aw," Ginger complained. "More driving!"

"Wait, you're leaving already? I barely met you guys!" Redd said from the window.

"Oh! I totally forgot you were still here!" Alexis exclaimed.

"Oh, it's fine. Hey, I have an idea! What if I come with you?" the little robin suggested.

"Wait, how? We have a van, not a truck, so you can't stay in the bed," Chidi said, racking her brain for how he could come with them.

"What do I look like, a turtle? I can fly, you know. I could just fly alongside your car!" Redd said happily.

"That's a great idea! You're a genius, Redd!"

"Right you are! I'm fond of you kids, so I might as well come with you."

"Hey," Tumbles said, "why don't we, after we're in our new house, build a birdhouse for Redd so that he doesn't have to build a nest and stuff? He could just live there!"

"Chidi? Alexis?" their father called through the door. "Open up!"

"Hide!" Chidi hissed to Redd. Redd slipped out the window. Alexis opened the door.

"Okay, get those pets in the van!" Mr. Parris instructed, closing the door tightly. The girls nodded, placing the animals in the trunk, once they got downstairs.

"Where are we heading next?" Chidi asked.

"Obviously, away from this creepy hotel!" Ginger exclaimed, pawing at the gates of her cage.

"I'm ready to go," Alexis said.

"Alright, we should probably get out of here," Chidi replied, an anxious look on her face.

....

11:34 A.M.

"Hey, Mom?" Chidi asked.

"Yes, sweetie?" Mrs. Parris replied.

"What are we doing for our birthday? We're moving and don't know any people or restaurants . . ."

"Oh . . . your—OH NO! I totally forgot! I have no idea how I forgot! I am so sorry, sweetie! Oh no!" Mrs. Parris cried.

"You forgot our birthday? How? We're turning twelve! That's just—just . . . ," Chidi muttered angrily, looking close to tears. Chidi stuffed her face in her pillow in silent angry sobs. Alexis sat there, stunned. She was far too surprised to move.

Wait. Is Mom kidding? How could she forget our birthday of all things? This isn't like her. She's probably putting on a show just to make us think she forgot, so we can have some sort of surprise birthday?

Her thoughts wandered when she heard Tumbles whisper something.

"Birthday? Is that the day with all the food and flying balls?"

"Yes, Tumbles, but the main food is cake, and the flying balls are called balloons," she said softly, so her parents couldn't hear.

"You're kidding," Ginger scoffed. "Your parents forgot about your birthday? That's crazy. Really—"

"Really, you could work on your character," Alexis said. Chidi looked out the window.

"Alexis, look!"

Redd was flying as fast as his wings could carry him, but he couldn't keep up with the car.

"Hey, Dad, don't we need gas? I see a rest stop. Can't we stop for a second? I'm—uh, feeling carsick. Please?"

Mr. Parris glanced at the gas monitor, then nodded. "We are getting low."

"Why do you want us to stop?" Alexis hissed. "Layla and Dexter and Jonathan will find us!"

"Because, we need to get Redd in here, fast! You get him inside Tumble's pet carrier, and then we'll go on. But poor Redd will probably fall down on the road if he doesn't take a rest. So—"

"Chidi, didn't you want to get out? I'm going to get gas."

Mr. Parris drove to the line, about three cars long.

"Alright, go in the pet carrier, Redd!" she whispered to the exhausted bird sitting on the top of the van.

"You want me to—" Redd began, shaking his head.

"Yes. Go in. Now. It's for your own good! You said you wanted to come with us, didn't you?"

"Oh, fine. I hope this isn't the biggest mistake of my life," he said, swooping in the pet carrier.

"Okay. I'll be right back," said Chidi, with Alexis following her. They divided—Alexis finding drinks; Chidi finding snacks.

She started walking into the station, holding a ten-dollar bill. "Peanuts . . . peanuts. Where are the peanuts?" she said to herself, walking up the aisles.

"Can I get you somethin', ma'am?" a clerk with a Texas accent asked. "I hear you sayin' somethin' 'bout wantin' a bag of them peanuts. I'd know where to get 'em. I got a hankerin' for one 'couple days 'go."

He led her to the snack aisle, where she saw there was a full selection of peanuts, mixed nuts, almonds, pistachios, and pecans. Chidi grabbed a bag of unsalted peanuts, along with a bag of sour cream and onion potato chips for her to share with Alexis. After she had paid and thanked the Texan clerk, she ran out to the car, where Alexis and their mother were waiting in the car.

Chidi slid some of the peanuts between the bars of the crate, letting Redd nibble on them.

"I want some!" Ginger and Tumbles whined together.

"Here, this shouldn't hurt you," Chidi said, giving each a handful.

"Alright, are you guys ready to get going?" Mr. Parris asked, buckling his seatbelt.

"Yep," Alexis said, ready to get away from the odd people in the hotel. She hoped that that was the last she'd ever see of them.

But that was wishful thinking.

Chapter Four

THE ATTIC (OF FUN!)

"We're in Arizona!" Chidi exclaimed, pointing to a sign by the highway.

Ginger raised an eyebrow as if to say, "Why is that important?"

Alexis motioned to Redd and Tumbles' cage, noticing that they were both asleep.

"Girls, we're going to stop at a hotel soon, then get to our new house tomorrow afternoon. Okay?"

The twins nodded, then Alexis snagged the bag of potato chips from Chidi's hand.

"Hey!" Chidi said, laughing. Then she snatched the almost-gone lemonade that Alexis had in her hand.

"Instead of taking two rooms, we'll get a large suite, where you can share a room, and your mother and I will take the other half. Okay?"

"Ooo, fancy. A suite!" Ginger called, waking the other pets up.

"Wait, where AM I?" Redd yelled, flocking around in the crate.

"What's that noise? Did a bird sneak into our car?" Mr. Parris asked. "Girls, look around."

"No random birds, Dad," Chidi said. It was the truth since Redd wasn't a *random* bird. He was a very special bird, with many talents. At least that's what the twins thought.

"Are you sure? It definitely sounded like there was a bird back there," Mr. Parris said, a hint of suspicion creeping into his tone.

"Let's just—er—get some rest!" Alexis suggested.

"Okay, good idea. We'll be at the hotel in an hour. And can you try to keep those pets quiet?" Mrs. Parris suggested.

"Yes, of course, Mom," Chidi said, giving Ginger, Redd, and Tumbles a hard look.

....

2:30 P.M.

"Hey, Chidi, I think Mom is asleep and Dad has his earbuds in. So now we can whisper-talk," Alexis whispered in a low tone.

"Okay. So I've been thinking, and if Mom forgot about our birthday, why don't we try to convince them to let us take scuba diving lessons? We'll be by the ocean anyway," Chidi suggested. She had always wanted to take scuba lessons ever since she read about sea creatures in an Animal Encyclopedia.

"But how could we convince them? I know that you love scuba diving, but I'm not too keen on it. So how?" Alexis asked.

"I don't know. I—"

"What are you girls talking about?" Mr. Parris asked, tugging his earbuds out of his ears.

"We're a bit hungry," Chidi said. "Could we stop for something to eat soon?"

"Yes, of course. What sounds good?"

"Burritos?" Mrs. Parris asked, waking up from her nap.

Alexis nodded. A few minutes later, the Parrises were in the Taco Chime drive-thru.

"What do you girls want?"

"Two burritos and water," Chidi said.

"How about freezies?" Mr. Parris asked, pointing to a sign. "What flavors?"

After Chidi had studied the menu, she asked for the blue raspberry. Alexis got strawberry.

"Thanks Mom! This is great!" Alexis said, taking a slurp from her drink.

"Is California by the beach?" Chidi asked, glancing up from her sea encyclopedia.

"Yes. We'll be up in Northern California. And California is a warm, sunny state."

"Cool. How long do you think we'll be able to stay there?" Chidi asked.

Mr. and Mrs. Parris had an adult-eye conversation.

"Well?" Alexis asked. "What is it?"

"We—" Mrs. Parris began, but the phone rang.

"It's Jenny," Mr. Parris said. "Put it on speaker."

"Hi, Laura. I'll see you guys tomorrow at your new house and pick up the twins. I'm so excited to meet them!"

"Hi, Jenny," Mrs. Parris said. "We'll be at the house at eleven-thirty. The girls will be excited."

"Okay. Bye."

"Who was *that*?" both of the twins asked.

"It was your Aunt Jenny," Mr. Parris replied calmly.

"What was she talking about, 'picking up the twins'?" Chidi said.

"Leh," Alexis added, her tongue out, looking for the reddish tint left behind from the strawberry freeze. "Anh weh haf un hunt? Hut hare hue hawking about?" She was still cross-eyed while looking for the red-ness. "Hue uve bun keping secrets fum us. Smell us tuh thrut."

In English, Chidi would have translated it to: "Yeah. And we have an aunt? What are you talking about? You have been keeping secrets from us. Tell us the truth." Loosely.

"You're going to live with her until we get this whole thing sorted out," Mrs. Parris admitted. "We've only been talking about it since those people came."

"What about Tumbles and Ginger and—" Alexis said, but Chidi glared, shook her head, and mimed slicing her throat.

"And who?"

"Just Chidi . . ."

"Well, the pets will stay with you guys. And of course, Chidi will be going with you, Alexis! Tomorrow, Aunt Jenny will come by and pick you girls up. Okay?"

Chidi nodded, wearing a fake smile.

....

The following day, 11:30 A.M.

"We're here, at our new house!" Mr. Parris announced.

"For three hours," Chidi mumbled to Alexis. "Then we'll be at our aunt's house."

After everything was unloaded from the car, the doorbell rang.

Ring-ring-ring!

"Mom, somebody's at the door," Chidi said.

"Will you and Alexis answer it?"

Chidi opened the door.

"Hello!"

The only thing Chidi could do was stare at the woman. Alexis' eyes shone with fear.

"I need to come in," Layla said with her sickly sweet voice.

"Um, no," Alexis said. She slammed the door shut.

"Uh, can somebody let me in?" Tumbles yelled from the backyard. Chidi scooped the pup in her arms and carried him to the kitchen, where Ginger was napping. Redd was on the windowsill.

Ring-ring-ring!

"Hello?" Mrs. Parris said, opening the door.

"Hi, I'm Layla. I'd like to speak with your daughters?"

"Alexis, Chidi! There's someone here to see you!" Chidi began to shake, but Alexis marched right to the door.

"What do you want? You already tried to capture me and Chidi, but you failed. So leave me and my sister *alone*!" Alexis yelled. She kicked the door shut.

"Who was that?" Mr. Parris asked, walking in and sipping his coffee as though a wannabee kidnapper hadn't just waltzed into their new house uninvited.

"That lady who tried to capture me and Chidi! And she's following us! I just can't do it anymore! Everywhere we move, they're going to follow us!"

"What?!" Mrs. Parris exclaimed. "She—"

"I'm here!"

"Jenny!" Mrs. Parris exclaimed, coming towards her sister at the front door. "We've missed you!"

"I've missed you too. Oh, are these your daughters? They've grown so much!" A short-ish woman with brown hair and maple-gray eyes, wearing ripped jeans and a plaid shirt, was in the doorway, smiling brightly.

"Yes, and they're all ready to go."

Alexis' jaw dropped and she stared at Chidi.

"Is she *kidding* me?" Chidi whispered.

"I don't think so, Chidi," Alexis whispered back. "I'm going to have a *lot* to write about in my journal."

Chidi rolled her eyes. "We are *so* not ready to go."

"Chidi, *you* know that, and *I* know that, but do *they* know that?" Alexis said with a nod at their parents.

"All right, get your things and load the car. Then we'll get going. Your parents are two hours away from the beach, but my house is just down the street from it!"

Chidi blinked. Yesterday she had been worried about her parents forgetting her birthday, and today she was worried about living with an aunt she had never met before!

"C'mon, Chidi," Alexis said. "Let's go."

The twins got to work, loading duffles and cardboard boxes into Aunt Jenny's blue car. Before leaving the house, Chidi snatched a notebook and two pens.

We can write-talk, Chidi wrote, handing Alexis the other pen.

Okay, Alexis wrote. What are we going to do? We're being shipped off to be with an aunt we don't even know!

Right? But I've seen movies about California, and the places right by the beach are REALLY fancy. But I'm super nervous.

We're not going to know ANYBODY! How long do you think we'll be with Aunt . . . Jenny, right? Alexis scribbled.

I can't believe Mom and Dad would let us go off like this? And I think her name is Jenny. Chidi answered.

"So, I'm sure you girls want to know where we're going," Aunt Jenny said, reading a sign she had passed. "We're going to my house. And right next door, there's a eleven, almost-twelve-year-old girl named Dalia Monroe."

"Um, will me and Chidi share a bedroom?" Alexis asked.

"Oh, no. I have a two-story house, so you girls can share the top floor."

Is she for real? Alexis wrote.

I have no idea. But this is really cool. And I wonder what this Dalia girl is like. Do you think she's nice? Or could she be snooty? Chidi quickly scrawled.

"Hel-lo!" Ginger whined. "I'm hungry!"

"Oh, Ginger, you're fine," Chidi said, then clamped her hand over her mouth.

How are we going to hide Redd from Aunt Jenny?

Maybe we can just tell her that he's one of our pets.

"Um, do you have any pets, Aunt Jenny?" Chidi asked. It felt weird calling a lady she hadn't known existed until yesterday her aunt, but what else could she call her? She couldn't call her Jenny, that was for sure.

"No. Why? I know that you have some sort of pet."

"Yes, we have a cat, robin, and dog. The cat is named Ginger, the robin is Redd, and the dog is Tumbles."

"Oh, I just love birds! They're so soft, and they're *very* elegant. Oh, where are my manners? What are your names? And what kind of food do you like? I don't keep much in my house, just some fruit and milk, so we'll have to go grocery shopping!"

"I'm Alexis, and this is Chidi," Alexis told Aunt Jenny. "When are we going to go grocery shopping?"

"Oh, after you're all settled in your rooms. Oh, and how old are you?"

"Um, we're turning twelve in two days," Chidi mumbled.

"Oh, really? Well, we'll have to celebrate, then! How about your first-ever scuba-diving lesson?"

"*Really?*" Chidi asked, wishing she didn't have the seatbelt on so that she could hug Aunt Jenny.

"What about you, Alexis? I know that scuba diving might not be your pleasure."

"Well, I like basketball, journaling, coding, and gardening," Alexis said slowly. "And Chidi likes volleyball and cooking. And we both would have wanted to go scuba-diving."

"All right. I'll drop you off at my house with your boxes, then go and buy birthday gifts."

"Oh, no. You don't need to get into all of that trouble just for—"

"Chidi, I haven't gotten you girls anything for twelve years. I have to."

....

8:00 P.M.

"What's your bedtime, girls?"

"Um, eight-fifteen."

"All right, and tomorrow morning, I'll make pancakes or something for you, and Dalia and her mother will come over."

"Uh, okay," Alexis said.

While they were getting ready for bed and unpacking their clothes, Chidi saw something.

"Hey, cool! Look at this!" Chidi called from her room, next to Alexis'. "There's a doorknob on the wall!" She twisted it, revealing a door to the attic.

"Oh, I have one too!" Alexis yelled back.

"Should we go in?" Chidi asked, leaning her head in the doorway.

"Yes, yes!" Chidi heard Alexis stomping around, so she sighed and entered.

"Whoa. This is huge," Chidi said. "And it isn't too low of a ceiling, either."

"Look at these chairs!" Alexis said, motioning to a set of four chairs and a table. The chairs were shaped like teacups, with a little swinging door attached to the side.

"This place is awesome," Chidi said.

"What's awesome? I wanna see!" Tumbles, Ginger, and Redd all fell inside of the attic.

"Oh, nice." Ginger was curled up in one of the teacup chairs in seconds.

"I'm going to ask Aunt Jenny if we're allowed to be up here," Alexis told her sister, already halfway out the door.

Alexis found her aunt in the kitchen, putting chocolate chips, bananas, strawberries, blueberries, and pancake mix on the counter.

"Hey, Aunt Jenny, me and Chidi found the attic, and there's some cool stuff up there. Are we allowed to go in there?"

"Oh, sure."

When Alexis returned, Chidi was poking around the other half of the attic, which had a small fan, two large desks, and a small coffee table.

"This is so cool! Oh man, it's so big up here! I love it!" Tumbles said, climbing up on top of the black desk and laying down.

"Hey, get off of there! This is not our house, so be respectful of it!" Alexis scolded.

"I want the black desk," Chidi said, dragging the two swivel chairs to the desks. "My watercolors won't stain it at all like they would on the brown one."

"Hey, we should go to bed before Aunt Jenny has to come up and tell us to do it. Oh, where should Redd sleep?"

"I have an old cupboard in my room. He could stay there."

After the animals all went sleepily to bed, Chidi looked around the attic. She also noticed a tea cart in the corner, so she rolled it over to the table, where a tea set was laid out.

Maybe Aunt Jenny will make us some tea tomorrow. And who would have thought I would get to go scuba diving? Everything is working out!

Chidi laid out some things and began organizing.

"Why're you still up, Chidi?" Redd asked, fluttering in. "I mean, Alexis was knocked out two hours ago, and Ginger, oh man, she wouldn't stop talking! I was about to steal Alexis' masking tape to keep her quiet."

"Oh, it's been more than two hours? I didn't realize. Maybe, since I can't sleep, I'll start putting my things on the desk." Chidi glanced over at the black desk. "Wait, why does Alexis have masking tape?!"

"Dunno. Can I help?"

"Oh, of course, Redd. Would you go into my room and open the box labeled **CHIDI'S ARTS AND CRAFTS**? It's right next to my bed."

Redd wasted no time opening the box, then Chidi dragged it into the attic.

"Do you mind if I hit the hay?" Redd asked.

"What does 'hit the hay' mean?" Chidi said, looking quizzically at Redd.

"It means go to bed."

"Oh, of course. I'll finish this tomorrow."

Chapter Five

THE BEACH

Alexis awoke early the next morning. She wanted to look out her window and see her first beach sunrise. To her dismay, the sun was already up and shining.

"Oh, Alexis, can I see if Ginger or Redd are awake?" Tumbles said quietly.

"Yes, Tumbles, but if they aren't, please don't wake them. You know how Ginger is in the morning."

Tumbles gave a happy little yip, then dashed through the attic.

Well, since I'm up, I might as well get unpacked, Alexis thought. She rolled the top of the desk up and slid open the drawers, filling them with animal-printed stationery and pens. Then she lined her journals and gardening books underneath a row of slots.

"Good morning, girls!" Aunt Jenny sang, climbing up the stairs. "Would you like to help me make pancakes, Chidi?"

"Oh, sure!" Chidi said, waking Ginger, who of course yelled, "What about me? Haven't you heard of letting cats sleep in? No one appreciates me in this house, I guarantee it!"

"Sorry, Ginger," Chidi apologized, rushing out the door.

"Can I please play in the attic with Redd?" Tumbles begged.

"Yes," Alexis said, heading towards the stairs. "I'll be helping Chidi with the pancakes."

"Hey, Alexis, can you pick the toppings we'll want?"

"Why not?"

Alexis observed the toppings: bananas, strawberries, chocolate chips, berries, and peanut butter.

That last one is really weird, Alexis thought. *I hope Chidi doesn't think I want any with THAT stuff smeared on it.*

Chidi began to add water, oil, and eggs to the mix.

"All right, you pour the batter on the pan, and I'll add the toppings."

"Oh, what about a chocolate chip and strawberry pancake?" Alexis suggested. "And Triple Berry: raspberries, strawberries, and blackberries?" After a while, they had a stack of different pancakes.

"Girls, Dalia is here!"

Slowly, Alexis walked towards the front room. Redd flew down the stairs and perched on her shoulder. Dalia had short, just-past-her-chin-length brown hair with a faint blue streak. Her nails were painted a similar shade. A pair of pink sunglasses were propped up on her forehead. Her mossy green eyes seemed to radiate coolness and seemed like the girl that would toss her hair and be popular.

She had a little dog in her arms, too.

"Mom, Oreo is getting impatient," Dalia complained as Alexis opened the door.

"Alexis, why don't you and Chidi show Dalia to your rooms?" Aunt Jenny asked.

Alexis gave a faint nod.

"Here, it's this way." Halfway up the stairs, Alexis heard Aunt Jenny tell Chidi to bring a stack of pancakes and some tea up to their room.

Chidi joined them in Alexis' room.

"Let's go to the attic," Chidi suggested.

"Hey, do you have any pets?" Dalia asked, leaning back in a chair. "And what's your name?"

"Yes. We have this robin, Redd, Tumbles is a dog, and Ginger is our cat. I'm Chidi."

"Tea?" Alexis offered. "I'm Alexis."

"Hey, what's your name?" Ginger asked the dalmatian pup.

"I'm Oreo."

"I'm Ginger!"

"I wanna eat something!" Tumbles cut in.

"Why aren't you unpacked?" Dalia asked, nodding at the boxes.

"Um, because we moved here yesterday?"

"What happened to your parents?" Dalia said.

Chidi and Alexis exchanged glances. Nobody knew about Layla and Dexter. Chidi's expression said, *Should we tell her?* while Alexis' said, *no way!*

"Um, they're . . . busy, so we're living with our aunt."

"Do you play sports?" Dalia asked, taking a bite of her pancake.

"Yeah. Alexis is a champion basketball player . . . ," Chidi started.

"And Chidi is a great volleyball player!" Alexis cut in.

"You play volleyball?" Dalia asked with interest.

"Yeah." Chidi nodded.

"My volleyball team is missing a player. You wanna practice down at the beach?"

"Uh, sure. Let's check with my aunt."

They came downstairs, where Aunt Jenny was chatting with Dalia's mom.

"Can we go to the beach?" Dalia blurted.

"Sure." Jenny shrugged.

"What if you invite Bella to come?" Dalia's mother suggested.

"No!" Dalia cried. "Not Bella!"

"We might as well let her come," Alexis said. "The more the merrier, right?" The truth was that even though she didn't want to meet yet another stranger, she wasn't very keen on the idea of sitting in the sand as she watched a ball being smacked around. It would be much better to have someone to sympathize with.

"Fine," Dalia sighed.

....

2:30 P.M.

Alexis poured a handful of sand into one hand, then poured it back. Where was Bella? Dalia had gone over to invite her, and she *said* Bella had agreed to come.

"I'm here!" someone called.

Alexis jumped up.

Bella was a tall, lanky girl, who almost mirrored Alexis' height, which was tall for an average twelve-year-old. She had blond hair that reached her shoulders and very interesting eyes—not blue, not teal, not green, and not turquoise. They were what could only be described as seafoam.

She adjusted her flowy shirt and smiled. Or smirked?

"Heya, girls," Bella said.

Dalia rolled her eyes at Chidi, then served the ball back, a little harder than she should have.

"Hi, I'm Alexis. I just moved here with my sister, Chidi. What do you do for fun around here?"

"I mainly boogie board or swim. Or I know this part of the beach where you can use these bumper boats."

"Cool!" Chidi said, jogging towards them. "Can we go?"

"Yeah. Normally you have to pay to rent them, but my uncle always lets me get a few for free. He runs the stand."

"I thought we were playing volleyball, Chidi," Dalia said, glaring at Bella.

"We were, but now we get to go on bumper boats!" she cheered.

"Follow me." Bella walked past a breakwater and motioned to a large beachside shack with a gardening shed behind it.

"Hi, Uncle Josiah. Can I have four bumper boats?"

Josiah motioned to a shed behind him, which upon inspection was full of brightly colored, foam-rimmed boats.

Bella claimed the yellow, Alexis the blue, Chidi the green, and Dalia the red.

"C'mon, let's get these in the water!" Dalia called, dragging her boat to the soft waves.

Alexis pushed her foot on the peddle and rammed into Dalia.

"Hey!" Dalia yelled. "Chidi, it's you and me versus Alexis and Bella."

Chidi slammed her foot on the peddle and bumped into Alexis, who retreated to talk to Bella.

"Ha! This is so fun!" Alexis said.

"Yeah, here, let me show you something!" Bella replied. Bella zoomed forward, and right as she was about to bounce Dalia out of the little boat and into the water, Alexis hit Bella away. She went spiraling away because of the force and drenched Alexis with freezing water, leaving her shivering.

"Hey, thanks, Alexis! That would have bounced me straight into the water!" Dalia said gratefully.

"No p-p-prob, b-b-but hey, Bella! That was a dirty trick you just attempted! The water is r-r-really c-c-cold today!" Alexis shouted as she turned her bumper boat around to face Bella.

"Whoa, whoa, whoa, you think I was *trying to hit Dalia?* C'mon, Chidi, defend me!" Bella said, giving Chidi a pleading, yet demanding look.

"Um, no. You literally tried to hit her into the water!" Chidi said, steering her boat to the shore. The others followed in her wake.

"Um, in case you haven't noticed, these are *bumper boats.* The whole goal is to hit them!" Bella stacked her boat in the shed.

"Not into the water! You were *obviously* trying to hit Dalia—HARD. Come on, Lexi," Chidi said, realizing that Bella's glare indicated that she was *not* a good person. She brushed wet sand from her ankles.

"Wait, you're ditching me? Just because I was trying to spice things up a little? Sure, Dalia is *pretty much my archenemy,* but hey, what are you going to do?" Bella asked.

"*Wait, Dalia is your archenemy?* We kids don't have to worry about things like archenemies and diabolical plans! And also, why?" Alexis exclaimed suddenly.

Dalia and Chidi looked at each other, and they exchanged glances that said, "*Is she always this dramatic?*"

"F-fine! I don't expect to see a-any of y-you ever again!" Bella sputtered, storming off into the beach-side neighborhood.

"Oh-kay? What just happened? Umm, I think I need a mental play-by-play of what just went on over here."

"Yeah, and an explanation of why you and Bella hate each other," Chidi said. "She seemed really nice."

"It kinda started in fourth grade. Bella had been sort of nice to me. We weren't best friends, but we weren't enemies either. Then one day, she started glaring at me. She did all these mean things, like making sure we weren't on the same softball team or whatever. It was really weird."

"Oh. I'm so sorry! Well, Let's take our minds off of this for a little, and try to decapitate the opposing team with a volleyball!" Chidi said, jogging towards the net.

"Uh, sure!" Dalia said awkwardly, not understanding half of Chidi's words.

"Okay, then. Might as well go on a walk," Alexis said to herself.

Alexis strolled down the beach path, listening to music. *Man, this place is great!* Alexis thought. *It is kinda cool that we can talk to animals, but man, this place is bustling!*

"Oh! I totally forgot to fill up Tumble's dog bowl! Better hurry back before he starts to whine his head off!" she exclaimed to herself.

Alexis ran to the house, but halfway across the beach, she ran face-to-face with a man.

"Oh, excuse me," Alexis said.

"It's fine, Alexis," the man replied slyly.

"It's you!" Alexis cried, looking up at the pale man. "Dexter!"

"Yes, I believe that's my name. And I also think that you should come along now, and follow me."

"Excuse me? No!" Alexis retorted.

"What?" Dexter lifted his eyebrows, almost amused.

"No, because you aren't my legal guardian. So just go away, okay?" she sputtered.

Alexis saw that a few lifeguards were looking at her, as well as a tall, dark-haired man in a sheriff's uniform who was standing near the lifeguard tower.

"I said, go away, and don't try to kidnap me!" she yelled as loudly as she could, pointedly looking at the sheriff.

"What's going on over here?" the sheriff asked, strolling over to them.

"This is just a man I've seen around, along with a few others. He seems to be following me."

"Really? What's your name, young lady?"

"Alexis Blaze Parris. My sister is here at the beach too. Her and our friend, Dalia. They're playing volleyball."

"What's your sister's name?"

"Chidi Ann Parris."

"Where are your parents?" Dexter sneered.

"Two hours away."

"So you're a runaway, huh?" Dexter smirked.

"No. I'm staying with a friend." Alexis knew she had to stop talking, since Dexter was right here. But if the officer asked where she lived, she would have to tell him, and Dexter would hear too!

"What's your name, sir?" the officer asked Dexter. "Full name."

"Dexter William Graham."

"Do you live in California?"

"Um, sir, Dexter has been following me in Texas, New Mexico, Arizona, and California."

"What state do you live in, Dexter?" the sheriff asked again, ignoring Alexis.

"California!" he barked.

"Um, I need to find my sister and get home. I'm sorry for the trouble." Alexis ducked out and ran towards her sister.

"Chidi!"

Chidi was so startled that she missed the serve.

"Dexter found us."

Chapter Six

THE TRUTH

"What?" Chidi asked. "Dexter's here?"

"Yeah, we need to go, now."

"Um, who's Dexter?" Dalia asked.

"Er, we'll tell you later. In the attic. But we have to leave now!"

"Hey, do you want to see if you can stay the night?" Chidi suggested.

"Sure, sounds like fun!" Dalia said happily.

Dalia followed the twins.

"Aunt Jenny!" Alexis said. "Can Dalia spend the night? I have a bunk."

"Of course." Aunt Jenny looked at Dalia's mother. "Is that alright, Emma?"

Emma nodded. "Sure."

"Yes!" Alexis ran upstairs.

"Okay, what happened with Dexter?" Chidi asks.

"I basically was walking along the beach, and I ran into Dexter. He told me to come with him, and I sort of had to talk to an officer to get away, but he looked at me like, *"This isn't the end, Alexis."*

"Um, *who in the world is Dexter?*" Dalia asked. "You guys aren't telling me!"

"Oh, sorry." Chidi settled in a teacup chair and looked at the ceiling like she couldn't find where to begin.

"So, we were just normal girls, sick of moving all the time," Chidi began, furrowing her brow. She couldn't quite remember how it had all gone. "Oh! And then our parents got us pets—Tumbles and Ginger—"

"What about Redd?" Dalia asked, tearing a hand through her hair.

"He's . . . not really our pet. I'll tell you about it in a sec. Anyways, Ginger pushed Tumbles down the stairs, and we learned that we can understand them." Chidi took a breath and glanced at Dalia. "Do you think we're weirdos?"

"Kind of . . . I guess." Dalia kicked at the base of the little table. "This is all just so *unbelievable*."

"Yeah. So then we were driving out of Texas and stopped at a hotel. Alexis and I had our own room, and we were just hanging out, then we heard these people outside our door.

"They were talking about capturing a mother and her two daughters . . . it was *really* creepy. And then they tried to get in. Then, later, a lady named Layla snuck in and Alexis was able to distract her until a man named Dexter caught her and forced her out.

"Then we headed to California. And we got sent to meet our aunt, whom, by the way, we never knew existed before yesterday. So . . . ," Chidi finished, "jealous of our lives?"

"No. No I'm not." Dalia sunk down against her chair. "But you didn't explain about Redd."

"Oh! We met him at the hotel, and then he followed us, but we didn't tell our parents. We told Aunt Jenny he was one of our pets."

"Why didn't you tell me before?" asked Dalia.

"Well, since we didn't know you very well. We didn't want to just give away all *our* secrets," Alexis said, re-entering with Oreo, Redd, Ginger, and Tumbles.

"Us kids don't have to worry about archenemies and diabolical plans!" Dalia cried. "Seriously, your autobiography would be a fairy tale!"

"Hmm," Alexis said. "Sounds familiar."

"Um, can we get back to the topic at hand?" Chidi said. "All three of us know that we're being chased by completely random people!"

"Calm down, Chidi," Dalia said. "Dexter can't know that you guys are staying here."

"Unless," Alexis said.

"Unless what?" Dalia and Chidi asked in unison.

"Unless, Dexter is somehow tracking us. Like putting tracking devices on our cars or something. Or on our bags." Something clicked in Alexis' mind. She ran to her desk, where she had placed the important business card. Alexis turned it over. It seemed heavy and thick. "I knew it!"

"What?" Chidi asked.

"There's a tracker in this card! That's why they put it outside our door!"

"How do you know it's a tracker?" Dalia asked, looking at the little card.

"Alexis knows her way around electronics!" Chidi said, grinning at her twin.

"This is a really good model," Alexis said. "But if I check something . . ." Alexis pulled out her laptop and began to hit keys. "Yes!"

"'Yes!' what?" Chidi said.

"This particular tracker can't pick up voices. So it only tells where we are, not what we say. And it also tells us that Dexter hasn't checked it in a few days. I can disable it. And also, we can link to Dexter's computer, so we can see his plans and stuff!"

"No way!" Dalia said.

"Way," Alexis said.

"Can you get us on?" Chidi asked.

"Yes," Alexis said, fiddling with the keys. "Perfect. We're on. Okay, boring files, where's his email? Perfect. We're in his Inbox. Let's see. What about . . ."

"Why don't you look at his notes?" Dalia suggested.

"Great idea. Let's see . . . remember to follow Chidi, Alexis, and Laura. Whoa. That's the one we're looking for. Why don't you text Mom, Chidi?"

"'Kay. Message sent. See if there's anything else. Has he sent any emails about the subject lately?"

"No, he hasn't. But . . ." Alexis punched in a few keys. "Whoa! This is a top-secret file. You need top-secret passwords and a username. Let's see, what about . . . Dexter?"

The machine buzzed. "Nope. Uh . . ."

"What about Dexterlicous?" Dalia joked.

Chidi laughed, but Alexis frowned and tried every username she could think of.

"If only we knew his full name!" Chidi said, exasperated.

"It's Dexter William Graham!" Alexis remembered, typing fast. "Yes! That's the username, what's the password?"

"What do you know about Dexter?" Chidi demanded, turning towards Dalia.

"He's always talking about zucchini. Weird, right?"

"It's zucchini!" Alexis cried. "Chidi, remember what Layla said? It has to be Zuincchi1s-3pic!"

Chidi's eyes widened. "YES!"

"Zoo-keenie ones three pic?" Dalia repeated.

"Yes, let's go!" Alexis dug through the file. "I'll come back later. This is going to take *forever*."

Chapter Seven

CONFRONTATION

"Are you kidding me?" Dalia asked. "I've known you guys for three hours and I already know that you just moved in with your aunt, you are being hunted down, *and* that a bad guy is after you? Is this all a joke? Are you in on a practical joke?"

"No, this is real. But I really wish it wasn't," Alexis replied as she rolled her eyes.

"This is so . . . insane! How am I supposed to believe a word you say? And I still have no proof that what you said is true!" Dalia cried.

"Dalia, don't be so dramatic! And you should believe us, we're not liars. And we haven't lied to you before!"

"What about when you didn't tell me that you were on the run from Dexter and Layla?"

"That wasn't a lie! That was just withholding information from a stranger."

"You think I'm a stranger? You guys are making—"

Knock, knock, knock. Bang, bang, bang!

Chidi flew down the stairs. Bella was standing on the porch.

"Hey, I just wanted to invite you and Alexis over to my house for dinner. I'm really sorry for being rude."

"Uh, thanks. We can come, I think."

"Great! Hope you like four cheese ravioli!"

"What was that?" Alexis asked, coming down the stairs.

"It was Bella. We're going to her house for dinner. We're having, uh, I think she said four cheese ravioli?"

"I wouldn't trust Bella," Dalia said. "She isn't exactly trustworthy. She's lied to me countless times."

"I know. But we have to go. We need to find out why she wants us to come over."

"Fine. But I don't trust her. She's acting way too nice," Dalia warned.

"We'll get going. Come with us, Dalia," Chidi said as she filled her green and white backpack with a bit of candy, some water bottles, granola bars, and other random supplies.

Then Alexis snatched her blue and green backpack and filled it with the cell phone and practically everything Chidi had, except that she added a small bundle containing her top-secret gadget that allowed her to hook up to any tech. "Never know if we'll need to escape," she said to herself.

"Whatever," Dalia said. "I'll join in on Operation Four Cheese Ravioli."

....

5:45 P.M.

"Hi, guys!" Bella greeted. "Come on in."

The trio walked into the living room.

"This is my mother, Mrs. Abigail Graham. Mom, these are Chidi and Alexis!"

Abigail Graham had chocolate brown hair and ice-blue eyes. Her hair was up in a messy bun with a few locks framing her face. She was tall and slender.

"Uh, hi, Mrs. Graham. Remember me? Dalia?"

"Oh, right! Bella tells us all about you!"

"All good things, I hope?" Dalia asked nervously.

"Um, sort of. Thank you for coming! The ravioli is almost finished. Mr. Graham is almost here. Why don't you show the guests the backyard?"

"Sure!"

The girls walked towards the backyard, skeptically surveying the rooms as they passed.

"ROAR!"

"AHH!" Dalia screamed. The other three stood staring at her.

"Um, really? With guests over? Ugh, you are so hopeless, Rankic!" Bella said to a boy, standing in the doorway of a room.

"Come on! Girls scream so much! You are no fun. Oh, hi random people I don't know. *Pardon my rudeness, your highness,*" he said, making an overdramatic bow to Bella.

"Come on, guys," Bella growled. The Graham's backyard was full of little kid toys.

"Those are my little cousin's toys."

A little girl toddled over.

"Well, hello!" Alexis said, crouching down.

"That's April."

"Benna!" April squealed, latching herself onto Bella's leg. "Did you find da bad girls? Do you want me da help? I can found—"

"Find," Bella corrected.

"—Find them. Dats what I said. *Find,*" April finished pointedly.

"Whoa, *bad girls?* What girls?" Chidi asked as she and Alexis locked eyes.

"Um, I don't know what she's talking about! April, where did you hear anyone say *anything* about bad girls?"

"You said dat! You said you get da bad girls for your daddy."

"Uh, What are you talking about? I never said that!" Bella resonated unconvincingly.

"Yeah, you did, Benna! You said dat I could help you get them! I found them and get them!"

"Okay, *enough.* Let's go see if dinner is ready. Man, I'm starving."

"Girls! Come in for dinner!" Mrs. Graham called.

"Yes! Right on cue!" Bella cheered.

During the conversation between April and Bella, Chidi and Alexis' worries had continued to grow.

"Yay! Dinner's ready! Dum de do ba ba," April hummed as she walked toward the house.

"Yum! Mom, your four cheese ravioli is so good!" Bella said.

"Four cheese ravioli? How dare you! Why would you possibly say that? I'm making *five* cheese ravioli!"

"Okay, by the way, who's your—" Alexis stopped cold when she looked up and into the house.

"—dad."

"Welcome. How do you do, Alexis? Chidi?" a tall, pale, black-haired man asked.

"Been better, Dexter. Why are *you* here?"

"This is our house. We're staying with my brother-in-law."

"You should wash your hands." Mrs. Graham smiled.

Dexter looked like a mostly average person except for one distinguishing feature. His skin. He was tall, skinny, and very, *very* pale. His eyes had a smirkish squint to them, but they looked like they could have had a softer side to them.

As soon as Dalia, Alexis, and Chidi were in the bathroom, Dalia exclaimed, "That's Dexter? I thought he was Snow White's evil brother."

"He does look a lot like Snow White, you're not wrong," Chidi said.

"This is no time for jokes! This was all a trick, just to get us right under his long nose! There is no way we are getting out of this!" Alexis was starting to panic.

"Oh, what have you two gotten me into?" Dalia muttered under her breath.

After the girls decided there was no point in hiding in the bathroom, they reluctantly, and slowly, walked down the hall. The dining room was large and mostly empty, except for the big, round table in the center.

"So. I see that you are the two girls that Dex was looking for. Please, take a seat, make yourselves . . . *comfortable*," Mrs. Graham said, sounding as if it pained her to say it. The friends all sat quietly down and stared at Dexter.

"Well. I have been looking for you two for a long, long, *long* time. Now then, please enjoy your food. I hope I don't make you . . . *uncomfortable*. We will get to business after we have eaten. Alright, *bon appetit,* you must eat," Dexter said.

That must be the signal to eat, I guess. Chidi thought. *Man, our lives have changed in the last few weeks.*

The whole family ate in silence, no one spoke a word. Even April seemed like she had tape over her mouth. After everyone was finished, Bella beckoned Chidi and Alexis to come sit on the couch.

"Now for *business.* I need you two to come with me. I am sorry, but I need to give you to my boss. He needs you for something, not that I care, but I want you to come without a fuss. If you make this hard for me I will be forced to do something . . . *rash,*" Dexter finished as he sat on the couch. "As for you, Dalia, you know too much already. I would *hate* to hurt anyone unnecessarily, *but I will.*"

"DAD! This was not part of the deal! You said I brought them here and you took what you needed, then let them *GO!*" Bella yelled. "BELLA! QUIET!" Dexter yelled back. Bella shrunk back into the corner of the couch. "Bella's actions have changed my mind. Dear, bring them to the basement."

Chapter Eight

THE BASEMENT
(OF DOOM)

The girls struggled as they were led down a dark stairway, their arms pinned, useless, by Dexter and Abigail Graham.

"Mom! Stop! Help!" Bella shrieked as she fought against her mother.

"She's your *daughter!*" Chidi cried. She felt a pang of homesickness. "Shouldn't you take care of her?"

Mrs. Graham stared at Chidi with disbelief. "I will do what my husband tells me! And you will tell me NO DIFFERENT!" she thundered. She shoved harder and they tumbled into darkness.

Dalia kicked Mrs. Graham and ran up the stairs.

"I'll be back!" she yelled to her friends. The door shut and the twins disappeared into darkness. Dalia ran as fast as she could out the front door, pushing and shoving her way out.

"GET BACK HERE!" Dexter yelled.

Dalia's mind was working like crazy, calculating how to find help and get back in time to save her friends.

"Think, Dalia, think!" she urged herself. She instinctively started running towards her house but quickly changed direction, heading for the twins' house instead.

Okay, maybe their pets can understand and help me? Do they understand anything? Dalia wondered.

"Hi, Ms. Kerifly. Can I borrow Tumbles, Ginger, Redd, and Oreo? I need to give them a little walk outside. Alexis said we should!" she asked, faking confidence.

"Oh! Even the cat? Oh, forget that, sure! Go right ahead," Ms. Kerifly replied. "How was dinner?"

"It was great," she yelled, running up the stairs. *I totally did not lie just now. Nuh-uh,* Dalia thought. *Oh boy . . .*

"Heeey, guys I hope you understand what I'm saying, but if you don't I need your help anyway. Chidi, Bella, and Alexis have been captured by an evil psychopath and his family. I need your help raiding the house and getting them back."

Oreo stared, seemingly emotionless, while Ginger and Tumbles seemed to gasp.

"Oh," Oreo said.

"Let's go!" Tumbles cheered.

"Mhm." That was Redd.

"All right, let's get Alexis and Chidi. But that Bella girl can stay in that place, for all I care," Ginger meowed.

All that Dalia heard was a chorus of barking, purring, and chirping.

"I'm not sure if that was a yes, but let's go anyway!" *And now I am hoping I am not insane, trying to deal with this myself instead of calling the cops. I CAN SO DO THIS. I know I'm not going to mess this up. Sure, I have no idea these animals can understand me, but I'm sure that they aren't going to doom us. Right?*

All the pets ran down the stairs with Dalia at the head.

"Good bye—" Dalia was already out the door and running to help the twins. *Please be there in time, come ON legs! Move FASTER!*

She skidded to a halt in front of the house and started to jiggle the handle of the door.

"ARGH! The door is locked!" Dalia muttered. Ginger purred a silly sound and stuck her claws in the old lock in the door.

Click!

The door unlocked, and Ginger pulled her claws out of the lock.

Ginger meowed and backed away. Shoving open the door, Dalia rushed in and started for the basement. She saw no one and stepped down into the basement. "Shh!" she whispered to her gang. She tiptoed quietly down the stairs, reaching the button soundlessly. She opened the door at the bottom of the basement just enough to peer through and saw Dexter, rummaging through a case of medical supplies. She could see Chidi and Alexis laying flat on cots in the back of the dimly lit room, eyes closed and pinned back with thick black straps.

"Okay . . . where is that one syringe? Ha, I am gonna have to practice my evil laugh after this. There! Found it! Ugh, stop feeling bad!" he said to himself as he grabbed the syringe and started towards the cots.

"On three. One. Two. Three!" Dalia's voice grew into a shout as she kicked open the door, and the pets flooded through the doorway.

"Huh? Dogs? But—but—oh no," Dexter cried as the dogs and the cat clawed and scratched him. All the pets pinned him to the ground, and he lay there, helpless. "Now," Dalia said, putting her foot on his chest. "Tell me what you did to them, or else I will tell my army to tear you to PIECES!"

"Army? Heh, I would hardly call this an—CAAAAAAT!" Dexter screamed.

"Aww, this wittle kitty cat? Does it scare you? TOO BAD!" Dalia mocked him in a baby voice. She picked Ginger up and set her on his chest.

"Okay! Whatever you want! Just get this cat off me!" Dexter yelled. "It was only a tranquilizer dart! They should wake up soon."

Dalia had no idea that his hand was slowly sliding across the floor to where he had dropped the syringe. "Now, let's see . . . WHY IN THE WORLD DO YOU WANT TO CAPTURE THEM IN THE FIRST PLACE? DON'T YOU DARE LIE, OR THIS LITTLE KITTY IS GOING IN YOUR SHIRT!" she yelled, spitting in his face.

"Don't get too hasty, now," he said calmly. In one fluid motion, he grabbed the syringe off the floor, and poked the tip into Dalia's ankle.

"Ow!" she yelped as she fell off of Dexter, trying to reach the syringe. All the pets jumped in confusion and loosened their grip on Dexter. He sat upright and shoved the dogs out of the way. He slid on his stomach to Dalia and snatched the syringe off the floor. He dashed to the cots, stabbed the syringe into Chidi's arm, then began to extract blood.

"Stop that! Dogs, ATTACK!" Dalia yelled, pressing her finger to her ankle to stop the bleeding.

The dogs bounded off the floor and bit at his legs. Dexter ignored the pain, finished filling the syringe, and plugged it into a machine at the foot of the cot. The machine took the blood out of the syringe and fed it through a pipe.

"What did you do to her?" Dalia yelled, and dove at Dexter's leg. She hooked her right arm around his waist and her left around his knee. She twisted with all her might and slammed Dexter into the machine. Dexter's head fell right on one of the many levers, and he dropped to the ground, out cold.

"Phew! It's been a while since I did that. Now, what monstrous things have you done to my friends . . . ," Dalia said, wiping sweat from her forehead and walking over to examine the cots.

Man, looks like some kind of restraining device! If I push this button here . . . and pull this lever like so . . . there! The clamps holding the twins retracted, and Dalia waited for them to wake up.

I wonder where Bella and her brother are? Arg, why do I care? She almost had us killed! I hope she is not fussy about me being down here. She BETTER NOT BE. Dalia started to search the room, looking for possible human-sized cabinets. She walked up to a black steel closet, and opened the door. "What do we have here . . . B-Bella?" Dalia stuttered as she saw Bella and her brother huddled in the corner of the cabinet.

"Dalia? You came? For us?" Bella started hopefully.

"Not exactly . . ." Dalia cut in. "But, even though your dad is an evil psychopath, I guess it's not your fault." Dalia smiled, and held out her hand.

"R-r-really? Are you sure? It's okay if you never forgive me, but thank you so much," Bella replied as she grabbed Dalia's hand, lifted herself off the floor, and dragged her brother behind her.

"Hey, Dail girl, thanks for helping us. And thank you for understanding," the boy said. "By the way, my name's Rankic, Call me Raggy. Oh, and Mom left like five minutes ago."

"Right. Name's Dalia, not Dail, by the way. Nice to meet you, Raggy." Dalia shook his hand.

"WHAT IN THE WORLD IS HAPPENING? WHY ARE WE IN A LABORATORY FILLED WITH SYRINGES AND TUBES AND RANDOM PEOPLE I'VE NEVER MET?" Alexis yelled as she sat up, and looked around like there was a flying gazelle in the room.

"Hey, welcome back!" Dalia exclaimed, laughing.

"I am so, so, so, so, so, so, so, sooooo—" Bella began.

"Yeah, cool it, girl. I get it. You're sorry. And I have no idea if I will ever accept your apology," Alexis interrupted Bella coldly.

"Let's get Chidi out of here, and discuss this *above ground*," Dalia cut in before Alexis could launch another verbal attack.

"Right," they all agreed. Raggy piggy-backed Chidi up the stairs and out to the beach.

"So. Glad. The. Beach. Is. So. Close," Raggy panted and set Chidi down on the sand.

"Hey, Dalia, can you *please* fill me in on why our pets are here and how in the world you saved us?" Alexis asked pointedly

"Ah, my little army is just what I needed," Dalia began. She told the whole story from start to finish as they rested on the beach.

"So, that walking octopus, Dexter . . . STABBED MY SISTER?" Alexis' outburst was just enough to wake Chidi.

"Arg . . . stooop," Chidi mumbled.

"Hey, let me handle this." Raggy walked over and glared at Chidi. "Hey, Chidi. We are all on the beach, and you need to WAKE UP NOW!"

"Huh? GET OFF!" Chidi yelled and socked Raggy in the gut.

"Owwww!" he complained. "You're stronger than you look!"

"Oh, sorry. Wait, who am I apologizing to and—MY GOODNESS YOU'RE ALL ALIVE."

Chidi grabbed Alexis into a hug. Alexis' face turned red from lack of air as her sister squeezed her tightly.

"Yup. All working and fully functional!" Alexis said breathlessly. "Well, kind of."

"Man, so glad. Goodness, my arm . . . ," Chidi said, hugging her arm close to her body. Ginger meowed and scooted onto her lap.

"Hey y'all, I have a hunch. I think my dad took Chidi's blood because it took some of her magic with it. I suppose he hoped he could use it for his own ends," Bella suggested.

"You mean both of your ends . . ." Chidi muttered.

"Wait, Chidi and Alexis have MAGIC?" Dalia exclaimed. "Man, I've known you guys less than a day, and I know that you guys have bad guys tracking you, parents who ship you off, AND magic powers? How many more secrets does your family have?"

"One. The power that we have, or at least that we know that we have, is that we can talk to animals. That's pretty much all that we know," Alexis told her friend.

Chidi turned to Bella with a scowl on her face. "I can't believe you would invite us to your house as if you were sorry, just to turn us in to your father so he could stab us with syringes and try to kidnap us!"

"Hey! I had no intention of helping him! If he is my dad, so what?" Bella cried "I can't believe you still don't trust me!"

"Sorry, Bella, but I kinda have to agree with them. We kinda lured them into coming to our house. We kinda are to blame," Raggy said, frowning.

"Okay, okay! Sorry. I didn't know he was going to capture you guys! Or that he was going to capture his own kids!"

"All right, sorry. That was a little bit harsh," Chidi said, then stoked Ginger's head.

"You said that Dexter took some of Chidi's blood, right?" Alexis asked.

"Yes."

"Maybe that extracted . . ."

"Some of her magic!" Dalia and Alexis said in unison.

"I JUST SAID THAT!" Bella exclaimed.

Okay, so if Chidi lost some of her magic, can she still talk to Ginger, Tumbles, and Redd? Alexis wondered.

As if reading her thoughts, Ginger asked, "Chidi, can you understand me?"

"Can I *what?*" Chidi asked.

"Wait. Maybe only some of the magic is gone. Chidi can half-understand our pets. Think of it like this: a person who just learned Spanish or French or whatever won't understand everything someone says in that language. So Chidi can only understand some things that they say."

"Oh!"

"Oh, yeah, the thing I've been SAYING FROM THE BEGINNING!"

"Okay, Bella, we get it."

So I'm only half magic? Chidi wondered.

"So, you're basically saying that Chidi is only, like, kinda magical?" Raggy said.

"Duh!" Bella muttered under her breath.

"Sorry! It's hard to keep up with you girls. You talk too much!"

"HEY!" Bella and Dalia yelled. Bella gave a small smile, which Dalia ignored and turned away.

"We've got to find a way to get Chidi's magic back," Alexis said, helping her twin stand up.

"Yep," Dalia said.

"No offense," Bella said, "but why does Chidi need her magic back? I mean, she's partially magic, right? Why does she need it ALL?"

"Chidi needs her magic back because without it, she's in pain!" Alexis retorted.

"And we need something to keep us from killing each other," Dalia added.

"I CAN'T BELIEVE DEXTER STOLE MY SISTER'S MAGIC!" Alexis screamed, hoping other people wouldn't hear. "We have to find a way to get her magic back!"

"Um . . . what's going on?" Dalia exclaimed as a bright violet light flew through and around Alexis.

"Cool!" Alexis chimed. She poked her head through the sparkle and—

"I feel like it's—calling me . . . ," she started.

"Alexis Blaze Parris, don't you *dare* do that!" Chidi cried.

Alexis turned and held her sister's gaze. "I *need* to. You'll be okay without me. I . . . can't stay. I need answers."

With that, she leapt through the portal and disappeared as the pets and friends were sucked in closely behind.

Chapter Nine

RAINBOWS AND UNICORNS, YUCK

"What just happened?" Alexis asked as they landed on a solid rainbow.

"I have no idea!" Chidi replied, just as startled. The group had brought a ton of sand with them from the beach as well.

Alexis spat out sand. "This is *disgusting.*"

"So, where are we?" Chidi asked, "And how did we get here? I thought Alexis was the only one who jumped in?"

Bella and Raggy nodded. "We didn't do anything!"

"Um, hello, unicorns?" Ginger meowed.

As a horned-horse was seen trotting in the distance, Alexis said, "I'm pretty sure, based on the rainbows and unicorns, we're in a magic world."

"Cool!" Bella said. "They're so pretty!"

"Creepy," Redd tweeted, perched on Alexis' shoulder.

"Couldn't agree more," Alexis said.

"Can't agree to what?" Chidi asked, not understanding Redd's chirps.

"It's creepy," Alexis explained.

"OH!" Dalia said. "What if Alexis tells us what Redd, Tumbles, Ginger, and Oreo tell us!"

"Oreo?" Raggy said, laughing. "OREO?"

"Yes. My brother gave him to me, and he was *already* named Oreo, thank you very much."

The dalmatian gave him a wounded look.

"Sorry about Raggy," Bella apologized.

"Who's your brother?" Raggy asked Dalia. "You have one, right?"

"His name is Nat. Nat Monroe," she replied.

"So, how do we find out how to get Chidi's magic back?" Alexis asked. "You know, now that we're stuck here."

"Um, isn't Aunt Jenny going to worry about us being gone?" Chidi asked.

"Maybe. But at least we can talk to her," Alexis said.

"How?" Bella, Raggy, Ginger, Tumbles, and Redd chorused.

"I hooked up our cell phone to Aunt Jenny's tech. Now I can control her phone, computer, camera, everything. Cool, huh? Oh wait. No signal."

"ALEXIS!" Chidi scolded.

"What? I did it with our house! If I'm going to live with my aunt, who, by the way, I didn't know existed until three days ago, I'm going to learn everything I can about her!"

Dalia sighed and shook her head.

Two unicorns approached them, both overly sparkly and far too fancy looking.

"Really?" Tumbles growled.

"Why, *hello* there," the unicorn greeted them. "I couldn't help but *notice* that you seem to be *lost*. Can I *help* you?" She tossed her green-and-pink mane.

"Yeah. You can help me by being quiet," Raggy muttered.

"*Excuse* me," the unicorn said.

"Miss—" another unicorn said, trotting up. "Ignore them. Two leggers." She shook her mane with disgust.

"Sorry, Miss?" Redd cheeped. "What's your name?"

"*Missy*. Miss *Missy* McMission *Missihorn*. So, *what* brings *you* here?" Missy asked.

"We need to find a place here that will restore my sister's magic," Alexis said.

"Oh, so you're looking for magic," the other one said, who was orange, yellow, and pink. She lifted her head.

"Uh, yeah!" Dalia said. "We just said that!"

"I'm Nasha. I can help you. I know where you need to go. Come with me, and you'll be fine."

"Just give us a moment to confer," Chidi said.

"What's up?" Raggy said.

"We just met talking unicorns! This is the best day of my life!" Bella giggled.

"No, we just met talking unicorns, this is the *worst* day of my life," Alexis corrected.

"I agree!" Ginger purred.

"Personally," Redd said, "I think we should follow them, but be careful. We don't know what they're up to."

"Alexis?" Dalia asked, pointing to Redd.

"We should follow them but be careful," Alexis said.

"Good idea," Chidi said, "They're *unicorns*, for Pete's sake."

"Unicorns are pretty!" Bella protested.

"No, they're untrustworthy strangers. But if we're going to follow them, we need some sort of an escape plan. You know, a way to get back here."

"Good idea, Dalia. What if we leave a trail?" Chidi said.

"Everybody, look for something you can use to leave a trail," Bella said. "Anybody have breadcrumbs?"

"I want breadcrumbs!" Redd tweeted.

"I have some food in here," Chidi said, motioning to her and Alexis' backpacks. "Maybe that can help us."

"Oh! You have that cool pen I gave you, right?" Alexis asked, digging into her pack.

"Oh! Right!" Chidi said. Then, to Bella, Dalia, and Raggy, she added, "it's called a 3-D pen. You can draw stuff and it becomes plastic. But I can do it wirelessly. But the point is, we can use it to set a trail! It'll work on trees and stuff!"

"Okay, whatever," Oreo woofed, drooping his tail.

"Pardon *me*, but are *you* going to *accompany* me and my *friend* Nasha? We will be *departing* soon. Thank you."

"Uh, Missy? We'll be coming. We'll stay behind you guys."

After Missy nodded, Alexis took the wireless 3-D pen from Chidi's hand. Every tree they went by, Alexis printed a plain arrow.

"Here we are!" Nasha announced. They were in front of a pile of dirt.

"Wow, I'm so impressed," Raggy remarked sarcastically. "I have never, ever seen dust before."

"Oh, don't *fret*. Nasha *knows* what she's *doing*," Missy said.

"These unicorns are annoying, right?" Raggy quietly asked Chidi.

"Like, duh," Ginger hissed. "They're weird."

"Oh, no. You don't understand. We travel *underground* now," Nasha said, dipping her sparkly mane.

"Um . . . how do we get down there?" Raggy asked.

Nasha laughed pitifully. "We dig."

Chapter Ten

DIG, DIG, DIG

This is so cool! Bella thought, scraping at the dirt with her hands.

"Why'd we even do this?" Alexis said, drawing an arrow on the ground to show the path.

"Because some gal just *had* to get *super* angry, and make the light teleport us here!" Chidi huffed.

"You teleported here?" Missy asked, suddenly stopping.

"Um, yes? We live on planet Earth, where there are no random unicorns or sparkly rainbows or complete weirdos!" Chidi snapped.

"Whoa, whoa. We are not 'complete weirdos,'" Nasha said. "Not even close. But you opened a portal? You're half Candyopolin, then!"

"What *is* Candyopolin?" Bella asked giddily.

"It's the place we've just arrived in," Nasha said from behind the children. She had Dalia dig in front, followed by Alexis, then Chidi, Bella, Raggy, then Missy. Nasha was in back to "supervise."

"Hey, what's this?" Dalia asked, cringing as her hand hit a sheet of metal.

"You have to knock in a special pattern," Nasha instructed. "Dun-dun-dun-dun, dun-dun!"

"Uh, whatever."

After she knocked, the sheet of metal that Dalia's hand had hit lowered.

"Now GO!" Nasha yelled. Missy butted her head against Raggy, who shoved Bella accidentally. The dominos continued to fall until Alexis plunged down.

"Looks as if we don't have a choice," Dalia said, and, with the pets, slid down the sheet of metal.

Chidi listened to the screams of Dalia—after all, peering down the slide, there *was* a huge drop—at least fifty feet. Bella slipped and slid her way down.

Raggy gazed at Chidi in awe as she got ready. "How can you just dive down there with no hesitation?"

She shrugged. "It's just the way it is. I've been through worse."

....

7:45 P.M.

They landed in a large meadow. There was vibrant green grass. Alexis bent down to inspect it, shocked when she realized they were emeralds.

There were flowers all over, made of more multicolored jewels. Alexis selected an opal flower, with a piece of amber set in the middle, with sparkling diamonds as drops of dew and slipped it into her pocket.

She glanced around. The trees were odd, with a bronze trunk and branches, while the leaves were made of silver, gold, and rose gold, while the fruits on them were obviously real.

"Where *are* we?" Raggy breathed, sweeping his shaggy brown hair off his forehead.

"*Obviously*, we're in Candyopolis!" Exclaimed Missy.

"OKAY, so WHY are WE here?" Raggy said, imitating Missy.

"*Excuse* me, young *man, are* you *mocking* me?"

"Of *course* not, *Missy.*"

"Harrumph."

"Stop it. I have a compass. We can use that," Chidi said, unzipping her pack. "Wait, what?" Her compass had changed to a round map, with five names—Candyopolis, The Golden Lands, The Mist Lands, The Dragon Realm, and Marina.

"Oh, so are you not *familiar* with the other *realms?*" Missy asked, eyeing them with suspicion.

"Other realms? Chidi, are you—Chidi? Where are you?" Alexis called.

"I'm . . . I'm right here!" As the group turned around, they saw Chidi sitting atop a scaly, reptilian horse, a look of trepidation on her face. "I was looking around, and I tripped off a small ledge and fell onto it . . . a little help, please?"

"My paws!" Ginger cried.

"We leave you alone for one minute!" Alexis huffed.

"What?" Dalia said, staring weakly. No one said a word, even the unicorns just stared.

"Nothing even surprises me anymore!" Raggy said, turning around and almost running into Nasha, who seemed to have doubled in size.

"Step back *children! This* girl is *dangerous!*" Missy snorted.

"What do you—" Chidi started, but the reptilian horse started to shake, making a clinking, rattling noise.

"Chidi! Get off that thing!" Bella yelled.

"I c-can't! I'm s-stuck!" Chidi froze, seemingly emotionless.

"*Charge!*" Missy yelled and ran at the scaly horse, horn first.

Nasha did as well, and her glistening, sharp horn stabbed the creature in the neck.

Nasha and Missy's horns looked to have impaled the horse, but it stepped back, its scales closing the wound. It turned around and started galloping towards a forest.

"Chidi," Alexis called "Come back!"

"*Now* then. *You* four will come with *us,* for *questioning,* and *cupcakes.*" Missy sniffed.

"Wait, questioning? Let *us* ask *you* a question first!" Raggy said, glaring at Missy.

"How did you get *so big?*"

"It is called magic. Magic is how we made Candyopolis! It is the most important part of our world!" Nasha neighed.

"Come now, children of the Black Orb, and let us detain you."

"Wait! Bla—" Dalia suddenly fell asleep, as did the rest.

Chapter Eleven

A LEGEND, A JAILER, AND A CUPCAKE

The foursome awoke in a large ballroom—surrounded by unicorns!

"*These* are the *children* of the darkness?" wheezed a unicorn in a vest. All around them unicorns and pixies were murmuring and whispering, looking worriedly at the kids.

"*What in the world? Chains? Really?*" Alexis whispered.   "*So* sorry for the . . . *rough* detainment. The *Unicourt really* doesn't like taking *chances*." Missy was standing behind them, her horn aglow.

"Let—us—go!" Bella yelled as she struggled against the chains.

"I am afraid not." A black and light gray unicorn stepped up to a pulpit.

"Now then. Tell us! The Black Orb! Where is it? Tell me!" she whinnied. "Tell me now!"

"Black Orb? Sorry, not gonna happen," Raggy replied coolly.

"What? Why?"

"Because . . ."

The whole court held their breath.

"We have absolutely *no idea* where it is, or . . . what in astrophysics you are talking about. So there."

The unicorn at the pulpit gasped.

"Take the boy away! HE *insults* the COURT!" Missy cried, pointing her sparkly horn at Rankic.

Three shaggy, brown unicorns with long ears, touched Raggy with their horns, and his chains clanked to the ground.

"Hey! Thank—whoa!" Raggy was lifted from the ground with telekinesis and soon disappeared from the room.

"Wait!" Dalia said. "Can you answer one thing for me, Miss?"

"*What are you doing?*" Bella hissed.

"*Trust me, Bella,*" Dalia whispered, and looked Bella in the eyes.

"Yes? What is it? Oh, and call me Jacky. Miss Jacky."

The unicorn sniffed.

"Miss Jacky, I'm new to this—uh—realm, and—"

"Get to the *point!*" Jacky pointed her horn at Dalia.

"R-right! We saw a greenish-blue scaly horse, and it took our friend! What was that?"

"You saw an Emerald-Scale Redemptor? What happened to your *friend?*" Jacky snorted.

"She . . . she . . ."

"She seemed to fall asleep with her eyes open?" Bella suggested.

"Fall asleep? In which direction did the Emerald-Scale go?" Jacky snorted

"The 'Redemptor' or whatever took my sister—" Alexis got cut off by Miss Jacky.

"THE GIRL WAS YOUR SISTER?"

All of the unicorns gasped at Jacky's outburst.

"Um, yes?" Alexis tilted her head.

"TAKE THEM ALL AWAY!" Jacky neighed. "I need a cupcake . . . sorry, children. It's nothing personal. It's just business. *Unicorn* business."

"Yes, ma'am," the brown unicorns said and used magic to pick up the girls, the same telekinesis that Raggy had been lifted with.

"Put us down! W-whoa!" Dalia yelled.

"Please be quiet and do not struggle," one of the shaggy unicorns said in a monotone voice.

"*Fine*," Bella huffed.

The unicorns put the girls down in separate pitch-black rooms with tiny pink stained glass windows.

When the unicorns left, Bella called, "Guys? Are you okay? Raggy? Are you there?"

"I'm up here! Look through the window!" Raggy called. "Up here!"

The girls looked through the small windows, and saw Raggy, hanging in a large bird-cage from the roof.

"Those stinky unicorns put me up here because I disrespected the judge or whatever nonsense!" Raggy laughed and asked, "How did you end up down here?"

"Well, some LOUD-MOUTH told Miss Stinky-horn that Chidi was Alexis' sister!" Dalia shouted. "And it was OBVIOUS that those horn-horses DO NOT LIKE HER!"

"Hey! I was telling her the truth! Don't be so rash!" Alexis shot back.

"*But those unicorns are so pretty . . . ,*" Bella whispered.

"So, you kids have come in contact with a Redemptor? *Or so I heard . . . ,*" an unknown voice declared. "*I am the jailer. My name is Autumn!*"

"Pixieeeee!" Bella squealed when she saw the little fairy- like creature.

"Yes, I'm a pixie. Whoa, you're a human! Whoop dee doodle do. Don't judge. It's not my fault."

Alexis, from her cell, studied the pixie. She had brown hair pulled up in a tight bun. Her eyes were blue and sparkled with excitement. She wore a dress like Tinker Bell's but in silver. She had an ice-colored hair band and matching ballet flats.

"Something seems familiar about you . . . ," Alexis pondered. "Nope, just a silly thought. Just like how I *had* to make the light go crazy. Like how I *had* to let Chidi out of my sight. Like how I HAD to tell those unicorns that I'm Chidi's sister! UGH! This is my fault! If I hadn't done this, Chidi wouldn't be in danger! NONE of us would be in danger!"

"Alexis—" Dalia started.

"This is all my fault! I should have never done this! I'm a terrible sister and a terrible friend! I—"

"ALEXIS!" Dalia yelled. "Autumn is going to help us escape! Stop laying everything on yourself! We need to get out of here and find Chidi!"

"Try to keep your voice down," Autumn muttered. "I'd rather *not* be caught."

"Um, Autumn, where are our pets?" Dalia asked. "I'm starting to worry..."

"Oh, do not worry! They are at the Hot Springs Of Elizabeth Sparkemane the First right now!" she stated in a heroic voice.

"*Thank goodness . . . ,*" Alexis sighed. "Miss Autumn? What is the Black Orb?"

"Well, the Unicourt, the court of unicorns, hehe! Well, they thought that you guys came from something called the Black Orb, or the Ebony Sphere, stop me, I have more . . . *any*way, the Orb is a ball made from a substance that, when it comes in contact with you, can *pretty much* make you evil. And they thought that, since you came from 'another dimension' you still have sanity and are trying to tell them the location of the Sphere."

"Who cares, Twinky-wings! Just let us out already so we can find Chidi!" Raggy grumbled. "We don't even know what we are supposed to be telling the Judge-horn!"

"Twinky-wings, eh? That sounds like my great-great aunt's twice removed cousins' third granddaughters' great great great great grandma's name! *Four times removed,*" Autumn teased, dangling the keys in front of Raggy's cage.

"Wait!" Bella pleaded "Please, please, please tell us what a Redemptor is!"

"Awww! Humans are so cute when they are begging!" Autumn said, flying in front of Bella's cell.

"Well . . . why should I? Hehe!" Autumn laughed, holding her belly, and rolling on thin air.

"Why you—!" Raggy took a small pebble from the floor of his cage and threw it at the pixie.

"Ow! Okay! Okay! I'll tell you! Sheesh!" the fairy grumbled, rubbing her arm, where the rock had landed. "Well, Redemptors have roamed ever since Malcora spied on Marina—and don't ask, that's a tale for another time. Well, at that time, Dragons were ferocious, the Unicorn Empire had an army, and the Pixies had their own government . . . genetically speaking.

"Redemptors were a hybrid, a bridge between Dragon-kind, and Unicorns. They had the unusual power of Freezing. Freezing is what it does when it finds a suitable rider. When the beast finds the rider, it is usually someone of royal blood, and—CUPCAKES!"

A heavenly smell wafted into the prison, and Autumn took off at top speed out the door.

"What was that?" Dalia questioned. "Oh, man! That smells so good! I didn't even get to finish my ravioli earlier!"

Bella leaned her head against the window, contemplating trying to break it.

"Hrf! Curpkics!" Autumn flitted into the room with a mouthful and platter of cupcakes. "Sorry, where are my manners? Have a cupcake, y'all."

She slid the treat through a little flap at the bottom of each of the prisoner's cells.

"One for you too, mister! *Even though you do not deserve it,*" she said as she flew up to Raggy's cage.

"Wow! These are so delicious! What flavor is this?" Alexis exclaimed.

"Magic! I am not kidding, it is literally a magic flavor!" Autumn giggled. "Sorry I rushed out on you! Now, where was I? Oh, yes! Freezing! So, if you are unlucky enough to be a suitable mount, and you actually find a Redemptor, it will use telepathy and tell you to mount it." She took a bite of her cupcake and continued.

"If you do, it will put a spell on you, making you unable to move until it wants you to. We still have not figured out how to reverse the effect without a Redemptor. Does that answer your question?" she finished. Even though no one answered, she said, "Good."

Autumn licked the frosting from her fingers and flitted out of the prison.

"Um, yeah I guess it does . . ." Alexis sank against the wall in her cell, fearing the worst for the pets and Chidi. "In a cell on our birthday . . ."

The group chatted for a little bit about what Alexis and Chidi were going to do for their special day, until—

"*Hello,* humans!" Missy trotted into the jail, her mane braided. "We will be *holding* your *trial* this *evening!* I would *suggest not* talking to that *repulsive fairy* anymore! She has been *found out* by our good friend *Nasha* Sparkehoof the *Eighth.*"

"Good *friend?* I *think* not!" Raggy shot back.

"Why, you are no longer going to need lessons in unicorn manners when I am done with you!" Missy snorted, pointing her horn at Rankic to lift him yet again.

"Let me down!" Raggy struggled as he floated in the air, and out the door.

. . . .

Meanwhile . . .

"Here you are, Ginger, Redd, and Tumbles," Nasha said, as the brown shaggy unicorns lowered the pets into a hot spring. "You're free from your evil masters."

As soon as the unicorns were gone, Redd hopped up.

"All right, troops! We're going to save Chidi, Alexis, Dalia, Bella, and Raggy! Chop-chop! Lickety-split! Let's go, let's go!" When Redd saw how everybody was still in the spring, he yelled, "Why aren't we going? We've gotta rescue Chidi!"

"Aye, aye, captain!" Tumbles yelped, bounding out in his playful way.

"Mmm. We just got here. Let's stay for a little bit," said Ginger, of course.

"GINGER!" Redd and Tumbles yelled.

Ginger leaped out of the water and meowed, "*WHAT?*"

"Get out! Don't you ever want to see Chidi again, or what?" Tumbles harrumphed. "I just wanna play with Alexis . ."

"I haven't known you guys for a long time, only like a few days," hissed Ginger.

"I know. So that's why we need to get going. GINGER!"

Ginger, as you might have guessed, had slipped away, playing in the warm water.

Redd flocked about, stretching his talons at Ginger.

"FINE! LET'S GO!" Ginger hissed. The pets started toward a large, lush forest. The oddest fact was that all of The Magical Realms were underground, but there was a never-ending sky, clouds, sun, moon, and stars.

"Well, Mr. Smarty-pants, where to? I am assuming you are leading us to fame and glory?" Ginger snickered, trying to look stoic and serious.

"The last time we saw Chidi she was heading to a forest like this, with that horse thing," Tumbles huffed. "So *yes*, fame and glory."

"Hey, guys? What is that?" Oreo woofed, as they came across a giant cave, going deep into the earth.

"A cave? Underground? Wow, this place makes no sense!" Redd cheeped, flying over to the entrance of the cave.

"Let's go in! Maybe we can find someone to help us in there!" Ginger purred, and ran to the dark tunnel, peering in. "Wow! There are gems down there! And little people!"

"Yeah, right! And we are not going down there! *I'm* the leader, remember?" Tumbles stated and shook his floppy ears.

"Oh, quit it! Just come look!"

"I'll . . . stay back here." Oreo stepped back and his tail drooped.

"Fine, just don't try anything, cat—hey! There is nothing down—AAH!" Ginger shoved Tumbles down into the inky blackness. "And *that* is for saying that you are the leader!"

She suddenly frowned, realizing that they now have to find help.

"Hey, now! Why did you do that?" Redd screeched.

....

2:45 A.M.

Tumbles tumbled down a steep incline, landing finally in a mud puddle.

"Ouch . . . why you!" He tried to climb back up, but his paws slipped, and he fell back down.

"AHH! Help! Can anyone hear me? I need help! Ginger! Redd! Oreo!"

Above him, Tumbles saw just the top of their heads.

"Help me get out!" Tumbles called.

"Um . . ." Oreo looked around. "I don't know how to. Maybe you can climb partway, and we can pull you up?"

Tumbles tried to climb but slipped down. "Nope." He frowned. "OH! Find Chidi, Alexis, Dalia, Bella, or Raggy! They can help me!"

"We won't leave you!" Redd cried.

"But you *have* to! After you find them, they'll help you! Redd, you can stay with me. But Ginger and Oreo, you have to find the others!"

"Oh, fine. I shouldn't have done that. Sorry, dog," Ginger said, and she actually looked sorry.

"Wait! Please don't leave me with her! She's mean!" Oreo complained.

Yeah, I don't blame you, Tumbles thought. "Just go and find help!" he called. "Hey, Redd, fly down here and explore with me!"

"Alright! Coming!" Redd's wingbeats echoed through the cavern, sounding like a hurricane.

"Let's go!" Redd chirped, and headed back into the cave. "Man, It's dark in here!"

"Yeah, I guess we could try—oh . . . wow!" Tumbles and Redd stumbled into a giant ravine, strewn with snow and Dragons perched on trees and in crevices.

A snow-white dragon with teal-blue wings waved a claw at them. "Bow, Bird. Dog." She tapped her claws against her golden necklace with a ruby set in the middle. She wore a matching tiara.

"Are you a—" Tumbles started, but stopped, and bowed with Redd.

"Now, *dog*, will you tell me what you are doing in my domain? I am Malcora, and you are not welcome here." The white dragon snarled.

"I am not 'Dog'—I am Tumbles! And we were just looking for my owner, Chidi!"

"Ah, your owner? A tall girl with black hair?" she replied and gave a purple dragon laying in a tree a wink.

"Y-yes, actually! Do you know her? Um—Miss Malcora?" Redd tweeted.

"Ha! Know her? I *have* her!" the dragon said, then whispered to a blue dragon, "Cue the evil laugh slash cliffhanger sound effects."

"DUN-DUN-DUN!"

"Mwah-ha-ha-ha-ha!" Two purple dragons made sound effects behind her.

Redd was covering his beak with his wing, trying not to laugh as Tumbles barked, "What did you do with her?"

"I did nothing to her! Xenex did!" Malcora beckoned to a figure standing in a crevice. The same horse thing that had taken Chidi stepped out and bowed its head to the dragon.

"You! Come closer and I'll tear you to pieces!" Tumbles growled.

"Come, now! You are guests, so no tearing and biting! Jerome, bring our visitors, and Xen to the Den."

Chapter Twelve

THE BAD GUYS

Wondering what happened to Dexter?

"AHH!" Dexter screamed. "Abigail, I was so close to getting those kids! I needed them! Bob's going to kill me!"

"Who's Bob, dear?" Mrs. Graham asked, putting the leftover *five* cheese ravioli in the refrigerator.

"He's my boss. Eh, I don't know what I should be doing. How can I get them?"

"Why don't you just tell him the truth, Dex?"

"The *truth?* I'm a bad guy! I can't tell the truth! I'm evil!"

"Well, then lie to him. If you can't tell him the truth, tell him the un-truth or don't tell him anything."

"Or . . . ," Dexter muttered. "I can tell him nothing! That's a great idea I just thought of."

"Yes, dear."

"I uh—need to get my things from the basement. And don't worry about Bella and Raggy, I'll find them." Dexter started toward the basement door. "Hey, make sure April is okay, would you? Thanks."

He stepped down the basement stairs and shut the door. "Now then. Time to make sure Mr. Bob got the dose . . ." He walked over to the computer sitting on the desk and punched in a few numbers. The screen crackled to life.

"Man, I need to get a new computer . . ." Dexter typed in the numbers 174-823-0837 and stepped back so the computer's video camera could see him.

"This is a pre-recorded message for Bob Brisket only. If you are not him, please ignore this. Hello, this is Dexter Graham, reporting from California. I was able to get a small dose of the blood needed, from target three. I have sent the syringe via tube transport and will arrive in HQ-Canada shortly. If you feel my *expertise* is needed elsewhere, please send a message via mail, via email, or via holo-mail. If not, I will continue my work pursuing targets one, two, and three. If a raise is needed, send it via check. Thank you."

The video ended, and Dexter shut the fizzing computer.

"Was that too many *via's?*" he muttered, walking towards the door. "Eh, better go check on April . . ."

....

In Canada, 11:00 A.M.

"Ah, finally! A report!" A short man walked up to a computer and opened a video message.

"Ha! Yes! Yes! Yes! Finally!" the man exclaimed. "Now for the dose!" He jogged and jiggled over to a machine that opened, revealing a medical syringe.

"Yes!" he cheered, as was his habit, and quickly punched a sequence of letters and numbers that looked something like this: Zuincchils-3pic.

"Commencing transfer . . . now for the tests! The media will scoff at me no longer! Haha!" He jiggled out of the room in joy.

"Xander! Get me Ophelia!" he shouted to a passing worker.

"Yes sir! Right away, Sir!" He dropped his clipboard and ran to the room at the end of a long corridor. The building, stationed in the highlands of Canada, was always cold, with its silver walls and silver floor. It was the only place that the man could find where he felt truly at home—and cold.

"Yes! Mr. Bob, Sir! What can I do for you?" A tall, lanky woman waltzed at top speed out of the end room, and joined the small man on his walk through the corridors.

"Oh, Ophelia, today is a great day! Dexter has *finally* succeeded! We have what we need to begin Project: ZUINCCHI!" The man laughed in delight. "Give the squid a raise!"

"Okay, Mr. Bob, Sir! We will send it to him right now!" the ever-stressed Ophilia scribbled something on her clipboard.

"Can we begin construction, Sir? And the tests?"

"Yes, yes, start them right away! All this excitement has made me hungry! Schedule my lunch break!"

....

In California, 12:00 A.M.

Where are the girls? Aunt Jenny wondered, peeking at her phone to see the fourteen unanswered calls she had made to try and contact the girls, plus multiple text messages. Eventually, she decided to call Laura.

"Hello, Jenny, is everything okay? Ben and I are at a 24 hour restaurant we found, we were so busy with the new house that we haven't eaten dinner. This was the only place open."

"Well, the girls went to the Grahams, and apparently, a man named Dexter lives there?"

"Dexter?" Laura cried. "Ben, Chidi, and Alexis are at Dexter's! We have to help them!"

"No, Laura," Ben interrupted. "If we go, we're just putting you in danger. And Jenny, too. And think of the girls! Jenny, are they alone?"

"No, they're with a neighbor named Dalia. They're all twelve. But I have to say, why don't you call them? It's their birthday, and you haven't said a single word to them!"

"Good idea, Jenny. I'm going to right now. Bye!"

"Okay. Oh, and—"

Beep, beep, beep.

"I don't believe it. She hung up! And I didn't even tell her that they're not responding to texts!" she gave an exasperated sigh, and started out the door.

Jenny was a tall, confident-looking young woman, with golden-brown hair. She usually wore black sneakers with a plaid shirt and jeans. She walked down the road and stopped at the Graham's house.

"Well, this is it . . . ," she said to herself, walking up to the front door. She knocked on the door and stepped back, waiting for a response.

The front door creaked open, and a blue-eyed, blonde-haired woman stepped onto the porch.

"Hello! Can I help you?" she asked, an awkward smile on her face.

"Actually, yes. I am Chidi and Alexis' aunt, Jenny. They came over for dinner a while ago, and I was wondering where they were?" Jenny returned the awkward look.

"Oh! Um . . . come on inside, they are, um . . . at the beach! By the way, I am Abigail. Nice to meet you, Jenny."

She stepped inside the house, beckoning for Jenny to follow. As they both sat down on the couch, Jenny asked, "At the beach, huh? They never came by to get swimsuits, and they are not returning my texts. I tried calling them, but—"

Bam! The basement door slammed open.

"Abigail!" a skinny man with jet black hair yelled, as he stepped up the stairs. "I just got a raise from Bob! I can't believe it! I guess convincing Bella to get Chidi and Alexis over here wasn't a bad idea after all!"

Jenny shot up and stepped away from the couple.

"What did you do to them? Where are they? And who *are* you people?"

"Looks like we have a guest?" Dexter said, looking at Abigail.

"I'm . . . I'm calling the police!" she whipped out her phone and started dialing 911.

"Hey! Stop!" he snatched the device out of her hands before she hit the last 1.

"Give—it!" She reached for her phone but tripped and fell back onto the couch.

"Now then! Why don't we sit and have a little chat, hm? Abby, make us some coffee, please."

Dexter plopped down on their couch and put his feet up on the ottoman.

Jenny eyed the door nervously as Dexter said, "The door is locked. Don't try it. Ooh, thanks!" He took a hot mug of coffee from his wife and smiled. "Alright . . . where to begin?"

Chapter Thirteen

A BIRTHDAY TREAT

In an ice prison, eating cold fish is not the ideal place to be on the day of your birthday. And yet, there she was, sitting on a freezing ice bench and eating with her hands. She heard the distant sound of a river, and she hoped with all her heart that Alexis would find her. Soon, a strange magma-scaled dragon clambered up to her icy prison.

"Hey! Kid, Her Majesty is requesting an audience with you in the Den. *Some odd dog and a bird stumbled into the Columns . . .*" the dragon trailed off.

Chidi bolted up from her bench, ran and slid to the front of the cell, and demanded he take her to them.

"Alright, missy. Follow me, and no shenanigans, okay?" He chained her to his black spear and started for the stairs.

As they walked by, Chidi could see other prisoners sitting in the back of their cells. One was even a dragon-like her captor, with back scales that had red, glowing veins running through them.

They walked through hall after hall, went up stair after stair, until they finally reached a golden-banded door. "Okay, in you go," he growled, as he unchained her from his spear.

"Can you take off my arm-and-leg chains? she asked innocently.

"No can do. Sorry, now *go.*" The dragon pushed open the door and shoved her inside. Chidi stumbled into the room and looked around for Tumbles and Redd. The room was spacious, with hard-wood flooring, a red velvet carpet, and four, giant chairs.

"Welcome. Please sit. I see we have found your friends, hmm?" Malcora breathed out a large plume of freezing smoke.

"Chidi! We were looking everywhere for you! Alexis is so worried, and—" Tumbles' yelping stopped suddenly.

"Oh wait, you can't understand us. Never mind . . ."

"Uh, what? Something about looking, and Alexis?" Chidi asked, then cringed. Malcora told Chidi what Tumbles had said and continued speaking.

"So, now that we are *acquainted*, I would like to know a few things. Do you know if you are of royal blood? Xenex here . . ." It was just then that Chidi realized that the creature she had mounted was standing next to Malcora's chair. "Tells me you have the scent of a Candyopolin Duchess."

"*What? Candy-what now? Duchess?*" Redd whispered to Tumbles, who was sitting on the chair with him.

"*I'm as confused as you are! Let's see what she says,*" Tumbles whispered back.

"I-I what? And you got *anything* out of that *thing*? The only thing he did was pick me up and run away with me!" Chidi retorted.

Malcora sighed another icy plume and said coldly, "Ah, you might not know it, but yes, I smell it on you too . . . the scent of the Candyopolins runs deep, and do you know what we do with the people with it?" A conniving smile grew on her face. "We DITCH them."

The dragons made their sound effects.

. . . .

Escape Time!

"Ugh . . ."

After three hours of waiting, Raggy finally floated through the door, looking completely exhausted.

"Now, stay *put,* and be *polite!*" Missy dropped him off, and trotted out the door.

"I was so worried! What did they do?" Bella exclaimed, as she ran to her cell window.

"Lessons . . . so. Many. *Lessons.* She was teaching me 'How To Be Polite and Proper' for *three hours!* It was like third grade math all over again!" He sat down on the floor of his cage and closed his eyes. "I'm—I'm gonna get some rest."

At around midnight, Alexis woke with a start. "Hm?"

"Hey! Alexis! Dalia!" a voice came from right outside the cells. "It's me! Autumn! I escaped, and I have the keys to the dungeon!"

"You came for us! Thank you! Now please let us out!" Dalia said nervously. "Before we get caught!"

"Okay, but promise me one thing first!" the fairy replied.

"What is it?" Raggy awoke with a start and was looking to escape as soon as possible.

"You have to promise that if you go looking for your sister, Chidi, that when you find her, you will bring her to me! I know a place that can restore her magic, but you have to bring me to Earth with you!"

"Bring you to Earth? Alright, we promise, now let's *go!*" Raggy whispered as loud as he could.

"Promise?" she said.

"Promise!" Dalia said.

"Okay, c'mon, the exit's this way!" she whispered as she unlocked the doors and their chains. "Follow."

The foursome followed her as silently as they could. They exited the dungeons and tiptoed across the courtroom floor.

"Keep following, I know a place where we can lay low for a little bit," Autumn said, as they exited the place and walked to a forest outside.

"Phew! That was scary! Thanks so much, Autumn!" Bella praised, "We couldn't have done it without you!"

"Aw! It was nothing! As long as you hold up your end of the barigan, we are still friends! Okay, y'all follow this path until you reach a small cottage. I'll catch up, but I have some business first." She motioned to a gravel path and gave them a wink.

"Don't worry, there's no one home. And good luck!" The fairy flew away.

"What kind of business do you think she was talking about?" Dalia asked as they walked along the path and through a forest with fall-colored leaves.

"I dunno . . . I just hope she stays safe! She rescued us!" Alexis replied, staring at the midnight sky.

"Hey, she was great and all, not that I didn't like her, but . . . do you think she was going back to snitches on us? Y'know, to *earn* her freedom by getting us back?" Raggy suggested.

"Hey! She wouldn't! Stop being so suspicious!" Bella protested. They kept walking in silence until they reached a clearing.

"Wow! What season is it?" Alexis exclaimed. The clearing was separated into four parts.

The first had dark clouds and was covered in snow, with large candy canes sticking out of the ground.

The next was covered in soft, green grass and lots of fresh, colorful flowers.

The third displayed a delightful array of colorful butterflies, a spring, with cool, running water, and sunbeams.

Finally, the fourth section showed a small cottage, with orange-brown grass, and fall trees.

"This place is amazing!" Dalia said, her eyes wide.

"I think this is the cottage! Wow, pick a season, any season!" Raggy joked. They walked to the cabin and opened the door.

"Unlocked, huh," Bella said. The interior had one set of fairy-sized bunk beds and a teeny little kitchen.

"Heh, regular exterior, fairy-sized interior!" Raggy snickered.

As Bella and Raggy started arguing, Dalia sat on the floor to rest, and Alexis went outside. She walked to the spring and sat at the edge of the water.

Chidi, where are you? Alexis wondered.

"Hey, Alexis?" Dalia said.

"What?" Alexis snapped.

"Whoa. I was just wondering if you could help me get Raggy and Bella to stop arguing, maybe?"

"Sure—sorry."

"But if she *did,* then why would she have let us out in the first place?" Bella yelled.

"*Guys!* Calm down! Stop arguing, and let's figure out how to get to Chidi!"

"Sorry, Alexis," Bella said, lowering her head.

"All right. Let's find the pets first. Then we can use their help to get Chidi. Remember, Ginger has those lock-picking claws. Now let's get *moving!*"

"But *why?*" Bella whined. "Why do we have to go *now?* I want to wait a little bit!"

"You need Ginger whining with you to make it effective. Let's take a vote. All in favor of leaving *NOW,* raise your hand," Alexis informed her friend.

Alexis, Dalia, and Raggy all raised their hands.

"*Fine!*" Bella grumbled. "Let's go."

Chapter Fourteen

DITCH = DUMPED IN THE CRAZY HOLE

"DITCH her! DITCH her!" the crowd of dragons cheered as they sat by a giant hole. It was surrounded by rows upon rows of colosseum benches, all filled with dragons. The Pit was in a super large cave, so no sound came out.

"Hello! Today's games will certainly be one for the record books! Please welcome, Chidi, of the 'Royal Candyopolins'! And, Maichi! The treasonous army commander of *my* army!" Malcora snarled. All the dragons in the crowd 'Boo'-ed when Chidi was announced. Chidi was standing on the edge of the pit, a green-brown dragon with wing binders standing across from her.

"Okay, Xenxex, Kako! Push them in! Two Redemptors walked to the prisoners and shoved them in the pit. "Let the games . . . BEGIN!" she roared.

"Aaaah—ugh!" Chidi yelled as she hit rock bottom. "What the—what—am—I—supposed to—do?" she yelled as she dove to the side, dodging the green dragon's tail as it whipped around.

"Be quiet and let me destroy you!" Maichi snarled.

"What? No!" Chidi dove to the side again, this time barely dodging his claws.

"Fight! Fight! Fight!" the dragons roared, and Malcora threw a sickle into the ditch. "Eliminate your opponent!"

Chidi grabbed the weapon, sweat running down her face. When he lunged again, Chidi stepped to the side and scraped Maichi's side with the edge of the blade.

"Ah!" Maichi fell to his side, and Chidi ran toward him, thinking, *it's him or me!* He tried flying out of the pit, but with his wings bound, he fell back down.

"Sorry!" Chidi yelled and caught his tail in the hook of the blade.

"Gah! Stop! Please! Stop!" Maichi begged. "Let me out!"

"Finish him!" Malcora roared, but Chidi did nothing. *He is a prisoner just like me,* she thought.

"Guards! Bring him to me," Malcora snarled. Her two sound-effect dragons flew down and grabbed Maichi. They flew him to Malcora, and she said,

"Treason is unacceptable. You know that better than anyone, hm? Well, I have a nice, cold cell waiting for you once you thaw out." Malcora opened her jaws, and a beam of below-freezing ice came out.

Chidi watched as the one who was trying to destroy her was frozen solid. All of the dragons cheered when he was taken away.

"The games are over. Bring *her* to the coldest cell, for not amusing me."

. . . .

6:00 P.M.

Chidi ate her fish, thinking about the day's events. "Frozen solid. . . ," she muttered.

"Hello, Chidi," Malcora snarled, sliding up to the cell.

"Um, excuse me, but why did you freeze Maichi? And what's DITCHing?"

"D-I-T-C-H. It's an acronym. Guess."

"Dude-I-Totally-Can't-Help? Or, Do-Insects-Talk-Crazy- Hippo? I give up."

"D-I-T-C-H. Dumped-In-The-Crazy-Hole. Or you could be DITCHED. Dumped-In-The-Crazy-Hole-Every-Day. That's the worst."

"Oh, brother."

"You, or the dog, could both be DITCHED, depending on how cooperative you are. Not that I really care about the dog, though," she said, coiling her tail around the freezing bars.

"Malcora? Why are you . . . well, my weird compass says we are not in the dragon kingdom?"

"Ah . . . you wish to know why I am not with my clan?" She smiled and breathed a plume of freezing smoke into the prison.

"I rebelled. I hated the way they ruled, and oh, how I tried to help . . . but they *refused!*" she growled, as she lashed her tail. "I gathered my forces and took the capital by siege. But, one of my prisoners, part of Clan Igneous, my sworn enemy, defeated me as I took my rightful place on the throne."

"Who was he?" Chidi asked. "Or her."

"Laven," she growled.

"Lava?"

"Never *mind!*" Malcora snapped.

She bowed her head down, so Chidi could see a broken horn, almost shattered to bits.

"So I left. With my honor gone, I flew as far as I could and ended up here. The few members of Clan Aqua catch fish from the river to feed us and our prisoners."

She finished, sighing.

"You said your rightful place?" Chidi started to ask.

"My father was the King of The Dragon Realm. I was the princess. After my mother died, he remarried, and they had my half-sister, Viola. She married and had a daughter, Isa, and in the dragons' culture, I could not assume the throne if I had a sibling who was married with another heir. Even though she was not royal, she was in charge!

"I knew that I was the heiress in my heart. I thought that the army of Marina was going to attack, and I remember my words. 'Father, my scouts say the army in Marina is ready to go to war; they are in fire-proof armor. Shouldn't we attack first?'

"But he brushed me off, saying it was nothing to worry about. But I pressed the matter, and he got so mad he locked me in my room for a whole week, feeding me only fish, to remind me of my idea.

"But, I think my patience has expired, as well as my hospitality. The dog will fight tomorrow, against a Gargoyle. I hope he loses. Sleep well."

"Wait, what happens if he loses again?" Chidi asked, hoping her assumptions were wrong.

"He . . . loses more than the game."

She slid out of the dungeons, leaving Chidi standing stunned at the bars.

....

On Earth

Jenny watched Dexter exit the couch after his very long explanation. She waited until he and his wife were in the kitchen, which was blocked by a door.

She jumped off the couch and shut the door, locking it. She then ran to the front door, feeling ridiculous when it easily opened.

Laura, I have to tell you something! she thought. She dialed her sister's number, but it went straight to voicemail.

"Laura, it's Jenny. Call me back ASAP. I met Dexter. He kidnapped them, and now they're missing. Come here *right now.* There are larger forces at work."

....

Meanwhile . . .

The group was on the underground road again, and Alexis was taking the lead.

"Do you think Autumn will be looking for us?" Bella asked, looking at a gray-purple squirrel scurrying by.

"I mean, If she wants to know where we are, couldn't she just use magic or something?" Dalia replied, shaking her head at the strange surroundings.

"Yeah, I guess she could," Bella said, "Do you have any ideas about where we could find the pets? We could be walking in the opposite direction for all we know."

"Yeah . . . I guess you're right. We would be super lucky if we were in the general area—" Alexis cut off and slapped herself in the face when Oreo and Ginger walked into view.

"Oh, come here, you!" Dalia rushed up to Oreo and gave him a giant hug as she knelt down.

Wow. How lucky! Alexis thought.

"Hi! We were looking all over for you!" Ginger meowed, rubbing on Alexis' leg.

"Hey, where are Tumbles and Redd?" she asked, worried about her pet.

"Oh, uh, Tumbles *fell* down a pit, and Redd went with him, and we need your help to get him out," Ginger said casually.

"*WHAT?* We need to go *now!*" Alexis took off in the direction the pets had come.

"Wait for *us!*" Bella, Raggy, Dalia, and the pets all ran after her. She ran and ran until she found the cave.

"Wait—for us . . . ," Raggy panted, stumbling into Alexis.

"This is it!" Ginger purred, who was riding on Raggy's back.

"Are you sure? I don't see them . . . ," Alexis mumbled, stepping into the mouth of the cave.

"They said they were gonna go exploring, so *obviously* they are not here. Careful on the way down. Tumbles said it was super steep," Ginger meowed.

Bella gave a questioning look to Alexis, who told them what Ginger had said.

"Okay, I'll go down first," Alexis said, "Then follow carefully, 'kay?" She slid down feet first into the darkness.

"Alright! I'm down! C'mon! Pets next!"

Ginger and Oreo slid down on their bottoms. They landed safely at the end of the incline. Then down came Dalia, then Raggy, then Bella.

"Okay, now that we're all together, let's go looking for them."

They crept along, carefully avoiding deep puddles.

"Hey! Redd! Tumbles? Where are you?" Dalia called. "Come on out!"

The gang searched and called until they found small paw-prints, barely visible in the darkness.

"Hey, guys? I think they went this way!" Raggy said, and they followed the prints until they found the ravine.

"Oh," was all Bella and the rest could say, when they saw the dragons.

"Hello. I have been expecting you. *Chidi* and Tumbles send their *warmest* welcome." The giant ice dragon was seated back on her rock, two royal-looking ice dragons seated next to it.

"Who are you? And what did you do to my sister?" Alexis yelled.

"And *what* are you?" Raggy took Bella's arm and stepped back, not wanting her to get hurt.

"Haha! Children are so naive! I am Malcora, *rightful* ruler of the dragons!"

The beasts around her cheered.

"W-why did you capture Chidi? And where is Tumbles?" Alexis stammered but regained her composure.

"Take them to . . . *see* her." Malcora nodded, and two white-and-blue dragons walked them through the stone walls of the domain.

Chapter Fifteen

AT LEAST IT CAN'T GET ANY WORSE

"STOP!" Tumbles barked. He was being dragged by his collar, down to a 'Training Room', the red dragon said. 'Training Room' or not, he certainly did not want to go there. Tumbles kept thinking about what he and Alexis would be doing, If they had not been separated, and it definitely was *not* this.

"Dog! Stop—struggling already! You're being Dumped In The Crazy Hole later, and I need to teach you how to fight a Gargoyle!" the crimson dragon grunted.

"*But I don't want to!*" Tumbles yelped. "Wait."

He stopped struggling, and walked in front of the dragon. "Fight a what-now?"

"A Gargoyle. In a nutshell, it's basically a goblin that turns into a statue," the dragon sighed, and shoved him into a room.

"W-why do I have to fight?" Tumbles asked, his tail between his legs.

"Because you are gonna get thrown in *the pit* later. And I want this to be entertaining. No one cares if you win or lose, but Her Majesty might spare you if you put on a good show. Oh, and call me Crim."

Crim motioned for Tumbles to follow him to an area in the room with statues and weights.

....

9:00 P.M.

"Now, show me what you can do. Attack the statue." Tumbles leaped off the ground and tried to tackle it against the hard tiles. Sadly, it was too firm, and he fell back onto the flooring, a bump on his head.

"That *hurt!*" he whined.

"Well, what did you think it was gonna do, fall over?" Crim sighed and told Tumbles to try again. This time, he jumped up and whacked the stone with his paw.

"YEOWCH!" he licked his paw and sighed. "What do I do?"

"You do this." Crim dashed forward, clamping his jaws around the statue's middle, locking his jaws closed, and smashing it into tiny pieces.

"Whoa! Teach me to do *that!*" Tumbles exclaimed.

"Nah. Your jaws are too small. Now, though you're small, if you attack from the back, you will get an opening . . . "

And so it went, until it was time . . .

....

The Hole, 9:45 P.M.

"DITCH them! DITCH them!" the crowd chanted once more.

"Welcome back to the games!" Malcora roared, "We have some special spectators today! These children are the friends and family of Chidi, who we saw fight yesterday. Now, as our competitors, we have, Galiro! My Gargoyle gladiator! And, Tumbles! The dog. Let the games . . . BEGIN!"

Alexis, Raggy, Bella, Ginger, and Oreo were watching from a pavilion, overlooking the Pit.

"Oh no! I hope Tumbles is okay . . . ," Alexis cried, craning her neck so she could see. The Redemptors shoved Tumbles and Galiro into the Crazy Hole.

"Oof!" Tumbles grunted, as he hit the floor. He got up immediately, just as Crim had taught him. As the beast lunged, he stepped to the side, waiting for the perfect moment.

"Wow! He looks like he's done this for years!" Bella exclaimed.

"Yeah . . ." Alexis couldn't help but worry for his safety, even though he wasn't hurt. As the Gargoyle jumped, Tumbles ducked underneath, and bit its belly. He shook his head, dropping Galiro. It shrunk away, even though he had not bit it very hard.

"Haha! Now this is what I call a show!" Malcora sneered.

"Very good!" Galiro jumped once more, and curled up to a ball, turning into stone. Tumbles stumbled out of the way just in time not to be squashed. He barked as loud as he could, and the beast stepped away, covering its ears. This 'fight' went on for a while, but the crowd cheered, and some laughed, seeing a dog beat a Gargoyle in combat.

"Alright! The dog wins! I haven't seen something like that in a long time!" Malcora sneered.

"Bring Galiro back to his room. He still put on a good show."

Raggy and Alexis breathed a sigh of relief.

"I knew he could do it!" Dalia said, high-fiving Bella. Bella blushed and turned away.

"What about me?" Tumbles barked. "I don't want to go back to the dungeons!"

Malcora sighed. "Bring him to one of the *smaller* guest chambers." She whispered something to a pale blue dragon sitting below her. Soon enough, the foursome was carried away, as well as Tumbles.

"More prisons! Can't we catch a break?" Alexis exclaimed angrily.

As they were shoved in yet *another* cell, a dragon said outside the bars, "Hey, I'm Crim. I helped Tumbles train. I honestly do not like Malcora, and I am willing to help you escape."

"Rrrright." Raggy rolled his eyes.

"Like we should trust you!" Dalia retorted, and Bella turned away.

"Trust me, we've had to deal with people like you all the time," Alexis said, glaring at the crimson-colored dragon.

"Okay, what do you want me to do to prove I'm trustworthy?" Crim asked, shaking his tail like a rattlesnake.

"You could find Redd, the robin; Chidi, the human; Ginger, the cat, *and* bring them back safely, and *then* let us go," Raggy offered.

"If I can, I will. I'll be back to sneak you some food."

"What's on the menu?" Bella asked, smacking her lips.

"Um, sardines and tilapia. Or, if you're not a fish person, I can get you some shrimp or lobster!"

"Uh, anything else?" Bella whimpered.

"Yeah, like a burger and fries?" Alexis murmured.

"What's a *burger?*" Crim asked.

All four children stared at the red dragon.

"You've never had a cheeseburger? Or a hamburger?" Alexis asked, dumbfounded.

"Uh . . . no?" he said, tilting his head. "*What* does a *burger* taste like?"

Alexis sighed and tried to explain. "It's like . . . bread, with cheese, meat, lettuce, and tomato in it. It usually comes with a sauce also."

"Mhm. Oh, and what are *frese?*" Crim asked, looking at them like they spoke a different language.

"Fries. Fried potato strips of goodness," Bella said, rolling her eyes.

"Oh. Well, I am sorry, but we only have seafood, and if you are lucky, vegetables. Our Aqua Clan dragons do all the food-related things," Crim finished.

"I'll have sardines! I love 'em," Raggy exclaimed, and all the girls looked at him strangely. "What? You girls like sparkles, I like sardines."

"Alright! Sardines, and . . . ?" Crim asked, pointing at Dalia.

"I'll have a little bit of lobster if you don't mind," she said politely.

"Tilapia, but without the skin, please. And cooked?" asked Bella.

"I'll have some lobster too, thanks!" Alexis smiled.

"Alright, be back soon!" Crim slid out of the dungeon.

"Gah! This is so terrible!" Alexis cried. "Separated, on our birthday, without our parents, *not going scuba diving!*" She sank against the wall, looking defeated.

"Yeah. It's bad for all of us." Dalia put her hand on Alexis' shoulder. Raggy looked between the bars, at something coming down the hall.

"Um . . . guys?" Raggy motioned for them to come and look. A white and gray dragon was walking another dragon down the corridor. The dragon was a dark red, which automatically made the children think he was an Igneous Clan dragon.

"Nothing to see here," the white and gray dragon said menacingly. "This here fellow tried to escape."

Dalia gasped and covered her mouth. The black-and-red dragon had a large spear wound on its side. It opened its eyes pleadingly but received a hard knock on the head.

"Oh . . ." Alexis looked fearfully at the dragon, wondering if he was okay.

When the white dragon left, Dalia said, "Is that gonna happen to Crim if he gets—"

"Caught?" Crim was standing at the bars, smirking. "Heh, I'm the master of sneaking! Here's your food!"

He handed Raggy his sardines, Alexis and Dalia their lobster, and Bella her *very burnt* tilapia without the skin.

"Thank you!" Raggy said.

"Yeah, and I'll find the bird, and make sure Chidi is okay."

"Wow! Thanks!" Bella said.

"Course! Oop! Time's up! Gotta go." Crim dashed out of the dungeons.

"Mmmm!" Raggy was eating his sardines. Bella shuddered and took a little nibble of her fish. "OOF—that's *burnt* . . . ," she complained.

"Huh, not half bad!" Alexis said, as she took a crunchy bite of her lobster.

"Yeah, I think Crim is actually a nice guy," Dalia added, "and I hope he can find Chidi."

"Hey, guys? You know that guy being dragged down the hall? Where do you think that wound came from?" Raggy asked, as he swallowed a bite.

"Hmm . . . maybe it was punishment for trying to escape? Or he was fighting or something?" Bella suggested.

"Or—" Alexis got cut off by a voice.

"Where did you kiddies come from? And why are you in jail?" a Centaur said from the cell opposite theirs. He was a half-human-half-horse hybrid.

"Uh . . . we came from Earth, and we honestly did nothing wrong!" Dalia exclaimed, "And now we are stuck in here, on my friend's birthday, with nothing to do except hope we live!"

"Ah. Earth, eh? They say it be a magical place with flying machines, and wondrous vehicles. And I, like you, did nothing wrong. I just wanted to see the world, but, as luck would have it, I stumbled into this here place."

The Centaur turned away and sat down.

"This place is weird!" Alexis whispered, and took another bite of lobster. At least a half hour went by until . . .

"I'm back!" Crim said, as he sauntered up to the bars. "Guess what?"

"What?" they all said.

"I found her! She is being held in the Ice Prisons though, so I don't know how long she'll last without a fire spell." Crim frowned, adding, "Oh, I tried to see the bird, but they locked him in the gladiator's room, so I didn't try to get in."

"Oh no, oh no, oh no!" Alexis cried. "She's gonna get hurt! We *HAVE TO FIND HER!*"

"I-I'm sorry, but I can do nothing until tonight. I will try to get the keys, but I cannot guarantee anything." Crim's eyes saddened. "Last time I tried to help someone escape this place, they ran and left me to rot."

Bella turned toward Dalia and started to speak, but she stopped.

"Who were you trying to get out?" she asked.

"Someone like you." He pointed at Alexis. "But he had magic. But he was silly, and nice, even though he possessed great power. He means nothing to me now, though. I will see you at midnight, if I succeed." Crim nodded, and took off.

The foursome ate in silence, finishing the last of their food.

"Let's get some rest. It's not like there is anything else to do. Except talk to the *locals*," Raggy said, and pointed at the strange Centaur.

"Good idea," Bella said and curled up in the corner farthest from Dalia.

Dalia looked at her strangely but lay down on the floor without a word. Alexis sat, her back against the bars, and thought, *someone like me? Wow, what a jerk. He left without Crim? I guess it can't get any worse.*

Chapter Sixteen

IT GETS WORSE

They slept until a scraping, clicking noise woke them.

"Mm. *Huh? Crim, is that—*" Alexis whispered at the bars.

"Ah, Crim was helping you? That will *surely* help our evidence of his . . . *tragic* demise." Malcora was holding a flickering candle in one hand and a small jewel in the other.

"What? Malcora, why are you here? And what did you do to Crim?" Alexis demanded.

"Wrong, I did nothing to Crim! I am sorry about this, as I should be. It is a shame you were so *attached* to him. He is right here." She held up the shining red jewel so Alexis could see.

"W-what . . . what do you mean? This is just a rock!"

"Wrong again. This is a Dragon Core. Something left behind when a dragon passes." Her eyes were saddened.

"N-no . . . you?"

Dalia, Bella, and Raggy awoke from Malcora's freezing breath blowing into the cell.

"How could you?" Alexis was trying to punch Malcora unsuccessfully through the bars.

"I did *nothing* to him, child! He was flying into the Columns and something knocked him out of the sky. Even though he was a traitor, he was a kind-hearted dragon." Malcora caught one of Alexis' flying fists that made it through the bars and looked her in the eye. "I do not care about you, or your friends, and you could easily be locked up in the Ice Cells just like your sister. We will have a day of mourning tomorrow, so do not fret about her. She will not fight."

"Chidi? *FIGHT?!*" Alexis screamed. She lifted her foot and kicked Malcora. "Why?!"

"Because she is Candyopolin."

Malcora walked out of the dungeons, leaving Dalia, Raggy, and Bella stunned and confused.

....

5:49 A.M.

"Where are they?! It has been three whole days since they went missing! I have looked everywhere!" Aunt Jenny yelled at a wall.

"Argh! Ben and—"

Ring ring! Ring ring!

Her phone rang.

"Yes, this is she. Still nothing?" she said. "I'm so sorry Laura, I—they did? Do you think? You will? I know, three days! No, she was banished, right? I think he hates us too? Nah, if they could've they would've. Missing on their birthday! Alright, I'll get right to it! Thank you, bye." Jenny sighed.

She wasn't a very tall woman, and her light brown hair was piled on her head in an extremely messy bun, with a pencil speared through it. Her eyes, a maple-gray color, were full of fear.

"Well, time to do it again," she said to herself, and thrust her left arm forward, pointing at the grass.

Aunt Jenny began to shimmer. Then, a bright lavender light zapped up her arm, and she disappeared. Jenny was concentrating on one name. *The Golden*

Lands! The Golden Lands! she thought over and over. The light dissipated, and Jenny appeared in a glowing forest, with fireflies flying all around.

"Ah," Jenny sighed. "Good to be back!"

....

The Gladiator Room, 6:00 P.M.

The Gladiator room was jam-packed with weapons. From spears to ball 'n chains, all sorts of weapons were hanging on the walls—even a knife chandelier!

Redd fluttered about nervously.

"What are you having me do?"

"Nothing, bird, just go in the cage," a greenish, bored looking dragon growled.

"Um . . . I'd rather not!" Redd flew out of reach and perched on a picture frame made of swords.

"Grah! Get down! I like birds when I am not hungry," she threatened.

"Oh, fine!" Redd flew past the dragon's claws and into the birdcage. The dragon shut the door and walked out of the room, carrying Redd. "Where are you taking me?" Redd chirped.

"You are our table centerpiece. Her Majesty likes birds if they are not *loud.*"

Redd gulped and shut his beak. They entered a large dining room, where Malcora was sitting at the head of the table. The dragon set Redd down and bowed.

"Rise, Grendell. Please, eat."

Redd studied the room. It was filled with small ice sculptures sitting on tables, mantels, and windowsills. He let out a surprised tweet when a slightly-chubby looking chef-looking dragon walked in.

"Y-your Majesty! Zere is ze commotion down in ze kitchen! An Igneous Clan Dragon is ransacking ze place!"

"*WHAT?*" Malcora roared. "Bring him to me at *once!*"

A few minutes later, two guards brought in the same Igneous dragon that had been walking down the hall with the white and gray dragon.

"*YOU. Why, why, why, why* can you not stay in PRISON?" she roared.

"I can hardly stay in one place. *YOU,*" he said, mimicking Malcora, "*Why, why, why, why,* did you try for the throne, anyway? Like, yeesh, this is a democracy!"

Malcora gave him a death stare and pointed at him. "You know what to do. If he wins, we get rid of her. If he loses . . . a win for me."

"Wait! No—" the Igneous dragon cried as the guards dragged him back out the door.

"Oh, no!" Redd chirped.

"GAH! A noisy bird too? Bring the bird elsewhere, and try not to disturb the evening more than you already have." Malcora motioned for the chef to take Redd.

"Yez, Your Highness" The yellow chef dragon sighed.

In the kitchen, Redd was set down on a marble counter.

"Wait, what are you?" Redd's voice trailed off as he saw the chef grab a long, sharp knife.

"Now," the chef cried, "I will no longer have to deal with ze evil flying creature!"

"Wait, you're a dragon! You fly, too!" Redd squawked.

"Zat is ze minor de-tail!" shouted the mustard-colored dragon.

"Whoa, whoa, whoa. If you're going to eat me, you might as well make me taste *good*. At home, I never would eat a worm or bug without properly seasoning it," he lied.

"Really? Vhat do ze suggest?" The chef looked intrigued. This little bird was offering to help him make itself into a good meal for Malcora.

"I need at least a bottle of ketchup," Redd said. "Oh, and also, at least six jugs of maple syrup. The real stuff, not the junky fake junk. And, like, a bucket load of salt? Maybe a pinch of pepper? Also, cover me with sugar, and I'll be a delicious feast for Malcora. Also, serve me raw. Covered with feathers. Oh, and add pickle relish. One last thing. Mint chocolate chip ice cream."

"Vhat?" She sneezed, very confused. "Vhat is *catch oop? And Ice Creme?*"

Redd smirked, his plan was working. "Ketchup is . . . uh, fermented tomato juice? And ice cream is milk, whipped and frozen, with mint extract and chocolate chips."

"Vill ze write ze recipe on ze paper?" the chef asked.

"Uh . . ." Redd looked down at his red feathers. "I can't write."

"Zen you will tell me ze recipe, and I vill write it down!"

"Uh, okay."

The recipe looked something like this:

The Recipe for Bird

Ingredients:

- One bottle of Catch-oop
- Six jugs of maple syrup (real, not junky fake junk)
- One bucket of salt (ish)
- One pinch of pepper
- Seven cups of sugar
- Mint Coco Chip Ice Crème
- Pickle relish
- Living bird
- Red feathers

Instructions:

Cover bird in catch-oop, maple syrup, and sugar. Roll around in salt. Smear with red feathers and pickle relish. Finally, top with Mint Coco Chip Ice Creme. Sprinkle pepper on Ice Creme. Serve raw.

"That's it!" Redd finished, "Now, you should start preparing the ketchup! Oh, and the Ice Cream! And pickle relish!"

"Yez, right away!" The mustard dragon rushed into the back of the kitchen.

"Don't forget to ferment the tomato juice! And whip the Ice Cream!" he tweeted.

"Yez, yez, I know what I am doing!" she called back.

Now that I have bought myself some time . . . Redd chirped to himself and started jiggling the door to the cage.

"Waz zat noise?" the dragon called.

"Oh, nothing!" he squawked, "just the window rattling!"

As the poor chef continued following Redd's terrible instructions, Redd popped open the door and flew to the top of the cage.

"Hey, I just remembered that Ice cream is *hot,* not *cold!*" he chirped, hoping to buy more time.

"Oh! Ozay zen."

Yes! She fell for it! Redd flew to the door, which was luckily cracked open. "*See ya!*" he whistled quietly. "Actually, I won't! Ha!"

"Bird?" the chef inside called. "I need to pluck your red feathers!"

Yeesh, Redd thought. *That kinda defeats the purpose of serving me raw.*

"Bird? I need to dress you in salt!" she called. "Gah . . ." Redd flew back into the kitchen, feeling bad.

"Vhy are you out of ze cadge?"

"I—I was bored? Don't you know a bored bird is bad for your digestive system?"

"Oh. No, I didn't. Anyway, c'mere I need to dress you in salt and pluck zere feathers," The mustard dragon sighed.

"Hey, uh, what's your name?" Redd tweeted.

"CornFlakes. Why?"

"Really? Your name is CornFlakes?"

"Well, the queen's name is Malcora. *Zat* doesn't seem to surprise you." CornFlakes turned and crossed her arms around her white apron that said, Cheese, Please, with a picture of a mouse with wild eyes scurrying for a piece of yellow cheese.

"Okay, then . . . *CornFlakes,*" Redd said it like a punchline, and added, "Do you really want Malcora to eat me? I mean, come on, 'This is a democracy!'" he quoted the dragon from earlier. *What does that even mean?* he thought.

"N-no, I zoo not," CornFlakes admitted, "I really like birds."

"Hey, why don't we go get my friends, together, and get outta here? You could come with us! We eat, uh . . . *good things.* And you could cook whenever you want!"

"Vow . . . really? Anytime?" CornFlakes clapped.

"Yeah! Now, whaddya say? Onward!" Redd perched on CornFlakes' shoulder, and they ran out the door together.

Chapter Seventeen

YET ANOTHER ESCAPE PLAN

"I can't believe we're stuck here! No more options either!" Bella complained. Alexis had not spoken since the devastating news last night and was now jotting in a notebook.

Dear Journal,

I'm so upset. Our friend, Crim, is gone. Not as in missing. Gone as in DEAD. I was able to wrestle the Dragon Core from Malcora.

Oh! Dragon Cores are gems left behind whenever a dragon passes away, apparently. I'm just so upset we weren't able to stop them.

Malcora SAYS that she didn't do anything—I don't believe her. But what can we do? We can't bring him back.

Our pets are missing. Chidi is gone. Crim is dead. We're in ruins. Friends are losing.

Based on all of these facts, I have come to a well-researched, carefully calculated, simple conclusion:

WE'RE DOOMED! WE'RE ALL GOING TO DIE!

Think about it:

HELP, we're going to die! Everything, everyone who could have helped us is either dead or missing! You know, I really don't think we can find our way out of here. Get out of a cage that is guarded by an evil dragon queen-person? Even for me, that's a crazy idea! (That's saying something, I'm wacko.)

My only hope is that my sister and the pets will burst through and save us. Alexis, get *a hold* of yourself! Get a hold! I have to get us out of here, before that demented ice dragon kills us too, or locks us in an *ice* prison. Change is coming, and we need to break out.

"Crim wasn't an option! He was a friend!" Dalia argued.

Raggy sat next to Alexis, his hand on her shoulder.

"Hey, do you think Redd and Tumbles, and Ginger—"

"And Oreo!" Dalia interrupted.

"Yes, and *Oreo*." Bella rolled her eyes, and sighed.

"Hey, Alexis?" Bella tapped her shoulder, but she shooed her hand away.

"Hey, leave her alone. We are all sad, and we need some time to revitalize." Dalia pulled Bella back, and gave her a look that said, *'And don't argue.'*

"Yeah, but we need to find all of them and get out of here as soon as possible!" Bella retorted, ignoring Dalia's look.

"Knock it off!" Alexis snapped.

"Whoa, Lexi," Raggy said. "I know you're upset—"

"And don't call me Lexi!" she snarled. "That's the nickname that I had when I was *a normal person*."

"Okay, *Alexis*," Dalia said. "You're sad. We all are. But you can't yell at Raggy. Or any of us, for that matter."

Alexis sighed, and said, "Well, what do *you* think we should do? I'm out of ideas and out of hope of ever getting out of here."

"Hey . . . I think I have an idea actually. What if we *try* to be DITCHed?"

"Thank you for the terrible idea, Dalia," Alexis replied, without emotion.

"No, no. We go in, but when they push us in, we grab onto the rim of it, and we climb back out?" Dalia said, clapping.

"With a bunch of dragons? And they wouldn't put us all in at the same time."

"Good point. Do you know of any other magic powers that you have?" Dalia said hopefully.

"Nope." Alexis shook her head.

"Well," Dalia said, plopping down next to Alexis. "I'm out of ideas."

Bella suddenly stood up.

"What—"

"Shh!" she whispered. In the distance, a chant could be heard.

"DITCH them! DITCH them . . ."

"What? She said that there were no games today!" Alexis shot up, as a voice was heard, saying, *"Again, we have Chidi of the royal Candyopolins! And Laven, our traitor!"*

"No! Chidi! Wait. Royal?"

Everyone looked at Alexis.

"HEY, GUYS!" Redd squawked as he rode in on the shoulders of a mustard-yellow dragon with an apron.

"How did you get out?" Alexis exclaimed, clasping the bars.

Redd explained quickly, while Alexis translated.

"And now CornFlakes here is gonna help us!" Redd finished.

"Yez. Zat is true," CornFlakes said in an Italian accent.

"Do you have the keys, *CornFlakes?*" Raggy snickered, receiving a hard look from the dragon and the bird.

"Yez, I do!" She unlocked the dungeon doors, and the group rushed up the stairs to find Tumbles and Ginger. They heard yelping and meowing from a room and slammed open the door. A white dragon was holding the small puppy by his collar, and Ginger by the scruff.

"What the—"

"HYA!" CornFlaked slapped the dragon in the face with a pan, catching Tumbles and Ginger as they fell

"Alexis!" they yelled and bounded into her arms. "Let's go rescue Chidi!"

....

Meanwhile...

While they were having a happy reunion, Chidi was sidestepping lava blasts.

"Sorry!" the dragon growled, as he shot another fiery blast.

"Ah!" Chidi was trapped, lava on either side of her. A spiked mace was thrown down, and she picked it up.

"Try it!" she yelled. "I dare you!"

Laven frowned, not wanting to hurt her.

"Hey, let's figure something out!" he said.

"Not a chance! If you were gonna stick to your word, you would not have tried to lava blast me!" she yelled back.

"Fine, then. I'm sorry!"

As he breathed another lava blast, she made a leap over the lava to her side. Chidi ran to *his* side and swung the mace, but he dodged the blow.

"I don't want to hurt you, but I will!" she yelled.

"AAH!"

She caught his wing with one of the spikes, making a tear. Chidi's next attack missed the mark, and he clawed at the ground. Laven jumped, tried to fly, but fell.

"Grr!" he growled, clawing at Chidi's arm. She fell back, cringing from the slice of his talons.

"Fight! Fight! Fight!" the crowd cheered.

"Stop right there!" a voice yelled. Alexis and the gang stepped into view.

"Seize them!" Malcora roared. As they fought back with pots and pans, Chidi nodded at Laven and ran over to him.

Unclipping his wing restraints, she said, "I'm sorry. Do you think you can fly? We can all get outta here!"

He nodded, and Chidi jumped on his back. The pair flew out of the pit, joining the gang.

"Get them!"

Chidi swung the mace, CornFlakes wielded a pan, Laven breathed lava blasts, and the rest held various kitchen utensils.

"Alright! Let's get outta here!" Alexis said, and they jumped on the backs of Laven and CornFlakes.

"Woohoo!" Alexis cheered as they fled the pit, flew up a rock tunnel, and left Malcora far behind.

She turned and looked at the ice dragon, waving her wooden spoon. "You haven't seen the last of *The Wooden Spoon of Destiny!*"

As they flew, Chidi told them what had happened, all while holding her arm and flying on a dragon.

"So, that's what happened! And now, here we are!" she finished.

"Wow! So, we are royalty, huh?" Alexis said, holding Tumbles in her lap.

"I'm just so glad we are back together!"

"Ve are going to zand! Hold zon!" CornFlaked yelled. The two dragons dived down, landing in the Four Seasons Clearing. The group all hopped off and let out a huge breath.

"Whoa, boy! That was fun!" Raggy exclaimed.

"Urg . . . maybe for you." Laven cringed, tucking his wing close to his body.

"Oh, man! Sorry about that! Ouch! We should both get patched up," Chidi apologized. They found bandages in the cottage and wrapped up Chidi's arm and Laven's wing.

"Hey—watch out!" Autumn flew into the clearing, and hovered in front of Alexis.

"Autumn! You're back!" Alexis hugged the tiny pixie, and asked, "What were you doing all this time?"

"Hehe! I was gathering all sorts of rare and precious ingredients! I wanted to make a delicious meal for all of you! Oh, and uh . . . who are *they?* And who's that girl?" She hid behind Alexis, pointing at the dragons and Chidi.

"Oh! She is CornFlakes, and she likes cooking, like my sister, Chidi! She's the girl with black hair and green eyes. And he is Laven—we have yet to find out *his* story," Dalia said.

"Oh, how come I can understand you guys?" she asked the dragons.

"We are like unicorns, we speak and don't need people with magic to understand us," Laven explained.

"Si!" CornFlakes agreed. "I zo love cooking."

Autumn shrugged and beckoned for them to come inside to eat. The dragons had to stay outside, but the five friends and the pets went inside and sat down.

"I made some soup, as well as mushroom biscuits and sponge cake for dessert!"

"Wow! Looks so good!" Raggy exclaimed, and they all dug in. Chidi brought some food out to the dragons, who complimented the chef and asked for more.

"Haha! Those dragons have quite the appetite!" Chidi laughed as she walked inside.

"CornFlakes compliments your cooking, Autumn!"

"I'm glad you like it! The special ingredient was Moon Mushrooms, which only grow on a full moon!" She gave a thumbs up and put more soup and biscuits on the dragons' plates. She brought them out, and they all laughed and talked until it was time for bed.

....

9:17 P.M.

"I'm gonna go wash my face, and then go to bed," Alexis said.

"I'll come with you." Chidi smiled.

"Me too!" Ginger purred.

"Okay!" Alexis picked up Ginger, and they went out to the spring together. Chidi sat by the pool, splashing water on her face and cut.

"Hey . . . do you think we are actually royalty? It kinda seems . . . I dunno, unlikely?"

"I don't know. Malcora is definitely untrustworthy, but do you think she would lie about that?" Alexis replied.

"This water is niiiice!" Ginger purred, and stuck her paws in the water.

"Silly cat!" Chidi stroked the soft fur on her head, then looked at the stars. "I don't think she would . . . not that I know her very well anyway."

"I really miss Mom and Dad. Dad only moves around all the time to provide for us! We were just being selfish."

"Yeah . . . me too."

"I miss them, and my food bowl, and my kitty bed, and the time where we were all normal," Ginger purrowed.

Alexis translated, and Chidi's eyes saddened. "Do you think I will be able to get my magic back?" She put her bandages back on and picked Ginger up.

"I—I'm sure of it!" Alexis said unconvincingly.

Chidi sighed, and walked back inside. Raggy was telling everyone hilarious jokes before bed.

"What path does a crazy person take?" Raggy smirked.

"Uh, the Dexter path?" Alexis joked.

"Seriously?" Bella rolled her eyes.

"The psychopath!" Raggy laughed, as did Dalia, Alexis and Bella.

"Let's just . . . go to bed," Chidi said, laying down in the 'guest room', which had tiny furniture.

"Wow, what a downer," Raggy whispered to Bella. They all lay down to sleep, turning out the lights.

....

The next morning, 8:15 A.M.

"What? WhereamI?"

Raggy awoke before all the others. He tiptoed quietly from the cottage and onto the dew-covered grass. Sneaking around the dragons, he sighed, breathing in the crisp morning air. Walking over to the spring, he saw something laying down behind the rock-waterfall.

"Who's there—huh?" A large deer, with big horns and glowing yellow eyes and markings, was laying in the grass. It raised its head and stood shakily.

"Uh . . . I didn't mean to disturb you . . ." He backed away, not wanting to frighten the ancient-looking being. It started away, looking back every once in a while to find Raggy still standing there.

"Weird."

"Hi," Laven said from behind him.

"KYA! Dude, don't sneak up on me like that!" Raggy yelled.

"Bro, calm down. What are you staring at?"

Raggy looked back in the direction the deer had run.

"Oh, uh . . . nothing," he replied.

"Great, uh, the pixie says that breakfast is ready. I'll see you there?"

"Yeah, sure."

Raggy washed his face and walked back to the house.

"Hiya! Breakfast is ready, y'all!" Autumn said cheerily as he stepped through the door.

"Great! What's for breakfast?" Raggy asked, rubbing his stomach.

"I got some homemade yogurt and berry bowls!"

"Sounds delish!" Alexis exclaimed, coming from the guest room.

"Great! Sorry everything is so small, it's all the right size for me!" Autumn apologized.

"It's all good, we'll just eat outside," Dalia said, following Alexis.

"Okay!" They got their food and sat on the small porch.

"So, Autumn, you said you know where to find magic?" Chidi asked, once seated.

"Yes, I do. The place is called the Tree Of Magic. Yeah, not kidding! You need to go there and speak to the guardian of the area. If he deems you worthy, he will give you magic." Autumn took a bite of a blueberry as she finished.

"Wow, that simple?" Chidi replied.

"The problem is getting there. The Tree is located in The Golden Lands, which has fallen from its former glory."

Raggy scooped a fairy-sized spoonful of yogurt, and asked, "How so?"

"Well, The Golden Lands used to be a large kingdom, ruled by some Valkyries, which are basically humans with wings. Then they replaced them with the Unicort, because they wanted a democracy, rather than single rulers.

"But now, some towns are crime centers and hubs for criminals! The tree is located somewhere in the center, surrounded by the Maze Forest."

Alexis said, "Whoa, Maze Forest? Sounds intense! And why does it seem like it's been a day and a half, even though it's been *three?*" She spooned a bite of yogurt, topped with blueberries, into her mouth.

"Haha! Lots of questions, eh? Yes, I have read books about your world, and time moves faster here, compared to where you're from," Autumn stated.

"Wow, this place is so different from Earth," Dalia said.

"Hello. Ve vere vondering vere ve will go next?" CornFlakes asked.

"To the center of The Golden Lands, I guess," Chidi replied.

"Oh . . . how do ze get there?"

....

A few minutes later . . .

"AAAAH!" Bella screamed, as they took to the sky on the backs of dragons.

"This is CRAZY!" Alexis yelled, clinging onto CornFlakes' neck.

"Alright, in three! Two! One!" Laven counted down.

"NOW!" He tucked in his wings, and dived through a metal shaft, followed by CornFlakes.

They sped out of the tunnel and into bright sunlight.

"Whoa!" Chidi exclaimed, after her eyes adjusted to the brightness. They were flying over towns big and small, rivers, and plains.

"I've never been this high in my life!" Redd cheeped.

"Amazing!" Dalia reached her hand up to brush the tip of a cloud.

"We are going so fast!" Ginger's eyes widened, and she clung to Chidi with desperation.

"Ze will slow down soon," CornFlakes assured her. The dragons slowed and started descending.

"WOOHOO!" Raggy yelled as they dived towards solid ground.

Autumn stuck her head out of Chidi's backpack when they landed.

"Man! That was scary, and I wasn't even looking!" She sqeaked. Alexis helped Chidi slide off of CornFlakes, and Raggy reached out to swing Bella and Dalia off of Laven.

"That was rough," he said, as the kids finally stood on solid ground. They had landed in a large plain, with a small town nearby.

"Best day of my life!" Raggy cheered. "That was awesome!"

"Yeah, but I don't see anything that looks like a 'Maze Forest' . . ." Alexis craned her neck to see, but found no sign of a forest at all, much less a maze one.

"I honestly have no idea where we are." Autumn shrugged.

"Well, we have never really been out here, so you tell us!" Laven tilted his head.

"Great. None of us knows where we are. Just wonderful," Bella muttered.

"C'mon, Bella! We're on an adventure! We're having fun together!" Dalia said, giving Bella a playful shove.

Bella blushed. "Oh, except for the fact that we could die at any moment if Malcora finds us. But, aside from that, this is fun!"

"Haha, yeah, thanks for the optimism," Chidi remarked.

"Guys, less talking, more finding out where we are! Let's go ask the locals." Autumn was flying towards the nearby town, not waiting for an answer. The group followed behind, giving each other skeptical looks.

"Hello, fine . . . folk?" Autumn stopped, as she saw the town was inhabited by dwarves.

"Ello'! What brings you fine . . ." The dwarf stopped talking when he saw the dragons. "T-terrorists! Run! Dragons!" He took off toward his house, as did all the other dwarves.

"O-kay? Hey, we just want to talk!" Chidi exclaimed, knocking on one of the doors.

A small child peeked out and said in a squeaky voice, "Can I elp' you?"

"Yeah, actually you can. Do you mind bringing your mommy so I can talk to her?"

"Sure! Mama! Ere' is a traveler who wants to talk wit' you!"

"'Ello?" she said in a soft, mother-like tone. "May I help you?"

"Um . . ." Chidi found it quite odd that a woman was shorter than her by a foot at least and about twenty years older than her. "Will you help us? Where are we? My friends and I—"

"Can I have all of your names?"

"Um . . . Chidi, Alexis, Raggy, Bella, Dalia, Tumbles, Redd, Ginger, Oreo, Laven, and CornFlakes. But the dragons are nice." Chidi pointed at each of them as she spoke.

"It's clear you haven't met the dragons *here*. They're—"

"Ere' terrorists!" the small boy cried. "Papa says we shouldn't trust 'em."

"Well, these dragons are *not* terrorists," Alexis said firmly.

"*All* dragons 'ere terrorists! Ye' will get chomped up in minutes!" A man came from inside the house and pulled his wife back inside.

"Taste my blade!" He charged out of the house waving a knife, tripped, and fell at Laven's feet.

"Urk . . . EEEEEE!" he screamed and ran back inside. Laven shrugged, and Chidi frowned.

"G'day," the woman said pointedly and slammed the door in Chidi's face.

"Well, that did not blow over well," Redd chirped. "Glad that's not *my* house."

"A HOUSE BLEW OVER?" Chidi exclaimed suddenly.

"No! The *conversation* did not blow over well!" Autumn translated and face-palmed. "And Redd is glad that's not his house!"

"We should find another town."

"Good idea. These houses are really tempting me to sit on them," Ginger purred.

"You like to sit on houses?" Chidi burst out again.

"*No!*" Alexis, Laven, Autumn, and CornFlakes chorused. Chidi sighed, and looked wistfully at Alexis.

"You're so lucky." Chidi frowned.

"No, just not unlucky," she joked.

"Guys! *Focus!* We need to get to the tree, right? So let's focus on *that* instead of *houses blowing over.*" Autumn eyed Chidi. "'Kay?"

"Okay," Alexis and Chidi agreed.

"So . . . we walk?" Bella asked, "Or something?"

"AAAAAAAAH!" Bella was screaming again as soon as they took off on the backs of dragons.

"Are ve finding *catch-oop* or *mint coco chip ice creme*?" CornFlakes asked.

"What's catch-oop and mint coco chip ice creme?"

"It is part of ze recipe from Redd," CornFlakes said.

"Oh, can I see that?" Raggy asked.

"Si." She handed Raggy a rolled up piece of paper.

Raggy read it over.

"Read it out loud!" Bella urged her brother.

"Uh, okay. Oh, dude, this is so weird!" Raggy exclaimed. "It's, like, something called 'catch-oop', maple syrup, SALT?! Sugar, pepper, *pickle relish?!* Even a living bird?!"

Alexis grabbed the paper. "'Cover bird in catch-oop, maple syrup, and sugar. Roll around in salt. Smear with red feathers and pickle relish. Finally, top with Mint Coco Chip Ice Creme. Sprinkle pepper on Ice Creme. Serve raw.'"

"Ew!" they all exclaimed.

When CornFlakes gave them a wounded look, Alexis said, "I mean, who *wouldn't* want to eat that!"

"Hey, we will be landing soon to rest and eat," Laven growled. "Don't scream, kid!" They flew for around twelve more minutes, then landed. Bella had to cover her mouth and close her eyes so she wouldn't yell on the way down.

"We're going down now," Laven informed them.

Although she tried to stop it, Bella let out a loud, "AAAAAHHHH! HELP! WE'RE GOING TO DIE!"

"Sure. Now *that's* a large possibility," Dalia said, rolling her eyes at the same time as Alexis and Chidi. Autumn was peeking out of the backpack.

"I'll make zome dishes now," CornFlakes said, when they landed. CornFlakes immediately started whittling a piece of wood with a topaz-hilted knife.

"Great! I'll help gather ingredients!" Chidi offered. "Or I can get the pot ready."

Autumn and Bella both decided to help, running to a nearby stream to look for stuff.

"Bella, I need lots of tomatoes," CornFlakes ordered. "I'm going to need tomato juice. Also, look for ze pickles and ze salt. I vill make ze bread. Autumn, you need to find me mint, syrup, cocoa, and sugar. If you can't find it, no worries, but zis forest should do juzt fine."

"Okay," Bella said, not piecing the ingredients together. Soon, all of the food was in a small area by CornFlakes. Chidi was going to cook with the chef dragon, and Alexis and Raggy were making a fire. Somehow, the forest contained all the ingredients needed, except for mint and coco.

"Hey, where are we going to stay?" Bella asked.

"Uh . . . I guess we could worry about that when we get there. Oh! I still have my backpack!" Chidi exclaimed. "I don't know why I packed a ton of stuff, but then again, we needed it!"

Soon, they all had a wood plate of something that was steaming deliciously.

"Yum!" Dalia said, licking her lips.

"That was good!" Bella complimented, running her finger along the edge of her plate to get the last bit.

"What was that?" Laven asked.

"That," CornFlakes said proudly, "was ze Improvised Recipe for Bird! No mint ice creme though, and not zo much salt and syrup."

"What?" Redd squawked. "I ate a fellow bird? I'm a cannibal! I can't live with myself!"

"No. I make bread, not bird!"

"EWW!" Dalia and Bella cried, pushing away their plates.

"Who cares?" Alexis asked. "Can I have seconds?"

"Anybody else?" CornFlakes asked. "No one? We will have leftovers!"

Not even Raggy wanted another bite.

"Why are you guys so freaked out?" Alexis asked, swallowing another spatula-full. "It's pretty good!" She licked her lips.

"Fifth helping?" CornFlakes offered.

Alexis sighed as she said, "Nah, I'll be good without it. I want some more for tomorrow. G'night!" She lay down, avoiding the stares of the others.

Chapter Eighteen

A-MAZE-D BY THE MAGIC MAZE

"I'm packing leftover Recipe for Bird!" CornFlakes announced.

"I'm *hungry!*" Ginger whined.

"What's for breakfast?" Raggy asked. "Not more Recipe for Bird, right?"

"I will make ze omelets," CornFlakes said, prying an omelet from the frying pan which had been heated by Laven.

"Yum!" Alexis called. "I mean, it's no Recipe for Bird, but—"

"Don't talk about that!" Bella wailed.

"Yeah . . . ," Autumn agreed.

"Okay," Alexis apologized.

"The idea is gross, but we all need to eat, right?" Chidi suggested.

"I guess you're right," Dalia agreed.

"Hey, we best get going! I scouted the area a bit, and it seems we are close to The Maze!" Autumn urged, "Chop chop! Let's go! Your legs ain't walking themselves!"

"I thought we were—" Chidi looked at CornFlakes, but Bella shook her head furiously.

"I am *not* doing that *again!*" she said pointedly.

"We walk. 'Kay?"

"*You* can walk, but if Laven and CornFlakes are okay with it . . ."

Laven nodded his head, and Chidi looked at Bella.

"Fiiiiiine," Bella sighed. "Let's go . . ."

Bella clambered uneasily onto CornFlakes' back, followed by Alexis and Raggy. Chidi, the pets, and Dalia climbed onto Laven, and they took off.

"Hey, how's your wing?" Chidi asked, once flying.

"It's doing okay. I'm still able to fly with it, that's what matters. Going up!" Laven suddenly swerved upward, into a cloud.

"Eek!" Dalia squealed.

"Haha!" he laughed and dipped back down.

"Almost there! I can see a big forest!" Redd chirped.

"Alright, alright, hold your dragons," Laven said.

Laven rolled his eyes as Chidi said, "Well, technically you aren't *mine*."

"Hold on!" Ginger meowed, as she saw CornFlakes diving down ahead of them. Laven followed, Chidi clinging to the pets for dear life. They landed roughly, causing forest dirt to fly through the air.

Achoo! Alexis sneezed.

"Bless you," Dalia, Autumn, and Chidi all said together.

"So, why exactly do we need to get through this maze?" Bella asked Autumn once she regained her composure. "I mean, can't we just go around it or fly over it?"

"Uh, *no*, we can't. Chidi has to prove herself, or you won't get your magic."

"Okay, okay. Sorry!"

"So, how long will it take to travel through the maze?" Dalia asked, surveying the tangle of trees and brush.

"About four hourz? But zat's if we take all ze right turns. Maybe zeven hours?" CornFlakes guessed.

"Well, better start going then! The sooner we get to the end, the better." Chidi started walking into the entrance of the maze.

"*You who enter the maze may never come out!*" Bella said in a spooky voice.

"Oh, cut it out." Autumn shook her head disapprovingly. As they walked farther in, the light got dimmer and dimmer.

"First junction!" Raggy cheered.

"Where do we go?"

"Hmm . . . right?" Alexis suggested.

"Are you sure? That might be the wrong way," Bella warned. Oreo and Tumbles both sighed.

"What? Oh, so what way do *you* think we should go?" Alexis frowned at Bella.

"Uh . . . my guess is right."

"You are probably much like your father," Alexis complained.

"Uh, Alexis, you may want to lower your voice and watch your step," Raggy said.

"Yeah, right! Bella thinks she is so—" Alexis stopped mid-sentence as she heard a click. She had stepped on their first booby trap!

There were some loud rolling sounds, and ginormous stones started to roll straight for them.

"AHH!" Bella screamed. Alexi didn't argue with her, because she was too busy screaming herself.

"What is with all of the screaming and yelling?" Chidi hollered, but upon seeing the giant rocks headed her way, she took off running. "HELP!" Alexis screamed

"Uh, guys?" Raggy exclaimed,

"RUN FOR YOUR LIFE!"

"Wait! Can you stop and—" Alexis yelled once she realized something.

"WAIT FOR JUST A MINUTE! The rocks aren't rolling after us anymore!" Raggy hollered.

"Huh?" Bella stood there with a dumbfounded expression on her face.

"Okay, then," Alexis said, wiping her hands off on her shorts. "We are fine." Then in a whisper, she added, "And none of you saw me running and screaming. *That did not happen.*"

"Uh, yes it did," Bella said snootily.

"Cut. it. OUT!" Chidi retorted.

"I guess this place has booby traps. Interesting!" Raggy exclaimed as he surveyed the walls.

"What's so interesting?" Redd asked. "We just entered a maze of doom that we're going to die in. It's not super intriguing if you ask me."

"What did you say? Mazes are to die for?" Chidi asked. "Doom is super intriguing?"

"Oh, don't even try to guess, Chidi," Alexis said sadly.

"Okay, guys. We're going to find Chidi's magic!" Dalia called, walking off.

"Wait for us!" Alexis exclaimed, running after her.

They walked for another twenty minutes, talking about random stuff. The pets were all making various noises, walking alongside the dragons.

"Another junction. Oh, hey, can we sit and eat? I'm starving!" Tumbles whined.

"Yes, one sec," Alexis told the group, and they sat for some lunch.

"Okay, ve have zome leftover rezipe for bird, and zome leftover omelets." CornFlakes took out the small wooden containers holding the leftover food. Tumbles, Alexis, and Chidi all took some "bird" and the rest had the leftover omelets.

"I'll go catch a lizard . . . or something," Laven said, eyeing Redd.

Chidi smacked her lips. "Yum! Recipe for Bird is my new favorite food! It's super filling too!"

Redd narrowed his eyes. *"This just got personal."*

"Redd just said, *this just got personal,*" Alexis translated.

"Wait . . . oh, because *you're* a bird," Bella said.

"Yes."

"What? Why is that offensive? Recipe for Bird doesn't even *have* bird in it. We can even change the name!" Bella exclaimed.

Chidi, Dalia, Alexis, Raggy, Tumbles, Oreo, Ginger, and Laven approached the junction and considered their options.

"I would suggest left," Raggy said.

"We should go straight," Chidi suggested.

"I think we should go *right*," Dalia proclaimed.

"What if we split up into teams?" Alexis asked. "We can go in different directions, and we can mark the way back here! If one of us finds the right way, they can come back and get the rest of us!"

Ginger huffed at the idea.

"Are you sure that's a good idea?" Chidi asked, joining the group.

"*I* think it could work," Bella vouched.

"Great. What are the teams?"

"Uh . . . Ginger, CornFlakes, Chidi, Autumn, and . . . Bella?"

"Uh, whatever," Chidi said.

"Alright, the other teams are me, Tumbles, Redd, and Dalia, and the other team is Raggy, Laven, and Oreo. Does that work?" Alexis suggested.

"Sure! At least I won't be with . . . *the Bird-Eater*," Redd said darkly.

"O-kay, then. My team will go right, Raggy, Laven, Oreo, you'll go left. The rest of you, go straight! But before we go, we need to mark the path. We can't get lost! Chidi, can you pass out extra 3D pens?"

"Uh, okay. And if someone hits a dead end, come back here!"

All of the teams departed into dangers unknown.

Chapter Nineteen

PROBLEMS BACK ON PLANET EARTH

"Why on earth did you trust Jenny to watch Alexis and Chidi?" Ben yelled.

"Ben! Yelling isn't going to solve this problem!" Laura exclaimed.

"But yelling makes me feel better!"

"Ben?" Mrs. Parris said, arching an eyebrow.

"Okay. How did they get captured?" Mr. Parris asked more calmly.

"Jenny says that they just went to some neighbor's house. After that, she didn't see them."

"Who were the neighbors?"

"The names were Bella Graham and her twin brother, Rankic Graham."

Mr. Parris spit his coffee out into the trash can. "Graham?"

"Do you recognize the name, Dear?"

"Yeah, who doesn't? Graham is one of the most common last names ever!"

"I meant, do you know someone *with* the last name?"

"Well, there's my friend Charles Graham, my cousin Martha Graham, someone I've been tracking with the initials D.G.—"

"Dexter . . . oh! He was on that business card that the girls found! Is he dangerous?" Mrs. Parris asked worriedly.

"Not really. But, still. Wait, get an internet-identity search going, Laura. Can't believe I didn't recognize him . . ."

"Uh, Dexter . . . Graham . . . okay, got it! His full name is Dexter William Graham. Apparently, he has two, no, three children, Bella Cassidy Graham and

Rankic 'Raggy' Danger Graham. Rankic and Bella are twins and twelve years old. He also has a sixteen-year-old daughter, named . . . Emmaline. I guess she ran away ten years ago and has never been found. His wife is named Abigail 'Abby' Ruby Graham, and is thirty-eight. Dexter himself is . . . forty-two. He works for a man named Robert 'Bob' Brisket."

"Anything else, Laura? Are you sure that they live here?"

"Um . . . yes. They live about three blocks away from Jenny. They are currently living with Abigail's sister."

"Who?" Mr. Parris asked.

"The Smith family, who are Josiah, Jessica, and their daughter, April, who is only four years old. Josiah runs a 'bumper boat stall' on the beach. Jessica is a teacher. She leaves April with Abigail."

"Interesting," Mr. Parris murmured, staring off into space while contemplating the information.

"The address is 148 N. Starhouse Drive. It's about two and a half hours away. Sorry. We should leave now if we want to find them," Laura told him.

"Okay. Pack us something, please."

Mrs. Parris stuffed baby carrots, dried fruit, and granola bars into her purse.

"C'mon!" Mr. Parris yelled from inside the car, "Thanks, hon!"

"Yes, of course. I believe it's time we pay this Dexter a visit."

....

In the Maze, 5:00 P.M.

"Are we there yet?" Ginger whined to CornFlakes.

"Don't worry, Ginger. We're going to be there soon!"

"What did she say?" Bella asked, scrunching her eyebrows together. "Are you sure we aren't going to get lost?"

"No, of course not," Chidi reassured her, marking an arrow on the ground. "If we *do* get lost, CornFlakes could fly up and trace our way back! We're going to be fine!"

"Oh . . . okay. If you say so." Then Bella stopped and put her head between her knees. "Sorry, we've been walking for a few hours. I'm feeling a little bit lightheaded. Let me rest for a few seconds. Then we can go."

"Okay. Don't keep going if you feel dizzy," Autumn told her, as Chidi dug through her pack. "Here's a granola bar."

"Thanks." Bella chomped on the chocolate-covered granola bar. She stood and swallowed the last bite. "Let's go, girls."

"All right!" Chidi laughed, giving Bella a high-five. "You know, I had my doubts about you, but I think you'll be a great friend, even though your dad is trying desperately to be evil and took away my magic and you helped him, you seem pretty chill."

"Wow. *That's really emotional. Great, but can we go now?*"

"What, Ginger? Wow, going is emotional? Can we go emotional now? That doesn't make any sense!"

"No, no. Ginger said that she wants us to depart," CornFlakes corrected gently.

"Oh," Chidi said, her shoulders slumping.

"Don't worry," CornFlakes said with a reassuring smile. We'll get your magic back!"

"I sure hope so."

⋯⋯⋯⋯⋯⋯⋯⋯⋯⋯⋯⋯⋯⋯⋯⋯⋯⋯⋯⋯⋯⋯⋯⋯⋯⋯⋯⋯

5:30 P.M., on the right side

"Not to complain," Dalia said. "But do we have any food? I mean, how can we live if we can't find food?"

"No worries," Alexis said. "I have a satchel of R-E-C-I-P-E F-O-R B-I-R-D and water bottles. Plus some dried fruit, granola bars, and, of course, half of our candy stash."

"Sweet!" Redd tweeted.

"Sweet," Alexis recounted to Dalia immediately.

"Great."

"Alright, let's get going," Tumbles barked. "We have more ground to cover!"

"Yeesh," Dalia said, after Alexis had translated his words.

"Hey, guys, don't you want to get outta here? Pick up the pace!" Alexis started jogging, but she suddenly stopped. "Chidi! Your team is on our side of the maze? Raggy, yours too?" The three pathways had connected into one big junction.

"Yup."

"What a coincidence!" Autumn shrugged.

Chidi nodded.

"Uh . . . guys? What is that?" A small hole opened up in the ground, followed by smaller chunks falling into darkness.

"Go back! The ground is breaking!" She motioned for them to run. More ground started falling, faster.

"Take the next turn!" Dalia yelled as she sped around a corner. They all stopped once the ground was stable again

"Oh, man! That was—a close one," Raggy panted.

"Where are we? I don't think we got too far off track, right?" Dalia slumped down to catch her breath.

"What's *down* there?" Tumbles bounded up to the edge of the trap and looked down. What had started as a small hole was now a dark, gaping cavern.

"Looks like there's water down there. Hey, throw a stone down, and see what happens!" Tumbles barked at Alexis.

"Okay, if you say so." She picked up a rock, and to Dalia's surprise, dropped it at Tumbles' paws.

"You wanted to see what would happen." He pushed it in, and a *kerplunk* noise was made when it hit the water. Dalia walked over to look as bubbles started to rise to the surface.

"Alligators?" Autumn exclaimed. Ten or more of the large, scaly creatures swam to the surface of the water, staring up at them.

"Let's get outta here."

....

Meanwhile . . .

While Ben was driving, Laura was worrying.

This is all my fault, she thought. *They don't even know that they are Candyopolin! I can't believe I didn't tell or train them! They're probably being forced to live in a jail cell!*

Laura's thoughts kept rolling around her mind like clothes in a washing machine.

"Honey, are you going to be okay? You look sick." Ben put his hand on her shoulder.

"I—I need to tell you something." Her whole body was shaking as she continued, "I—we, me and our daughters, have magic blood. I came here from a magical world, escaping from my responsibilities. I am a duchess from that place, and I never told them. I thought it was unsafe."

Ben sighed and rolled his eyes. Pulling over into a parking lot, he said, "I know you have a lot on your mind, but just think about it, what is realistic? Is what you said realistic?"

"Ben, you have to believe me! Fine, I'll prove it." She got out of the car and walked behind a large rock, taking Benjamin by the hand.

"Laura—" His eyes widened. Laura had covered the rock with blooming hibiscus flowers with a wave of her hand

"Laura, what is this? Is this some sort of trick?"

"No, Ben, I'm not lying to you. This is my magical power, power over plants and growth. I really am a Candyopolin duchess. When I turned eighteen,

I snuck through a portal that I was able to create and turned my back on that magical world. I met you and had our children with no intentions of Alexis and Chidi having magic. I didn't know! I'm so sorry! This is my fault!" Laura began to sob. "I didn't mean for them to be lost!"

"It's alright. Alexis is the tough, bodyguard-like person, and Chidi is the smart one, they'll be okay."

"Excuse me?" a man in a bright orange-and-yellow uniform asked. "We'll be doing some construction in here, and we ain't wanting some emotional couple walking in the fresh 'n wet *cee*-ment!"

"Uh, sorry, sir." Ben pulled Laura away awkwardly.

Once they were in the car, Laura said, "You—actually believe me?"

"How could I not?" Ben shrugged like it didn't surprise him, easing the car back onto the road.

Laura and Ben drove in awkward silence until they reached the beach.

"Okay . . . let's see, 148 N. Starhouse Drive, here it is," Ben said, climbing out of the car.

Ben tells Laura "I think it would be smart if we pretend not to recognize Dexter from the hotel so that he might let us into the house." Laura smiles and says, "That sounds like a good idea."

Knock knock! The couple waited for an answer, and when the door opened, a man grumbled, "Whatever it is you're selling, we ain't buying it!"

"Um, actually, sir, we have evidence that our two daughters disappeared at your home," Mr. Parris informed the man.

"Wha'?" the man said. "Alright, come on in. Abby! Bring out something to eat, please!"

"Yes, dear."

"Come in, come in," the man said.

"Thank you," Mr. Parris said, stepping into the house.

The man pointed to the couch. "Sit down. I'm Dexter. There's my wife, Abigail. Our children are running around somewhere," he said, a hint of worry in his voice.

"Bella and Rankic?" Mrs. Parris asked coldly.

"Yes," Dexter said with a smirk. "What are your names?"

"I'm Ben, and this is my wife Laura. We have two twin daughters, Chidi Ann Parris and Alexis Blaze Parris, and I believe that you had them over for dinner last evening?"

"Yes. They went to the beach after they explored our basement."

"Alrighty then," Ben Parris said, straightening up. "Let's have a look at that basement, Dexter."

"You can't do that!" Dexter yelled.

"I can."

Ben holds up his badge and says "I'm investigating the disappearance of my twin daughters. I'm a police detective, and I can and will search your house. You do realize, Sir, that you can be held responsible for my daughters' disappearances?"

Ben glares at him, deciding to drop the nice act.

"I'm going down there," Ben said sternly. "And I would suggest you follow me."

They went down.

"Hello, Laura!" Abigail said cheerfully.

"Abigail! I haven't seen you since high school! Remember, we were on the school paper together, and we did that play—"

"And you wanted the lead role but I got it!" Abigail finished.

Both ladies laughed.

"So, married to Snow White's brother?" Laura asked.

"I guess so! Everyone says they look alike. I mean, Dex really *is* pale. And you! A police detective, am I right?"

"Yes, I guess so! I've missed you! We were good friends," Laura agreed, slowly sinking down on the cushions.

"Do you want a coffee? Or maybe some broccoli?" Abby offered.

"I'm not the sugary coffee type, but I'll have some greens."

"Good choice! I'll get us some carrots, peas, and some sliced apples, too! For whatever reason, my children absolutely *hate* green vegetables! Raggy, my son, he's twelve, says that green vegetables are children's public enemy number one, and sugar is a child's number one friend. Isn't that hilarious?"

"I know! Chidi would always eat some, just to be that little favorite, but Alexis always turned up her nose and refused. She's a wild thing. She's the sporty one, and *very . . . powerful*, if you get what I'm saying." Laura paused and smiled at her friend. "But Chidi is very nice as well."

"What's Cheater—I mean Chidi like?" Abby asked Laura.

"She's quieter, but she's a smart kid. She loves school. Alexis is more into basketball and gardening. Chidi likes cooking, photography, sewing, and drawing. Oh, and painting. She's the artistic one, and Alexis is more strong, determined, and fierce. But enough about my kids, what do your kids do?"

....

In the basement (of doom)

"Um, Dexter, why are there tubes, wires, and restraining devices in your basement?"

"Well, Ben, I guess you could say I'm a collector," Dexter said, patting Ben on the shoulder. "You know, the kind that has all kinds of things all over the place. I'm not really an organizer!" Dexter laughed a little too hard. "Ah-ha-ha-ha . . . ha."

"Are you sure?" Ben asked with a smirk. "Are you sure there's nothing that you're hiding?"

"Um . . . yes. I'm sure. Except for Christmas gifts!"

"Hilarious. I'm going to check your latest sent messages."

"Oh, I don't think you have to . . ." Dexter looked embarrassed.

Ben leaned over a computer and typed in a series of commands. Like his daughter, Alexis, he knew his way around a computer.

"Alright . . . let's watch this last recording." Ben hit the play button. It made a few little noises before it began. When it did, it changed everything.

Chapter Twenty

WE'RE IN HOT WATER (LITERALLY!)

"Seriously? Alligators?" Bella cried.

"Not alligators," Raggy told his sister. "Crocodiles."

The group had joined back up, all of them looking down the hole at the hungry animals.

"So, either way, we are *not* going down there. Right?" Autumn looked nervously at Alexis.

"Of *course* not. I'm not some crazy person! Let's just keep going, okay?" Alexis replied to Autumn's look.

"Alexis? Raggy? What do you make of *that?*" Chidi pointed to a large stag with red eyes and glowing markings that had just appeared at the edge of the woods

"Hey! I've seen something like that before!" Raggy exclaimed, pointing at the majestic animal.

"W-what's it doing?" Dalia cried as it started charging toward them.

"Hey—AAAH—"

Splash!

The stag charged into the kids, dragons, and pets, sending them flying off the edge of the chasm and into the water with powerful force. Under the water, Alexis swam frantically toward her friends.

"Guys! Are—you o-okay?" She gasped as she came up to the surface once she reached them.

"I'm—okay, but I can't say the same for the dragons! We need to help them!" Raggy exclaimed as he swam toward the group. The crocodiles were swimming and snapping at the dragons, hoping for a feast.

"Get back, kid!" Laven was using all his strength to stay afloat.

CornFlakes swung her pan at the nearest crocodile, crying, "Laven! Get ze kids to ze shore! I'll handle ze beasts!"

"What shore—oh, okay!" Laven turned as CornFlakes pointed toward a black-sand shore and swung her pan again.

"C'mon! Let's go!" Laven swam with the kids to the small sandbar.

"CornFlakes! Come on!" Dalia called to her. CornFlakes beat her wings, making her move faster through the murky water. They all plopped down on the sand, realizing how exhausted they were once they were safe.

"That—was a—close one . . . ," Bella panted, wringing out her hair. Raggy rubbed his chest and said, "I hope that thing didn't make me break a rib!"

"Yeah. How are we gonna get back up?" Ginger made an inaudible squeak, not wanting to move.

"Ginger wants to know how we get back up," Alexis translated.

"Yeah, I'm wondering that myself . . ."

Oreo barked, "Hey! Where's Redd? And the fairy?"

The group looked around, but they were nowhere to be seen.

"Redd? Hey, where are you?" Dalia called.

"We're up here!" They heard a faint tweet coming from the edge of the chasm above them. "That thing missed us!" Autumn called.

"Are you okay? I can see—ALLIGATOR!" Redd squawked frantically.

"Hey, glad you're okay! Can you guys fly down?" Alexis called back.

"Coming!" Redd and Autumn flew down, eyeing the water uneasily.

"Under the floor is surprisingly dark!" Raggy joked.

"Calm down." Laven closed his eyes, and the space between his scales started glowing.

"How—"

"Igneous Clan trait," Laven cut Bella off, looking at her like she should know what that means.

"Can't we just *fly* back up?" Bella asked, raising her eyebrow.

"I need to recover ze little bit first." CornFlakes shook the water off her wings.

"She's right. Even though it's a small distance, swimming really hurts. Remember? Magma dragon?" Laven pointed at himself.

"Hey, how do you heal so fast? You had that spear wound just a few days back," Chidi asked.

"Heat helps. I can just splash some lava on my back, and it'll heal pretty quick."

"Ouch!"

"Meh, not too painful. Just hot. And I'm used to it, so it's *fiiine*."

Dalia looked nervously at the water and said, "Hey, we should try to get outta here before *they* come back."

They nodded in agreement and looked through their soaked backpacks.

"Nope. Nada. Nothin'. Zilch. There is nothing of use except soaking granola bars and an almost broken 3-D pen," Alexis stated.

"Well, *that's* not gonna help us," Ginger meowed, and rolled her eyes.

"She says—"

"She's right. I can't help," Chidi interrupted Alexis.

"Guys! Let's just focus on getting out!" Bella examined the floor—now the roof—from below. "Hey, is there another sandbar or something? We could explore down here while the dragons rest up." Raggy said.

"You really think that's a good idea?" Dalia pointed at a crocodile/alligator or whatever it was.

"What should we call them? We don't know if they're crocodiles or alligators!" Chidi shrugged.

"How about . . . an allidile?" Raggy offered.

"No," Chidi argued, "It should be a crocogator!"

"CROCOGATOR?" one of the crocogators yelled. "I'm named JIMMITHY!" The pets sighed.

"Of course," Autumn shook her head.

This is normal now, Tumbles thought.

"Nice to meet you, Jimmithy!" Alexis called.

"*You are talking to a crocogator that tried to kill us,*" Bella whispered.

"Who in the dragon's stinky fire breath is *Jimmithy*?" Dalia exclaimed.

"Hey, Cheryl! Come over here!" Jimmithy hissed.

A more gray-ish-looking gator swam up beside him.

"I'll translate," Alexis stated.

"Thessse are those sssskiny kids?" 'Cheryl' rasped. "Hardly even worth my time."

"But *they* can understand us."

"The only question is, 'Can we eat them.'"

"No."

"Yes."

"No."

"Yes—"

"Hello? Can you understand what I am about to say?" Raggy called. "You! Can! Not! EAT US!"

"They say, 'Fine, then get out of here,'" Alexis said.

"Uh, we WOULD IF WE COULD!" Raggy yelled.

The soaking Oreo, Tumbles, and Ginger—along with the dry Redd—rolled their eyes and covered their ears.

"'We don't want you here. We'll call some friends to take you away,'" Alexis translated, sounding bored.

"Okay, sure thing. GET US OFF THIS ROCK!"

"Okay, okay! Alligators have very sensitive ears!"

"Wait, you're an alligator?" Alexis asked, disappointed. "I thought you were supposed to be a crocogator!"

"Fine," Jimmithy said, "I'm a crocogator. Is your heart singing for joy now? Going 'whoo-hoo'?"

"No, not really. Say it again." The crew looked at Alexis strangely, wishing they knew what was happening.

"Whoo-hoo. Yay. I'm a crocogator." Jimmithy slapped his tail on the surface of the water, splashing Laven.

"Owch!"

"That feels great!" Alexis called, who had been equally dosed.

"Yuck!" Autumn dried her silver hair on Alexis' shirt.

Laven shook his head like a dog. "Yeah, great."

Meanwhile, CornFlakes had encouraged Bella, Dalia, and Ginger to hop onto her back.

"C'mon," she whispered. She launched herself into the air. Chidi was the only one who saw it happen. The others were busy yelling at the 'crocogators'. Soon, CornFlakes flew back down to scoop up the rest of the group.

"Bye, Jimmithy! Now let's go." Alexis started walking after saying goodbye and dismounting.

"Is that deer still here?" Oreo woofed to Tumbles.

"Don't think so."

"We should be close," Autumn said.

They kept walking until the path started to widen. "Hey, I think she is— right."

They walked into a large clearing, overflowing with wildlife and plants no one recognized.

A giant flower filled with crystal-clear water stood at the center of the clearing. It looked like a large hibiscus flower, but the center—where the pollen should be—was filled with water. All around the flower were more deer-stags, does, and fawns alike—all with different colors, all bright and vibrant.

One stag was standing on one of the giant flower's petals. It had pure-white eyes and somewhat short horns with gold speckles on them.

"Uh, guys?" Raggy said. "For you girly girls, this is all super cool, but for a normal human like me, I want to get out of here, as soon as possible, before another booby trap is set off!"

"Boo," a voice said from behind them.

"AAAAAH!" they screamed, but it was just a baby deer.

"Wait, you talk?" Raggy yelled. "You actually scared me! No one can really do that! Obviously, I was just pretending. *Nothing* can scare *me*." He wiggled his eyebrows.

"What about a giant wasp with stinging poison?" The deer trotted over to a lever and acted like he was going to pull it and release a giant wasp or another creature of doom.

The older deer sighed and stared expectantly at Chidi and Alexis.

"Ah! Don't let that thing near me! Help! Don't pull that lever! Whatever you do, *don't pull that lever!*" Raggy screamed in terror.

"Raggy, that's nothing. C'mon, let's just go."

They walked up to the flower, looking for the 'tree of magic' that Autumn had told them about.

"Chidi. You come here seeking magic?" the white deer said in an ancient, creaking voice.

"Y-yes, Sir?" she replied.

"Good. Then come with me."

Chapter Twenty One

NEVER DID I EVER

"What are you saying?" Chidi asked, kneeling by the flower's water. They were talking to the deer and trying to figure out what was going on.

"You girls are special. Alexis, you possess the power of lava, heat, fire, etc., etc. Chidi, the power of Summoning, but another power lies deep . . . hold still. By the way, my name is Tree."

Tree, the deer, shook his head, and a white light shot out of his forehead and enveloped Chidi with a shimmering yellow light.

"Magic problem solved."

"You—gave me my magic back?" Chidi looked around, startled.

"*What?*" Alexis' voice was barely a whisper as she looked at her hands, eyes wide.

"Summoning?" Chidi asked.

"I shall train you both. Now Chidi, close your eyes. Where are you?"

Alexis gasped as her sister disappeared with another flash of light.

....

Somewhere . . .

Chidi opened her eyes.

"WHOA!"

She was in a dark, murky cave. She peered closer into the darkness, but she couldn't see anything.

Somewhere, deep in her heart, she heard a voice say, *"Look inside yourself . . . find yourself . . . be yourself."*

Myself, Chidi thought. She closed her eyes, and a warm, golden glow surrounded her. The air grew thick and enveloped her with light.

She allowed the warmth to seep into her, warming her from somewhere deep inside herself. She wrapped her arms around herself.

A feeling of . . . hope . . . filled her. As if there was a chance for them to stand against anything. But, at the same time, she was scared. Threats loomed above her, along with unanswered questions.

Will we ever get home again?

Will we ever see our parents?

Are we going to be here forever?

"Never," Chidi whispered. "Never."

Suddenly a vision appeared . . . like she was watching a million images on a TV screen. But it was her family.

Bella, yelling at them with a hurt and angry expression on her face.

Raggy, glaring at Alexis and holding a bowl of something.

A younger version of Laura, standing with a teenage Jenny in front of a violet portal.

Dexter and Abigail, huddling next to a teenage girl, looking tearful and upset.

Dalia, kneeling at the foot of a turquoise bed, sobbing.

Ben, standing in the midst of a wildfire and looking grief-stricken.

Chidi, herself, crumpled on the floor and clinging to a framed photograph.

Alexis, laying on a white cot with lots of bandages around her midsection.

"Why?" Chidi asked aloud. "Why are all these horrible things happening?"

The light breeze of the cave stirred and became like a storm.

A phrase flashed through her mind, flickering like a dying flashlight.

Never Did I Ever.

"Will anything good ever happen?" Chidi shouted into the wind.

More images came.

Bella, smiling as she linked arms with Chidi and Dalia.

Raggy, sitting at a wooden table eating a hamburger and chatting with Chidi, beaming.

Laura, surrounded by her family—Jenny, Ben, Alexis, and Chidi—clutching them close as if she had lost them before.

Dexter and Abigail, holding Rankic and Bella and telling them something.

Dalia, surrounded by her friends, each looking ready to help her through whatever she was faced by.

Ben, beaming as Alexis, grinning, held a ball of blackness.

Jenny, talking with an elderly woman and man, looking happier than ever.

Chidi, laughing at something Rankic had said, both of them talking over one another.

And Alexis, talking with a girl Chidi didn't recognize who had dark hair, freckles, and glasses, while settled in a blue, red, orange, and yellow room.

"I get it," Chidi said. "We'll have hard times and then good times. But can't we just . . . have a normal life?"

"It will never be the same," a little voice whispered . . . but not like the other one. This came from her head, not her heart.

"No," Chidi answered, her voice coming out as a squeak.

She tried to pull an answer from her heart. But, all that came to mind was a motto of her late grandfather, based on a Bible verse:

"In this world, you will have tribulations. But take heart; I have overcome the world."

The *I* in the verse referred to Jesus Christ.

"He has," she said, her voice strong and clear. "And I can face the day."

Something made her add, "Never Did I Ever."

As she spoke the words, a dot of white appeared in the distance. It came closer, growing with each step.

The first thing she saw was a strong, white paw. It was an Albino lioness.

Chidi touched the lioness' back, expecting it to jump at her and maybe swat a large paw. But instead, the lioness purred like a house cat.

Chidi sank to her knees, the lioness curling up beside her.

The lioness let out a low, throaty growl, and the sound turned in Chidi's mind until it formed one word: *Crystal.*

"Crystal?" she asked.

In response, the lioness leaped up and played with a rock.

"Crystal, no," Chidi told the lioness. It obeyed.

"All right . . . ," Chidi mumbled. "What to do? Well, I'm going to call you Crystal for sure . . . but, what do those images mean? Will they actually happen? Are they warnings?"

Instead of answering, the lioness—Crystal—swatted at a dove flying through the sky.

"Okay."

Chidi touched the images that glistened, hanging in the air. They were still there, bordered with colorful lights.

"Are there more?" she wondered, hoping she would see an image of her, Alexis, Dalia, and maybe Bella hanging at the beach or in the attic. But instead, one video flickered into place.

It was the most beautiful thing Chidi had ever seen, although not too happy.

Chidi was standing in the middle of a battlefield.

Dalia was holding a large stick and beating a cloaked figure.

Bella was *flying* with a burst of wind and attacking the figure.

Raggy was chucking rocks at the mysterious person.

Alexis was shooting dark blue flames.

And Chidi was standing on the sidelines as her friends and sister fought. All while a voice whispered, *"Do I belong?"*

But then it skipped on and went to a voice clip of Raggy: "Chidi, you will always belong to the fearsome five."

Then Bella: "Don't forget that you're different—you fit in because you stand out."

Alexis: "You're my sister. I love you. Don't change yourself—you're Chidi Parris, and you're different, and that's why everyone loves you."

Rankic again: "Chidi, you're awesome—one of my favorite people ever. Just . . . never forget that you belong with us."

Alexis again: "Chidi, you are a *Parris*. Adventure will find you . . . let it in. You're the best person I've ever known, and . . . I love you."

And then Dalia, leaving Chidi with the best message of her life: "Chidi, you're my best friend . . . and you'll be perfect for whatever you do. Remember that you're our *family*. We'll do anything for *you*."

Then Chidi thought, *Maybe I belong here.*

. . . .

Present Day . . .

Chidi blinked and reappeared back in the odd forest.

"What did you see?" Tree asked.

Chidi didn't want to share her discoveries. They were too . . . private. So she explained about Crystal, and Tree seemed very pleased. But Alexis seemed suspicious.

"Very good. This is your special animal. Unique, strong and courageous, but weak without your pack." Tree smiled.

"Crystal. That'll be it's name," Chidi whispered. She was getting used to her magic again.

Suddenly a violet light struck out of Chidi's outstretched arm. In the mist, a white lioness stood, the same as Chidi had described.

"WHOA!" Alexis exclaimed.

"What the—" Chidi ran over to it, shaking her head.

"So cool!" Alexis exclaimed.

"Would you like to be trained as well?" Tree asked.

"One thing first. So, *you* are the 'Tree of Magic'?" Alexis asked skeptically.

"Yes. I do kind of look like a tree, as is my name."

"Uh-huh."

"So. Do you like spicy things?"

"Uh . . . yes? Why?"

Tree laughed. "Do you doubt me?"

"No? You gave Chidi her powers back, so—"

The stag stepped back. "One second."

"O-kay?"

"Hya!" Tree rammed into Alexis, sending her flying backward.

"What was that for? That *hurt!*" she exclaimed, rubbing her ribs.

"For now, the only way to trigger your fire is to make *you* use it. I can train in controlling it, not making it."

"So you're gonna hit me over and over again?"

"Well? What do you think?"

. . . .

Meanwhile . . .

"Don't you think it's crazy how he just zapped her powers back?" Raggy was sitting with Bella on a large rock.

"Yeah, but I guess that's how these things work. I can deal with talking to Crocogators, seeing my life flash before my eyes, and getting imprisoned by a dragon. But I'm kinda jealous right now!" Bella watched Chidi talking to the pets and lion happily.

"Yeah. I get you." Raggy was watching Alexis sparring with a deer, one of the funniest things he had seen in a while.

"Hey, y'all!" Autumn flew over from talking to Dalia. "So . . . y'know you can go home after this, and I am still expecting you to hold up your end of the deal."

"You mean taking you to Earth?" Dalia asked.

"Yes."

They all sighed. They knew bringing a magical creature into the real world wasn't a good idea. They had read about it lots of times.

"Who are you going to stay with?" Bella asked. "It *probably* wouldn't go well with our family. And Dalia's parents don't know *anything* about magic."

Dalia looked at Bella and rolled her eyes.

"What? My dad knows more about it than yours!" Bella shrugged and continued. "So, are you gonna stay with Chidi and Alexis?"

"Yeah, I guess—do you smell something burning?" Autumn flitted higher so she could see.

"*Whaaaa?*" Autumn flew down, a look of sheer surprise on her face.

"Hey. Uh . . . did you know Alexis could shoot fireballs?"

"*What?*" they all yelled in unison.

"Uh-huh. Uh-huh uh-huh uh-huh." Dalia looked around Autumn, and sure enough, there was Alexis, standing next to the deer, a fireball in her hand and terror on her face.

"Yeah, I guess that doesn't really surprise me. They're *royalty,* so why not give them cool *MAGIC POWERS!*" Dalia shook her fist at the sky.

"Darn you, Destiny!"

"Rrrrright," Raggy said and continued the conversation like nothing had happened.

"This is normal," Ginger purred.

....

Malcora's Lair

"Where are they?" Malcora tore apart yet another map.

"I have searched everywhere!" A short black dragon with glasses stood with her.

"Not everywhere, the Palace has not been—"

"THE PALACE? Are you crazy?" Malcora roared.

"Uhum, n-n-no?" the black dragon stammered.

"We are *not* going to the Palace!" Malcore sighed.

"Void, how much do you want to be the number-one cartographer?" she sneered.

"V-very badly, Miss!"

"Good. Would you like to use your old mapmaker again?"

"What are you suggesting M-miss?"

"My . . . *counterpart* is arriving soon. We will take back what is rightfully ours!" A ferocious gleam was in her eye as she blew out a candle.

....

The Dragon Palace . . .

Princess Esmerelda looked at the mirror. Most of the dragons didn't wear clothes, except for the staff and royals. She curtsied in her floaty green dress.

"Thank you, thank you! I love being your queen!" she told herself.

"Princess Esmerelda?" a rose-colored dragon asked.

"Oh! Um, Floid, hello! What are you doing here?"

"I came to tell you that your mother requests your presence down in the dragon hall."

"Thank you, Floid," Esmerelda said.

"Of course, Your Highness." Floid bowed and then scampered away.

Esmerelda sighed. Her eldest sister, Isa, was going to be crowned queen that night. Her dreams of being a queen were close to over. She was the fifth eldest of eight.

I DON'T WANT TO BE A PRINCESS! I WANT TO BE A QUEEN! Esmerelda screamed in her head.

"Maybe," Esmerelda murmured, "I could try to take it by . . . *force*." An evil grin spread across her face. "Enjoy it while you can, Isa. Enjoy it while you can!" And with that, she let out the evilest cackle ever heard.

"But," Esmerelda said quickly. "I can't do it on my own. I need an expert." She tapped her talons on the floor. "Malcora!"

"M-m-alcor-r-ra?" Esmerelda's friend, Pixie McKenna, fluttered out of a small, birdhouse-like room hanging on the wall. "You surely don't mean Malcora, the former queen, do you, Esmerelda?"

"Of course, I mean Malcora, fool!" she snarled. Then she regained her posture. "I mean, of course, I meant Malcora, McKenna."

"But why, Esmi?"

"Because," Esmerelda replied, "We need to take the plunge. For the *whole* kingdom."

Chapter Twenty Two

MALCORA STRIKES AGAIN

"Alexis?" Chidi asked her sister. "Do you think Dexter is the real boss?"

"Huh?" Alexis turned towards Chidi. "What do you—AHH!" Tree had rammed into her again.

"Alexis! Another fireball!" The stag shouted.

While Alexis dodged Tree's blows, Dalia, Bella, and Raggy were thinking.

"Y'know, we could ask for magic, too," Dalia said.

"What? You think that tree-deer is going to just give us magic powers?" Raggy asked.

"Well, why not? I mean, Chidi didn't even ask and she got all of her magic restored!"

"Restored . . ." Bella leaped up from her place on a log. "I've got it! My dad has Chidi's magic in that syringe, right?"

"Uh-huh."

"So if we go back, we can inject ourselves with it and get powers!"

"Uh, slight problem. Not to point out the obvious, but we're trapped here!" Dalia said, exasperated. "Also, I'm not *that* desperate for magic!"

"Excuse me?" Alexis said, walking over with Chidi at her heels.

"Well," Dalia began.

"Why do you get the magic? I mean, you are royalty, *plus* you have magic powers! It's not fair! If we inject ourselves with your magic, Chidi, *we* could have good things happen, too!" Bella shouted.

Raggy stared at his sister in surprise. "What? You're crazy! Dad always was . . ."

"He is terrible! He *locked us in the basement.*"

"Of doom."

"Yes, of doom. But, he doesn't worry about us! You guys have each other, *plus* good parents, *plus* a caring aunt, *plus* great pets, *and* you're royal! You have everything I've always wanted! And with magic! We get the worst part of things, and we just want one thing to go our way! Don't you get it?"

"Yes, Bella. I just . . . I can't believe you would take *my* magic and use it. It's . . . ," Chidi trailed off.

"Well, you already have your perfect life back!" Bella screamed.

"Fine!" Chidi shouted back.

Raggy defended his sister, and Dalia sided with Chidi. Alexis went to Tree.

"Hey, Tree?"

"Yes? Are you ready to resume?"

"Uh, in a minute. Can you maybe give my friends some magic powers? I mean, they're really, really jealous. Please?"

"After you do one task," Tree told her, a sly gleam in his eye.

"What is it?"

"Try this," Tree said, leaning in to tell her something.

Lexi looked pained, but decided, Chidi guessed, to try it. She went into the forest with Tree, then reemerged, looking flustered.

"Okay, now give my friends magic, please!"

"Fine."

Soon, Tree had all of the kids around him.

"Bella, I grant you the power of wind. Raggy, you can now control metals and rocks."

"What about me?" Dalia asked.

"Oh! Well, whaddya wanna do?"

"Um . . . could I have invisibility magic?"

"Yup!" Tree nodded his head. "Dalia, you can turn a group of people invisible."

"Uh, alright."

"Bella, you can control the wind."

"Whatever."

"Raggy, you can control stone—"

"Got it," Raggy interrupted.

"Well." Tree straightened up. "That's all! Oh, and your powers will be weaker than Alexis and Chidi's magic."

"I guess we go on?" CornFlakes asked.

"Yeah, I guess so," Alexis said.

"Uh, Alexis?" Chidi said. "Do you remember what I asked earlier?"

"No."

"Do you think Dexter is the real threat?"

"Excuse me!" Bella called. "I know he's a lunatic, but he's also my dad!"

"Yeah, I see the resemblance," Dalia said, rolling her eyes—something she did so often that the twins wondered if her eyes were loose.

"So, is he?" Alexis asked Raggy and Bella.

"Well, he works for a guy named Robert Brisket," Raggy began.

"Robert?" Alexis raised her eyebrows.

"No, just kidding. Bob. Bob Brisket."

Alexis blinked one time and then burst out laughing.

"Bob Brisket!" she managed between howls. She wiped tears from her eyes.

"It's not *that* funny," Dalia said.

"Try saying it aloud!"

"Bob Brisket," Dalia said in a monotype. Then she lost it. "Ah-ha-ha-ha! Aw, man, that's *awesome!* He is named after part of a *cow!*"

"I know!" The two girls repeated the name over and over between giggles.

"Let's go! We can fly through the maze, taking breaks at parts, since we don't have anything to prove." Laven said finally. "Girls, go with CornFlakes. I'll take the guys."

Raggy, Tumbles, Redd, and Oreo boarded Laven while Alexis, Chidi, Ginger, Bella, and Dalia climbed aboard. Autumn napped in the backpack.

"Whee!" Chidi squealed while Bella screamed, "AHHH!"

Dalia and Chidi settled into a conversation about volleyball. Bella looked at Alexis with a hopeful look on her face.

"So," Alexis said. "Uh, what do you like to do?"

Bella stared at Alexis with the blankest expression on her face. "I like gardening. I have a patch of strawberries that I grow."

"Really? Cool! I garden. A little. I've never tried strawberries, but I've heard they're hard. Who taught you? Your mom?"

"No. My grandpa," Alexis replied.

"Is he . . ." Bella trailed off. She didn't want to seem rude or impolite.

"Yeah. It's fine," Alexis said with a sad smile.

"So, what about you? Besides gardening."

"Um . . . I love technology. I like to think I'm good at it, but I'm really not. Also journaling. I wish I had my journal. I just have a notepad." Alexis told her.

"Well, you could always write on that, Alexis."

"Yeah, I guess so." She straightened her olive green T-shirt with little gold palm trees.

"I wish I had a change of clothes!" Bella said, motioning to her short pink-and-yellow flowy shirt. "It's so . . . formal for this adventure! You're dressed for this kind of thing." She pointed toward Lexi's T-shirt and blue leggings.

"Yeah, but I'm *so* ready to go home, know what I mean?"

"I know, right?" Bella began chattering away about clothing.

Alexis sighed. She unzipped her pack and pulled out a multicolored ballpoint pen and notepad. She began to write.

Dear Journal,

I'm writing this from on top of a dragon. I know, it sounds crazy. My friends, Bella and Dalia, are with me and Chidi. I can't believe what's happened! Chidi got her magic back, and she can summon a lioness named Crystal! I have the power over lava, heat, and that sort of thing! Also, Bella, Raggy, and Dalia also got powers! Raggy can control stone, Dalia invisibility, and Bella can control wind! It's so cool! Ginger is with us on top of CornFlakes.

CornFlakes really lost that whole, "Zoo are going to become food!" kinda act. Also, she isn't struggling with talking normally. It's only when she's excited.

Dalia is super fun and adventurous. She's always optimistic. She's really fun, but she seems to be closer to Chidi since they both play volleyball. (Probably better than my basketball. They're both super talented!)

Raggy is twelve, just like all of us. He's Bella's twin brother. He's nice enough, I guess. He hangs out with Laven (whom I will talk about soon!) and argues with Bella all the time. It's pretty obvious that they are siblings.

Laven is another dragon. He is an Igneous dragon. Apparently, he and Chidi had to battle in an arena, like those gladiators from Rome or Greece. One of those ancient places. He is nice, from what I can gather. He and the other boys are having fun together.

Autumn is a pixie and an amazing cook. Her Dim Sum, as well as mushroom biscuits, are delicious. She's really fun. She also made us promise to take her back to Earth with us. I have no idea what to do. But I guess we'll have to tell Mom and Dad what happened. Let's hope they don't think we've gone crazy in the head.

Bella is my closest chance of a friend, I think. She likes gardening and is pretty nice. But she just seems so girly! She loves pink, unicorns, and rainbows.

Plus, she cares about clothes a whole lot more than I do. But . . . I don't know. I somehow actually *get* Bella. Although, Bella and Chidi are good friends too.

Oreo is Dalia's dalmatian puppy. He's really cute and shy. And as expected, Chidi and I can understand him. He and Tumbles are friends. Plus, Ginger and Redd are close with them.

Alexis stopped writing and slipped it into her pack.

"Hey, I'm gonna try my power!" Bella exclaimed. "Uh . . . how do I do this again?" she asked Alexis.

"Concentrate really hard. Focus on what it would look like when it happens," she instructed.

"And don't forget to be calm and kind," Chidi added. "You want to coax it, not to force it."

"Good advice," Alexis told her sister.

"Kay." Bella squeezed her eyes shut. "Hmm."

A small sphere of swirling wind appeared in her hands.

"Whoa!" Bella lost focus, and the ball zoomed out of her hands, flying into a cloud.

"Wowzer!" Autumn exclaimed from the backpack.

"That's cool!" Alexis laughed.

"Yeah, I guess." Bella shrugged.

"Ve are going to stop for a rezt!" CornFlakes called and started descending.

"EEK!" Bella shut her eyes and wrapped her arms around Alexis' waist. They landed in a cloud of dust, still in the maze.

"So that's when I spiked it over the net . . ."

Dalia was telling Chidi about one of her games. "And when the other kid bounced it back, I got it over for the winning shot!"

Raggy was telling Laven about video games and some of his favorite ones. Alexis smiled as she walked over to a corner of the maze with no bushes.

"C'mon . . . c'mon!" she urged herself and made a ball of fire. She examined it, thinking, *Man. This could be so . . . dangerous. Especially if it got into the wrong hands.*

Bella walked over and asked, "Whatcha doin'?"

"Oh. Nothing," she replied calmly.

"Nothing? *Playing with fire* is *nothing?*" Bella smirked.

"Hey, I'm not playing! Just trying to figure out my lava and sun powers. Tree only taught me fire."

"Uh-huh. Looks like it's not going too well." She rolled her eyes.

"Like you're one to talk . . ." Alexis muttered.

"Chill! Not judging!"

"Whatever."

"So . . . wanna snack?" Bella held out the biggest, juiciest strawberry ever.

"Thanks! Where did you get that?" Alexis took a big chomp out of it.

"Tree filled Chidi's backpack full of fruit!" She laughed and held out three peaches.

"Ha! Well, no wonder he was staring at her backpack!"

"Yeah." Bella's eyes filled with sadness.

"Hey, you okay?"

"Just, well . . . homesick I guess."

"Same. I really miss my parents, especially my dad. I wish I could say sorry."

"Sorry about what?"

"Just . . ." Her flame flickered out. "I was being really disrespectful. I was letting my anger be my boss."

"Anger about what?" Bella asked, and sat down next to Alexis.

"Moving. We had moved so many times, Chidi and I just lost it."

"Oh."

"Hey, guys? Where did Dalia go?" Chidi walked over.

"I dunno. I thought you were talking to her?" Bella shrugged off the question.

"I'm right here!" an invisible someone exclaimed.

"AAH! Oh, you went invisible!" Alexis snapped her fingers.

"Hey! We are departing soon! Earth-bound!" Laven called, as Raggy walked over.

"What did you teach him?" Bella asked.

"*What*? I *might* have told him about some retro-space video games."

"What am I gonna do with you?" Bella cried, as she hopped on CornFlakes.

Dalia reappeared and jumped on behind her. Alexis sighed, mounting as well.

....

The Dragon Hall

"Esmerelda! This is truly a wondrous occasion, isn't it?" Esmerelda's mother, Queen Viola, was a tall dragon, with purple scales and pretty brown eyes.

"*Yes*, Mother . . ."

They were walking down the white-quartz hall. The windows gave natural light to the majestic room. Statues and paintings of the Dragon Queens lined the walls. They stopped by the newest one, a sculpture of Princess Isa.

The sight of it made Esmerelda's blood boil.

"What is wrong, Dear? Oh, isn't it just *beautiful*? Like the sun gleaming through a crystal shard . . ."

Esmerelda tuned out her mother's poetic outburst, looking down at all of the statues.

"Mother!" she interrupted.

"*Yes*, Esmi?"

"Uh, I need to go and . . . uh, check on Prince Noon. He wanted to, um, talk to me?"

"Esmi, you need to know that it is simply not *proper*—"

"Okay, bye!" Esmerelda took off down the long hall and turned a corner into her bedroom. She flung off her dress, grabbed her tiara, and snatched McKenna up in a tight grip.

"EEK! Where are we—" Esmerelda silenced her with a stern look and ran to the landing. Dragons were flying in and out, making it easy to be lost in the crowd. She zoomed off the balcony-like platform and into the sky. She stretched out her wings in the blue sky, zooming fast over the Dragon Kingdom.

"*Now* will you tell me where we are going?" McKenna squealed, losing her breath in Esmerelda's iron grasp.

"We are going to find Malcora! I cannot stand this anymore! 'Esmi, you aren't proper!' 'Esmi, do this!' 'Esmi, curtsy like this.' '*Darling*, isn't this statue of your older sister who-took-your-rightful-place *BEAUTIFUL?*' And I think I know where she is," she roared.

McKenna gave her a sorry look, and she was silent the rest of the flight. Diving through a metal shaft, Esmerelda swooped at high speed into a cave, her wingtips brushing the walls.

"Ungh!" she grunted when she landed.

Two blue dragons stepped behind her to block her exit, once she stepped out on a big ridge.

"Who are *you?*" Malcora was eating a large bird, again, on her rock.

"I-I am—" She put on her tiara, and continued, "I am Princess Esmerelda. And I have a business proposition for you."

"Well, well, well. If it isn't the little princess. Why are you here? For 'peace'?" Malcora sneered.

"Exactly the opposite. I want to declare war upon soon-to-be Queen Isa!"

Her announcement shocked Malcora. "You want to *what*?"

"Declare war on Isa, my . . . ugh, sister. She's not supposed to be queen, *I AM!*" Esmerelda yelled.

"That is the exact thing I thought . . ." Malcora smiled.

"Then we are in agreement?" Esmerelda said uneasily.

"Yes. Yes, we most certainly are!"

Chapter Twenty Three

BOB IS BACK

"WHAT did you do?" Bella screeched at Raggy. "Why did you bring a *video game* with you, and *why on earth* would you give it to *a dragon*?" His tiny console was only about as large as his pocket, and he carried it with him everywhere.

"Well, he wanted to know how 'Knights and Dragons' worked, so I let him."

"Wait," Autumn said. "Isn't 'Knights and Dragons' about knights trying to *defeat* dragons?"

"Oh . . . yeah." Raggy hung his head. "Best take it away from him."

"Wait, they just locked the dragon into a *cage*?" Laven asked. "That's so sad!" The game fell from his claws and hit the floor. Raggy swiftly picked it up.

"Well, you can always pick the dragon as your character," Chidi said gently, stroking Ginger.

"Uh-huh," Alexis said, trying to make another fireball.

"Ahh!" Dalia cried. "Why is there a fireball on my jacket?"

"Oh . . . sorry. I was practicing my magic."

"Well, please practice it on your *own* jacket."

"I'm sorry. I'll buy a new one?"

"No . . ." Dalia shook her head. "It's not destroyed. I mean, the ball didn't scorch it, just, y'know, made it hot."

"Isn't that the point of a jacket?" joked Raggy.

"Yeah, very funny, court jester!" Dalia exclaimed, holding the jacket like it had a deadly virus on it.

"Let's just get out of here. It should only take one more flight to get out of the maze!" Chidi exclaimed optimistically and hopped on CornFlakes' back.

"Yeah, yeah. Let's just go already," Bella said and snatched the small device from Raggy's hands.

"*I* will be taking *that!*" she said snootily and hopped on behind Chidi.

Alexis just sighed and slid onto Laven's back. She was the only one on him, and once he had taken flight, she said, "Hey, Laven?"

"Yeah?"

"How, exactly, do you control your magic?"

"I guess I just go with the flow."

"What?"

Laven tilted his head as they soared around a cloud. "It's like this. If I don't think I can make a volcano, I just make a blast of lava. You're lucky, you have lava *and* fire and heat and stuff. I only have lava."

"Oh. Laven, do you think I can suck *away* heat to make it cold?"

"You mean, like power over ice and snow *with* your heat powers?"

"Yes."

"Hard to say. I don't know if you can. I don't know much. Probably not though."

Alexis concentrated on making a ball of fire. She made it bigger and bigger. Finally, it was as big as Laven himself. Then, as a final test, she reached her fingers towards it.

Chidi, riding on CornFlakes, saw her sister. "LEXI! Don't touch the fire!"

"What? I wasn't going to touch it!" Alexis lied.

"Alexis Blaze Parris, you are *not* going to lie to me!" Chidi yelled.

"Okay, okay!" Alexis called.

"Ugh, you're so reckless!" Chidi shouted in frustration. "And I do *not* think you can control the cold, so do *not* try it!"

"All right, all right," Alexis mumbled.

....

In Canada . . .

"How are the tests going?" Bob demanded. He was standing next to a lab worker, in a large room filled with odd machines, levers, and giant test tubes.

"S-sir, the essence is still unstable, but if the construction team is ready, we can inject it now." The nervous worker was typing as fast as his fingers could go, doing binary and multiplying square inches at the same time.

"Why are you so lazy?" Bob shouted. "You aren't doing anything!"

"Yes, s-sir. I-I'm so s-sorry. I-it won't happen again."

"It better not!" roared Bob. "I want that portal ready for me! I want the magic done *now!*"

"Mr. Bob?" a lady named Ophelia said, standing tall and poised. "You have an unexpected visit with Mr. Graham."

"All right, who's that?" Bob had forgotten who Dexter was. After getting directions, he walked down many halls and into an almost empty room.

"Ah, Bob." Dexter was sitting at the head of a long table.

"DEXTER? What are you doing here?"

"I just wanted to be given my . . . fair share."

Bob seated himself in a chair. "What do you mean, fair share?"

"Um, Mr. Bob, you *did* promise Mr. Graham would get half of the area you'll overtake."

"Oh. Yeah. Well, go home! I don't want you to get it, and if I don't want to give it to you, you don't get it."

"Well." Dexter rose and gave Bob a stern stare. Bob was only thirty-one, while Dexter was forty-two.

"Good-bye!" Bob slammed the door.

Out in the hall, Dexter began to think. *I think Bob's just using me. Maybe Bella was right. Maybe the good path* is *the right one.*

....

In the Magical Kingdom

"Can . . . we . . . take . . . a rest?" Raggy wheezed as he trudged along a path.

"Sure. Also, *where* are we going? I mean, we already have Chidi's magic back. Why would we need to go to a specific place?" Alexis asked, conjuring a smoky cloud.

"Hmm." Bella thought as she unzipped Chidi's backpack and snuck a granola bar.

"I don't know, but we need to find a way home, ASAP," Chidi said, simultaneously snatching the granola bar out of Bella's hand and stuffing it into her pack.

"You need to see the Unicort for that," Laven told them. "They're in charge of the Golden Lands."

"Yeah . . . slight problem. We kinda got locked in jail there three days ago."

"Wait, what?" Chidi exclaimed.

"Yeah, that's where we met Autumn. She was the jailer. Missy and Nasha were the ones who brought us there."

"Oh. I guess that's where we're headed?" Chidi said quizzically.

"Alexis! Chidi! Are you here?" a woman's voice called. "Girls?"

"*Aunt Jenny?*" the twins exclaimed.

"What a coincidence!" Jenny laughed.

"What are you doing here?" Alexis exclaimed, running over to her.

"And how?" Chidi added, wrapping her aunt in a hug.

"Oh, hey, Mrs. Kerifly," Dalia added cooly.

Aunt Jenny sighed. "Girls, we need to talk."

Alexis twisted her mouth up but followed Jenny and Chidi to a set of tree stumps.

"I'm *from* here. I mean, well, I—um . . ." Aunt Jenny cleared her throat and sat up. "What I mean to say is that your mother, who is my older sister, and I were Duchesses of Candyopolis.

"I loved being royal, but your mother was very tired of it and wanted a better life. She was able to find a portal to Earth and decided to leave. She told only me her plan, and because I adored her, I followed her. We made a new life. Anyway, we had to start a new family of secrets, but it was worth it," Aunt Jenny finished.

"Whoa, whoa, whoa. What's Mom and your powers?" Alexis interrupted.

"Alexis!" Chidi hissed. "Don't be rude!"

"It's all right, Chidi," Aunt Jenny said with a laugh. "I have teleportation magic, and Laura has plants and growth."

"So," Raggy said. "Can we get home now?"

"Wait!" Everyone turned to Jenny. "I haven't been to Candyopolis in years! Can't we at least visit?"

"All right," Autumn said.

"So, how long does it take?" Dalia asked Aunt Jenny.

"Oh, about ten seconds." Jenny closed her eyes. "Close your eyes, everybody!"

....

At Earth, 2:00 P.M.

"So, you have no idea where they went?" Mr. Parris asked Dexter. He had let him go, telling him to talk to Bob Brisket, face-to-face. He agreed and came back with news.

"*Plus*, he won't give you the land and money he promised?" Laura cut in.

"*Plus*, he is working on something big that could bring an end to the so-called 'Magical World'?" Mrs. Graham shook her head furiously like she struggled to believe it.

"Y-yes . . . all those things are true." Dexter slumped, realizing the destruction he could cause.

"I have *every* reason to arrest you right here and now."

Ben took Dexter by the shoulders, staring intensely into his eyes. "*But, I need both* of your help. To find *all* of our kids."

Dexter and Abigail both agreed, worried sick about Bella and Rankic. They were on the beach, walking to the Parris' car.

"So, you have *magical powers,* huh?" Mrs. Graham muttered, staring at Laura.

"Yes, I do. You really want proof?" she replied coolly.

"I'm struggling to believe it myself," Ben said with a nod.

Mrs. Parris sighed, closing her eyes. She pointed at the Graham's planter and traced an invisible line in the air with her index finger. The parents were all standing behind her, blocking anybody from seeing. Flowers of all colors shot up from the ground, making the word, "Magic".

"Wow . . ." Abigail ran over and traced her fingers along the M, as though she didn't believe it was real.

"W-w-we believe you . . ." Dexter stepped back, almost looking scared.

"Good," Laura said, as she opened the car door. "Now let's go save our kids! And possibly the whole magical world!"

. . . .

Meanwhile . . .

"OOOOOOphilea!" Bob called. He was standing in a large hanger, a giant circular metal ring in front of him.

"Y-y-yes Mr. Bob? W-what seems to b-be the matter?" Ophelia rushed in with her trusty clipboard.

"Hahaha! Nothing, Ophelia! Just *look* at it! The portal in all its glory!" He laughed. "I can finally achieve my dreams! Tell Juniper and his team to start the test run! And prepare my Goblet as well!"

"S-sir, I have a meeting, and I need to—"

"Just DO IT! I don't CARE if you miss your meeting! DO IT NOW!" he thundered, cutting Ophelia off.

"Y-y-yes . . ." She rushed out of the hangar, bumping into a formal-looking man as she passed.

The man walked over to Bob, putting his hands on his hips. He wore black sunglasses, a navy-blue suit, and the same shade beret.

"*This* flimsy thing is the 'portal'?" he said with an icy voice, speaking with authority.

"Mr. Jackson, Sir, I *assure* you, this *will* work. I have . . . ahem—never mind," Bob trailed off, the man lowering his glasses.

"Brisket, *what* were you going to say?" He gave him an intimidating stare.

"I was—*oh, look,* the tests are about to start. Follow *me.*" Bob jiggled up to a set of stairs, leading up to a glass room.

"Go ahead, Mr. Jackson."

Jackson gave him an angry grunt and practically flew up the stairs.

"*Bob,* why don't you join me up here," he said. It sounded like a statement, not an option.

"Urg—coming." Bob moved up the stairs with some difficulty, grunting and huffing.

"Come on inside, Mr. Bob, and Mr. Jackson, Sir."

A thin woman dressed like a flight attendant bowed and opened a white-steel door for them.

"Start the tests!" Bob thundered once he sat in a large, white, swirly chair.

"Yes—Sir!" the scientists echoed, sitting in front of a giant machine. One of them hit a large red button that plainly read, 'START'. The metal ring began to shake and flashed with green light.

"After all your failures . . . I am undoubtedly surprised," Jackson said. He grinned. "Excellent work, Brisket."

Chapter Twenty Four

WELCOME TO CANDYOPOLIS

"Jennifer," Jenny told the guard at the gate. "Duchess Jennifer."

"Your Grace, I must ask why there are all these . . . commoners about you," the guard said with a sniff.

The dragons had left for some sort of a dragon ceremony, and Autumn was with the kids.

"Why I oughta—" Raggy raised his arm, ready to give him a *very* rough argument.

"Rankic!" the four girls shouted.

"These are my nieces Lady Chidi Ann Parris and Lady Alexis Blaze Parris and their friends." Jenny smiled warmly.

"Please, enter, M'Lady."

The guard opened the gate and bowed as Jenny, Chidi, Alexis, Bella, and Dalia passed, along with the animals, but when Raggy walked by, he straightened. "You should know that I am a high official. I am of royal stature. I—"

"Yeah, whatever. Buh-bye!" Raggy ducked under the arm that he held out to stop him.

Dalia gasped as soon as she saw the village. There were gingerbread houses, decorated with every kind of candy imaginable. Gumdrops, lollipops, candy canes, you name it. The town was covered in a force field, making everything look delectable.

The clouds were cotton candy, the sun was a lemon drop, and the rain was probably soda.

"What is this place?" Alexis asked in wonder.

"Oh, this is just the town. We're going to the palace." Aunt Jenny led the way.

"THAT'S THE PALACE?" all of the children exclaimed in unison.

The bricks of the castle were blocks of solid milk chocolate. The roof tiles of the turrets were brownie brittle. The window frames were dotted with gumdrops, and the flower boxes were peanut brittle. The dirt was chunks of dark chocolate, and the stems of the flowers were green licorice. The flower itself was made of round, fruit-flavored candies.

Raggy snuck over to the window and shoved a flower into his mouth.

Bella and Alexis looked at each other, and then Bella nibbled a slice of peanut brittle.

Alexis wasn't content with the candy down there, so she broke a small piece off the wall, hoping no one would see.

Chidi and Dalia showed up to scold them, but even they got distracted by the cotton candy tree.

"C'mon, guys," Aunt Jenny said with a chuckle. "Let's go inside. I am glad you are enjoying yourselves. The candy will reappear in about . . . one minute?"

"Wow . . . ," they all gasped as they stepped inside.

The interior looked majestic, the large domed hallway they were standing in was lined with paintings of Kings, Queens, and landscapes.

The picture frames were lined with gumdrops, red ones for the Kings', yellow for the Queens', and mini multicolored ones for the landscapes.

"This is . . . wow!" Dalia was examining a photo of a pink-and-blue bird.

"You *lived* here?" Raggy asked, gazing at the end of the long hallway.

"Yes, I did." Jenny nodded shyly.

Chidi realized how hard it must have been to leave and wrapped her arms around her aunt.

"Aw, Sweetie . . ." She hugged her back, as Alexis walked over to a cotton-candy shrub. It was in a pot, next to a painting, and Alexis struggled to figure out how *cotton candy* was growing.

"Hmmm. We might need to taste it to figure it out," Dalia said with a grin.

"Oh, calm down. I know you're hungry, but this is a *palace!* Mind your manners, Dalia." Alexis took her by the hand and led her back to the group.

"So," Jenny started toward the door at the end of the hall. "I am going to say hello to my parents and try to explain everything. You will *all* stay in my extra room, alright? Please, *please* behave."

They nodded and followed her. They passed through a large ballroom before ascending the stairs and into a room with a gold-banded door.

"This is it!" Aunt Jenny exclaimed, as she gently opened the door for them. "I'll be back in a little bit! Stay *out* of trouble, okay?"

"Er, yes, Ms. Kerifly," Bella said.

"Oh, just call me Aunt Jenny." She smiled and shut the door.

"Alright," Raggy said. "Let's check out this room!"

The pets had been left outside the palace, but Autumn was allowed to enter.

"No way! Lady Jennifer said to stay here and *out* of trouble, okay?" Autumn said.

"Oh, brother. We don't need a babysitter! We're almost teenagers! C'mon, let's see what this place has!" Raggy exclaimed.

"Well . . . as long as nobody is going to do *anything dangerous*. I'm talking to you, Raggy!"

"Okay, why don't Autumn and Dalia stay here, and Raggy, Chidi, Alexis, and me go and look around?"

"It's 'Alexis and *I*,'" Chidi corrected. "I'm going to stay with Dalia and Autumn."

"Well, come on, slowpokes!" Alexis called, racing ahead.

"How . . . are you so . . . fast?" Bella huffed.

Alexis shrugged. "I play a lot of sports. I'm just athletic, I guess."

"You must win, like, every game," Bella said, her eyes big.

"Let's explore!" Raggy interrupted. "Hurry up!"

Bella rolled her eyes at Alexis, who just laughed and sped ahead.

"Watch out!" Bella cried.

But it was too late. Alexis crashed right into a *very* elderly man with a gray mustache.

"Oh, excuse me," she said politely.

"Hmm." The man looked down his nose at Alexis. "And who are you?"

"I'm . . . er—Lady Alexis Blaze Parris." Alexis held her head high. "And these are my friends, Raggy Graham and Bella Graham."

"La-dy my foot," he snapped. "If you're going around pretending to be someone important, at least be something lower. Why *are* you here, Young Missy?"

"I am here with a woman who used to live here. You may have heard of her," Alexis replied with a smirk. "She goes by the name of 'Duchess Jennifer.'"

"Well," he said, though his eyes had grown wide. "You are interrupting a tour of our friends from the Mist Lands. Out of the way, child. We mustn't waste this day."

"Oh, Sir Barnaby," a young woman said. "You most certainly do not care for children!"

All of the other important people laughed like she had told them the funniest joke.

"Well, we'll be on our way," Bella said to Sir Barnaby. "Good day."

"N'yes," Sir Barnaby said grudgingly.

"Oh, boy," Raggy whispered as the three children hurried off.

"That guy was *so* snooty," Bella added.

"He was all, 'I'm *so* sophisticated and important!'" Alexis said with a chuckle.

"*Hello,*" Raggy said, imitating Sir Barnaby. "*I am a certified important person!* MadAmMm," causing the girls to burst into laughter.

"Hey," Alexis said, stopping. "That's Aunt Jenny!"

"Oh, man. We better hide," Raggy said. "Um. Uh."

"There's that big cotton candy shrub! Let's hide there!"

They all squatted behind the plant that somehow had that sugar candy that nobody really likes growing on it.

"Yes, I'm on my way to find my father and mother," Jenny said.

"Who is your father?"

"My mother is the Dowager Duchess Charlotte, and my father is Sir Grimwood. My grandfather is Sir Barnaby."

Raggy, Bella, and Alexis all stared at each other.

"*Sir Barnaby is—*" Raggy began to whisper.

"SHH!" Bella whisper-yelled.

Jenny looked around. "What? Who was that?"

"I don't know, your Grace," the servant she was talking to said.

"Oh, I don't care. Find my relatives, if you please."

"Let's go into that room," Bella said, pointing to a slightly ajar door.

"Hurry! Quietly," Alexis whispered, doing the army crawl into the room.

"Perhaps they are in Duchess Laura's room," the servant said.

"Yes, let's go," Jennifer said. And to Lexi's horror, stepped into the room.

....

In Jenny's Spare Room

"You know, I'm kind of worried about Raggy, Alexis, and Bella," Chidi said.

"Huh?" Dalia asked, her mouth full of sticky taffy. She had found it in the form of an extra purse.

"I'll look for them," Autumn said. "You guys stay here. And Dalia, don't eat her Grace Jenny's things!"

"Things, sminges. This is the *extra* room!" Dalia exclaimed, scooping some coffee ice-cream off a chair with her hand.

"At least use a spoon, Dalia!" Chidi said, rolling her eyes.

"Be back soon!" Autumn called as she zoomed off.

"C'mon, Crystal," Chidi whispered, closing her eyes. Pretty soon, Crystal had arrived.

"Ooh, should I turn us invisible? Then we can figure out where Alexis, Raggy, and Bella are!" Dalia offered.

"Even so, we might get caught."

"I don't think Autumn can save them on her own," Dalia said doubtfully.

"Neither do I. If she's not back in twenty minutes, we'll go."

"Hm?" Dalia had gotten distracted by the candy again.

"You *love* candy, huh, Dalia?"

Crystal growled, and shook her furry head.

Dalia was still chewing, but she nodded energetically.

Three minutes had passed, and Dalia had moved on to the kitchenette.

"This place is crazy!" exclaimed Dalia. "Like, *everything* is edible!" She looked intently at the chocolate teapot and lifted the lid. "Hey, there is some tea in here, still warm too! Lavender, I think. Want some?" Crystal's eyes brightened, and she sniffed the counter.

Chidi accepted some for her and her lion, looking for the teacups.

"Found the cups! They are in this cupboard. Ooh! Cinnamon sticks!" She pulled two teacups and two cinnamon sticks out from the pantry.

"Thanks!"

She poured the tea, and Dalia put her cinnamon stick in it.

"This is good."

"Yeah, especially for being made and served in chocolate cups! Autumn would love this!" Chidi sipped her tea again.

"So, what do you plan on doing when you get home?" asked Dalia.

"I guess we'll see if we're going to live with Mom and Dad or Aunt Jenny. Honestly, this literally ruined the word 'secret' for me though."

"I wonder what your sister and the Grahams are doing," Dalia said, sipping her tea.

"Oh, probably eating the walls of the hall."

"LUCKY!"

....

In Laura's Room

The trio had the same thought, at the same time. They all dashed under the bed, narrowly avoiding being seen by Aunt Jenny.

"What was that?" the servant exclaimed.

"Hmm . . ." Jenny scanned the room, looking in all the nooks and crannies. "Suspicious. Tell the guards to be on high alert. There might be a thief among us."

It was hot and stuffy under the bed, and Bella accidentally banged her head against the underside of the bed frame. She would have yelled if Raggy had not clapped his hand over her mouth.

"*Shh!*" Alexis pointed to the pair standing in the doorway and shook her head, indicating not to be caught.

"I should go check on the royal patio." Jenny dismissed the servant and exited the room. Alexis was not listening to the conversation. Instead, she stood looking at something hanging on the wall.

"*PHEW—*" Raggy clapped a hand over his own mouth when Jenny suddenly slammed the door open.

"Huh . . . nobody . . ." She closed it again, and they heard her footsteps leaving.

"Let's get back to the room, and *fast!*"

They dashed out quietly and retraced their steps all the way back to the room.

"We're *baaaaack!*" Bella called in a sing-song tone.

"Good! We were starting to get worried—hey, where is Autumn? She went looking for you three cray-crays!"

Alexis stood up abruptly from her spot on a comfy-looking gummy armchair.

"Ooh, that looks tasty!" Dalia said, rushing over to the chair and ripping off a chunk.

"Dalia! You're going to get a stomachache! You are going to get *so* sick." Bella shook her head.

"We need to stay *here*," Alexis said. "We can't risk anyone seeing us. Especially not *Sir Barnaby*."

"Yeah, your great-grandpa!" Bella said. "We saw a family tree in your mom's room."

"Wait, what?"

Alexis sighed. "Sir Barnaby is an old man who hates kids, and he's our great-grandpa."

"Seriously, Alexis? Don't be rude! Hey, at least we have a magical great-grandpa, or something . . ." Chidi stroked Crystal's white fur.

"I guess we should—"

"Kids!" Jenny burst through the door. "Come meet your grandparents, the Dowager Duchess Charlotte, and Sir Grimwood."

"Uh—alright?"

They started towards the door, waking Crystal, who was sleeping lazily on the carpet.

"Oh, and no lions or anything. We are trying to be *respectful*. Kay? Now follow me." Jenny led them out the door and up a series of stairs.

At the top, was an outcropping where two tall people stood.

"Is that them?" asked Raggy.

"Are they them, and yes," Jenny said.

The woman, with a pointy nose and a thin face, didn't smile but said, "Wonderful."

The man, who was a somewhat large man with a great big smile and a jolly look, was wearing a fashionable captain-like hat, and a blue, almost black vest with a red velvet cape. "Hello, children!" he boomed. "I am Grimwood."

Personally, Raggy didn't think 'Grimwood' was a good name at all for the jolly man. Perhaps 'Gary' or 'Garath'.

"I am Duchess Charlotte," the woman said, arching her raven-black eyebrows. "You may call me Lady Charlotte."

Bella, a lover of fashion, observed Charlotte's outfit. She was wearing a green-colored gown, dotted with amethysts. She wore a golden tiara with emeralds and amethysts. Her black-like-Chidi's hair, though streaked with gray, was up in a tight bun with a few locks framing her rosy face, and her emerald-colored eyes practically glowed, and she had posture so straight that it made stiff poles seem to slouch.

Grimwood had reddish-brown hair also streaked with gray and Lexi's blue eyes that sparkled with anticipation.

"So," Grimwood said. "Let's do something exciting!"

Chapter Twenty Five

THE RETURN TO CANDYOPOLIS

"Remind me how we get to the 'Magical World' again?" asked Dexter.

The adult gang was jam-packed into the car, talking as Laura took the wheel.

"We are driving to the Fresno County Museum of Art. I *happen* to know of Bob's supposed 'break-through'. A portal, to, and I quote, 'Another Dimension'. It is being showcased there, and if we sneak in, we might be able to use the portal to teleport to the magic world." Laura said as she drove the car to their destination trying to look confident.

"Whoa, whoa, whoa! How did you know about this? And what if it is not stable and we get zapped into non-existence! *Plus,* it is a high-tech *specialty* showcase for important people! It will be almost impossible to get in! *Plus,* Bob will be there! He's bound to notice me!" exclaimed Dexter. "And we'll get arrested if we are caught! *Plus,* I can't face Bob! I am way too guilty of *stabbing your kids* to get the magic already!"

"Hey, we're here. So choose now. Come with us, and we have a better chance of saving all of our beloved family. Don't, and well, you will have to live with that guilt and more for the rest of your life." Mr. Parris' eyes narrowed as he faced Dexter.

Abigail nodded and stepped out of the car. She had chosen to save her pride, and more importantly, her children.

"I, um—I'll . . . ," Dexter stuttered. He gave a long and exasperated sigh. "Let's go." His eyes had a gentle, yet defying gleam to them, as he stepped out of the car, and towards their uncertain future.

Abigail followed Laura after watching Dexter, the pair silent as they walked to the tall, looming museum.

"Where is this exhibit?" Ben asked, standing at last, inside the large lobby. They examined the room and saw a large mass of proper-looking people crowding to get to a ticket booth.

"*I am assuming that is where we need to go,*" Abigail whispered, stepping away from the crowd of people.

"How are we gonna sneak in?" asked Dexter.

"I—I am still working on that."

Mrs. Parris sat down on a bench and started to think. "Hmmm . . . no, that is too obvious . . . and *that* is way too dangerous. No, we need his help . . ." she muttered.

They waited until the flood of people had dissipated.

"We need to sneak in *now,* if we are going to at all!" Dexter exclaimed, looking very worried.

"Alright, I think I have a plan." Laura began telling them what to do.

"Okay! Who has a sticky note? We also need . . . never mind. Dexter, you guard the door, and make sure nobody gets in. Abby, go distract the person at the ticket booth so I can get close. Ben, you need to block off the escalator, so no one sees what we are up to. Okay, go, go, go!"

They didn't ask what she was going to do, and they all took their respective posts.

"Hiii! Uh, I need to know where the—uh modern-art exhibit is. My—um, uh . . . *brother* is waiting for me there," said Abigail, strolling over to the ticket agent.

"Miss, you can ask the—"

"No, he is—uhm . . . on *break*," she interrupted the bored looking agent.

"Ma'am, he is *not* supposed to be on—mmmph!" suddenly a large green root burst out of the ground, and wrapped around the agent, binding his arms, and covering his mouth.

"C'mon! Let's get our kids back!" Laura was crouching behind the man, her hand on the floor. "He'll be fine."

They all dashed down the hall, slamming open the door to the specimen room. A large metal ring stood in the middle, blue-and-purple light whirring inside of it. The room was gigantic, and the important-looking people sat in an enclosed room, not far from the portal.

"It's now or never, guys! Time to save our kids!" Ben led the charge, running full speed towards the swirling light. Bob spotted Dexter running to his invention and grunted in angry surprise.

"You! Stop right now!" He burst out of the room and caught Abigail by the shirt collar.

"Lemme go!" She struggled, and Bob put her arms behind her back.

"Stop NOW!" Mrs. Graham had jabbed her elbow into Bob's protruding belly. She ran back to her husband, taking him by the hand, and dashed into the swirling light.

"Here we go!" Ben and Laura ran after the couple and disappeared into the portal.

"NO!"

Bob Brisket stood dumbfounded at the edge of his invention. The onlookers watched, as he stormed out of the giant room.

"NO! IMPOSSIBLE!" he raged, slamming open a door across from the specimen room. "AARGH!" He shut the door behind him, almost breaking the hinges.

The room was a small, custodian-like one, with only a safe.

"Oh, c'mon!" He turned the safe's dial until it clicked. He pulled out a golden goblet, filled with sparkling clear water.

He turned around, careful to not spill the water, and locked the door behind him. "Alright. Now let's see . . ." He tapped the water's surface with his index finger and stared intently at the liquid.

"Mal, can you hear me?" he said, expecting a reply.

Abruptly, the dragon Malcora's face appeared like a reflection inside the goblet.

"Yes. Is something the matter? I am in the middle of planning a battle!" she hissed.

"I am coming into the world with you! Some *random* people BROKE IN, AND RAN THROUGH THE PORTAL!" he yelled.

"Alright. The time has come!" sneered Malcora. "I have found us some allies as well! She is our ticket *straight* to the Dragon Kingdom!"

"Good. I will be there shortly. Goodbye, comrade."

The dragon gave him a sly smile, and the image dissipated. Bob put a clear lid over the goblet and opened the armoire. He took out a satchel and put the golden cup inside. He also took a bag of "ration" food.

"Time to go."

. . . .

Soon . . .

"AAAAAAAH!" Laura was the first one to fall out of the sky. She hit the ground with a thump and let out a surprised "Owch! Man, that *hurt!*"

Dexter fell from the sky just seconds after her, landing in a bush.

Ben landed on his bottom and rubbed his neck. "So is this how you got to Earth?"

Abby plummeted to the ground and landed on her hands then did a flip to land on her feet.

"At least there aren't any more people falling from the sky," Laura said, studying the surroundings.

"LOOK OUT BELOW!" a short man bellowed.

"BOB?" the four adults shouted.

Bob had followed them into the magical world.

He landed roughly on a gelatin bush and bounced face-first into a rock-candy rock. Bob was out cold.

"Huh."

"So, Laura, what kind of place is this?" asked Abigail.

"Let me see," Laura interrupted, pulling out a compass-like object.

The grown-ups peered over her shoulder.

"What in the world *is* that?"

"It's sorta like a map of this magic kingdom. See the little dot? That's where we are."

Abigail squinted at the tiny words. "So we're in Can-dee-o-polis?"

"Yes!"

Ben's eyes grew wide as he studied the forest they were in. The snow on the ground was candied shredded coconut, and the trunk of the trees were candy canes with smaller candy canes for the branches and pine needles. The flowers were made with gumdrops and lemon drops, plus green licorice.

Dexter grinned and chomped into a fallen 'branch'.

"Dex! Don't eat the wildlife!" Abigail scolded.

"Well, not all forests are like this, some are normal, and just have weird wildlife and stuff." Laura shrugged.

"Well, what are we going to do with *him?*" Ben growled, angrily picking up the tiny man.

"Well . . ."

"I have an idea! It has to do with him and a VOLCANO!" Ben thundered, cutting Dexter off.

"Ben! Calm down! He might be evil, but he can be useful!" Mrs. Parris ordered, shaking her head.

"If anything, we tie him up and force him to walk wherever we go."

"*Fine*, but don't expect me to be even remotely kind to that—"

"Wha—?" Bob woke, wiggling and squirming under Ben's strong arm.

"Let me down! Kidnapping, I say! Kidnapping—"

Ben hung him up on a tree by his tux, hissing, "Kidnapping? You told *Dexter* to kidnap our kids! Our daughters! We are *only* here because of *YOU*, and you had better behave because you have another thing coming if you try to run!"

Bob's face turned pale, and he nodded furiously, knowing that Mr. Parris was *very* serious. Ben slipped him off the candy-cane tree and brought him over to the group. "Does anyone have some rope?"

But when he was ready with the licorice vines, or what would suffice as rope, Bob was gone.

....

In The Columns

"Remind me *how* many dragons are going to help you?" Malcora was sitting at a desk, with a large map, and Esmerelda sitting across from her.

"About thirty-five, why?"

"We need to know what area is best to attack from! The soldiers are ready and waiting, but we need this specification first! Have you *never* planned *anything* in your *life?*" Malcora retorted, angrily pointing her talon at the princess. "You have no idea *how long* I have been in control of an *entire army of dragons*," she hissed, "So I need *absolutely NO* advice from you."

Esmerelda was quite shocked, as she had never been treated like this before. "Whatever area we attack from, my sister's coronation is soon! And if we don't attack *then*, we don't attack *ever*. This is a time crunch. I say we start the assault *here*," she tapped a forested area with her claw on the map.

"It is wooded, so we will have cover. Also, this river runs inside the castle, and to the basement, where they purify it, so if you can get a few dragons to swim up . . ." She traced the nearby river into the palace. "You can ambush from below."

Malcora stared, stunned at the realization of the princess's smarts.

"So be it. I shall ready my troops. My comrade is not here, so I assume we will see him after I—ahem, *we* win the battle." The icy dragon started for the door, and just as she was about to go out, she breathed something barely audible.

"You think this is about *you*, princess. This is something *much* bigger. You will never get the chance though, to change your ways, because you have committed to this alliance. You are *one of us*. But trust is a fragile thing. This is a warning, girl. Try anything, go ahead, but I assure you, this world will be a distant memory once I am done with it. Power comes from strength, so if I were you, I would listen to the *strong*. As for the weak," she whipped her head around to stare Esmerelda in the eyes. "*Well, legends are never forgotten . . .*"

The queenly figure exited the room, leaving Esmerelda alone with her thoughts . . .

....

Candyopolis

"What's your idea?" Raggy asked.

"Hush, child!" Charlotte snapped. "Grimwood knows what he is talking about!"

"Hush, child—" Raggy muttered, frowning.

"Raggy!" Alexis shook her head.

Sure enough, Charlotte had turned and was frowning at her.

"Whatever is the matter, Allison?"

"Uh, my name's *Alexis*," Alexis told her. "And—"

"I can call you what I want, Allison," Charlotte interrupted. "Chidi, dear girl, we simply *must* discuss the wonders of Candyopolis!"

Clearly, she had found a favorite.

"Ooh! Like what? Maybe the candy forests, or the fact that Candyopolis is literally made of candy?" Chidi looked over the royal garden from the balcony, which was flourishing with gelatin flowers, gumdrop-holly-hedges, and chocolate trees, to name a few.

"Ha! *Those* are not wonders. This palace's architecture is simply amazing! Fun fact—the walls and roofs are made from solid cake!" Charlotte gave Chidi a loving squeeze, Alexis glaring at the back of her head.

"*Why does she like Chidi so much?*" she muttered, walking across the balcony to Jenny.

"So, shall we go on an . . . *adventure?*" Grimwood wiggled his eyebrows and gave a jolly smile.

"First of all, nowhere lame. I'm not six, for the record. *And second,* no dragons, we have two—" Raggy was interrupted by an outburst from the Duke.

"DRAGONS? WE HAVE NEVER MET ONE WE HAVE NOT—" he stopped, realizing he was yelling at children. "Never mind."

Charlotte gave an exasperated sigh and asked, "Have you all ever been to Marina? Jenny has not."

"Where is *Marina?*" Alexis asked, still annoyed.

"Oh, ho ho! It is one of the realms in this world! It is a Kingdom flooded entirely by water!" Grimwood snickered.

"*Water?*" Alexis said. "We've been to the Golden Lands, Candyopolis, and a place with a dragon called . . . *Malcora.*"

"Malcora?" Grimwood said with a chuckle. "Malcora is no danger to us! Ice dragons are deathly afraid of sugar or candy!"

"We have two great friends who are dragons," Chidi informed Charlotte. "CornFlakes and Laven! CornFlakes cooks, like me, and Laven and Alexis can both make fire!"

"Magic powers, Allison?" Charlotte said.

"*Alexis* can make anything that has to do with heat," Bella jumped in.

"And Chidi can summon a lioness named Crystal!" Dalia put in.

"Do show us, Chidi, dear," Charlotte said, ignoring the mention of 'dragons', and assuming it was just their imagination.

While Chidi summoned Crystal, Raggy muttered, "If Chidi couldn't do anything, *Duchess Charlotte* would be completely amazed."

"At least Grimwood kinda favors Alexis," Bella whispered.

Ever since our adventure together, Alexis thought, *the Graham twins have kinda had my back.* She smiled. *This is kinda fun!*

"Not really," Alexis said.

"What do you think they're talking about?" Dalia hissed to Chidi.

"I don't know!"

"Hey, since you practically own the place, can I have an itsy-bitsy snack?"

"Dalia!"

"Friend of yours, Chidi?" Lady Charlotte asked with an amused grin.

"Er, yes, your Grace," Chidi said. "Should I call you your Grace, or Grandma, or—"

"Just call me *Grandmère*," Charlotte said.

"Okay, your—I mean, *Grandmère*," Chidi fumbled.

"Um, can my friends call you that, too?" Alexis said, marching up to the Duchess.

"Can *you*?" Charlotte said, arching an eyebrow.

"Why, yes, I can," Alexis argued.

Chidi closed her eyes and rubbed her temples. "Oh—never mind," Chidi muttered.

"Call me *Grandpère* or Grandpa," Grimwood added.

"Alexis!" Raggy called, motioning her over to the railing.

"Wow, look at that!" Bella said. "The entire MOUNTAIN is one GINORMOUS piece of candy corn!"

"Ugh," Alexis said. "Candy corn is disgusting!"

"No way!" Dalia said, joining them. "If it has sugar, it's delicious!"

Alexis gave Dalia a mock punch. "You sure do have a sweet tooth, huh?"

"I think all twenty-eight of my teeth are sweet!" Raggy joked.

"*So,* shall we depart momentarily?" asked Duke Grimwood. Jenny nodded excitedly, and Charlotte gave a dainty sigh.

"Uh . . . yes? Your Highlyness?" Alexis cringed, knowing she mispronounced the title.

"I shall call the transportation!" Jenny proclaimed.

"Uh, can't we just take a taxi?"

"You goofball!" Bella shouted, disheveling Raggy's hair.

"Hey, I am not a goofball! Don't call me that!"

"Stop it!" Alexis hissed. "Or the perfect Duchess Charlotte will put you on time out!" she teased quietly.

Charlotte seemed to decide right then and there that she *absolutely* did *not* like children.

She sniffed and took Duke Grimwood's arm.

"We shall meet you at the front!" he exclaimed, winking at Alexis. They exited the balcony and left the kids standing alone.

"They are nice!" Chidi smiled, Crystal rubbing against her leg.

"Sure, they're super nice!" Dalia chimed in.

"Calm down, Lex." Bella put a hand on Alexis' arm. "I think we're going on 'the adventure of a lifetime.'"

"Yawn," Raggy said. "Wake me up when it's over."

Alexis had to agree with Raggy. *If it has royalty,* she thought, *it probably WILL be boring.*

Grimwood re-entered the balcony. "So," he said, his blue eyes sparkling like fire. "Who wants to go on a wintery ride?"

Chapter Twenty Six

DIVE FOR YOUR LIFE!

"Sledding?" Chidi couldn't hide her disappointment. When she had heard, "wintery," all she could think about was the normal, same-thing-at-home sledding.

"Who said anything about sledding, dear?" Charlotte said, resting a hand on Chidi's shoulder. "We will be riding polar bears!"

"Cool!" Raggy exclaimed.

"Oh, and your *humble* pets shall stay at the palace with Jennifer," Grimwood added.

"These bears are probably the marshmallow ones," Alexis muttered.

"Two adults can fit on a polar bear or three children," Grimwood said.

"So, uh, who will ride on each?" Chidi said quickly.

"Chidi, dear, you and I will go together, Grimwood will go with Rock, and Allison, Dalia, and Bethany will go on one. Jenny will stay at the castle and govern for now."

"Cool, let's go!"

"That's the spirit, Alexis," Grimwood said, giving an unneeded chuckle.

They exited the palace and went to the royal stables. Charlotte and Grimwood walked past pegasi, Catchalopes, and more, but stopped when they reached three polar bears, which were indeed made of marshmallows.

They led them to the edge of the forest and helped to seat the children.

"Wait, are we supposed to steer this thing?" Alexis said, holding the licorice reigns in her hands.

"Yep!" Grimwood said, with "Rock" sitting behind him.

Before Alexis could ask him the question, "How do we steer them?" Grimwood had already set off, calling, "Giddyup, Coco!"

"Um, giddyup?" Alexis said.

The bear stood still.

"Ooh, try pulling the reigns!" Bella said.

"What do you think I'm *doing?*" Alexis snapped, jerking on the licorice.

"Oh, for crying out loud!" Dalia dug her heels into the bear's side, and it reared up like a pony and set off in the coconut-shred snow.

"EEEK! This is crazy!" Bella laughed.

"I c-can't c-cont-trol thi-is c-crazy thi-ing!" Alexis cried.

"Allison, try to actually *use* the reins? And call Vanilla by her name!" Charlotte advised, steadily riding after Grimwood.

"Uh . . . Vanilla! Follow them!" The polar bear's ears perked up, and it trotted along after the Duke and Duchess.

"This is fun!" Dalia commented, once riding in a comfy position.

"Yeah, but what do you think Marina is going to be like?" Alexis asked her.

She shrugged, unconcerned.

"Ooh! Look at that cool bird!" Bella pointed out a large flying thing in the sky.

"Wait . . . that is not a bird! And that is more than ONE!" A giant mass of dragons flew overhead, armed with spears and clad with armor.

"What in the world?"

Charlotte and Chidi rode on, catching up to Grimwood and Raggy.

"What *ARE* those things?" Dalia screamed. By now, Charlotte and Chidi were out of view and hearing range.

Hearing Dalia's startled cry, Vanilla turned abruptly and tromped over to the frozen lake.

Vanilla charged onto the lake with such force that the ice cracked and broke free, and the bear and the three girls were stuck on an iceberg, which was steadily moving farther from the snowy shore.

"HELP!" the three shrill cries came, all thoughts of what they had just seen in the sky quickly replaced by paralyzing fear! And they didn't stop screaming as Alexis slipped into the murky water. "ALEXIS!"

....

At the edge of Marina

Chidi and the Duchess were riding fast, speeding through a dense forest. Suddenly, the dense greenery dissipated, and they were sitting at the edge of a giant waterfall.

"What is *that?*" Chidi whispered, completely mesmerized by the sight of it.

"Ha! Even though we are underground, Marina still shares our barrier! This is no mere waterfall, it is actually the entrance to the Ocean World!" Charlotte dismounted the polar bear with ease and walked daintily over to the wall of water. Chidi clumsily slid off the mount and walked over to Charlotte's side.

"Wow . . . it's so pretty!" she reached out a hand, and touched the water, sending a ripple up it.

"Laura and I used to come here for a picnic. She loved it. She always wanted to go to new places and see new things. 'Having a picnic with my mother!' she always laughed and told all the butlers about our 'adventures.'" Charlotte looked wistfully out into the deep blue water.

"It must have been nice, seeing her all the time."

Chidi was enchanted by the beautiful swimming creatures. "How many cool animals have you seen swimming around here?" she asked.

"Oh, quite a few! Chidi, my girl, have you ever seen a Seakie?" asked Charlotte, grinning. "They are half-mermaid-half-horse, and they are actually quite dangerous." They talked for a few more minutes, then the Duchess began to get worried. "They should all *be* here by now." She paced back and forth, then added, "Especially Grimwood! He is always so fast!"

Chidi agreed, knowing that Alexis would never get lost. "Something is *not* right . . ."

....

In the frozen lake . . .

Alexis was knocked senseless by the freezing water and struggled to swim up. She gasped for breath, her head breaking the water.

Suddenly, something clenched around her ankle.

"HE—" She was pulled underwater again before she had time to yell for help.

Losing all feeling in her limbs, she struggled against what was pulling her under. Making a small ball of heat to protect from the cold, she looked down at her feet. A gang of black-and-red penguins was wrapping their fins around her ankle, trying to drag her down.

Alexis' eyes widened, expecting something much worse. Kicking and pushing her feet, she broke loose of their holds and swam frantically to the surface.

"ALEXIS! Grab hold!" Bella and Dalia unhooked the reins and threw them into the water.

As Alexis grabbed the reins, holding on for dear life, they pulled her up onto the iceberg. The gang of about ten-to-fifteen penguins popped their heads out from the water.

The largest one—probably the leader—had kelp-looking bushy eyebrows and a large, fat beak. Alexis crouched, panting on the iceberg, and practically hugging a fireball.

"S-stinking-g p-penguins!" she gasped, Bella and Dalia looking very concerned.

"Stay away from us!" Dalia threw a chunk of ice at the penguins, narrowly missing the leader's face.

"Hey, watch it!" he wailed, in a Scottish accent. He swam closer. "What's your problem?"

"What's yours? You tried to drag me underwater!" exclaimed Alexis.

"What'd he say?" Dalia hissed into Alexis' ear.

"He asked 'what your problem is,'" she murmured back.

"What's your problem?" Bella retorted.

Alexis conjured a fiery blanket and wrapped it around herself.

Then Bella made a strong breeze that carried her, Vanilla, and Dalia to the shore, and Alexis made herself a fire path.

"Wait!" the penguin called, as he swam madly towards the shore.

"We ain't tryin' to hurt ya! We just haven't seen *hoo-mahns* in so long! I'm Thurston, and dis' here is my gang. We were just curious, Madam-s."

"Hmm." Alexis sat on the coconut ground and thought. "What's everyone else's names?"

"This is Jim," Thurston said. "And this is Matt and Andy and—" He went on and on. Alexis let most of the names fly by. "John, and last but not least, it's Carrie!"

"Aww!" all three girls said. "She's so cute!"

Carrie was a little baby penguin, with big, brown eyes and the most adorable face. *She* was the only normal-colored penguin.

"Yes, yes, anyway, can you please give us something to eat? We have not eaten anything except fish for this whole generation!" Thurston begged as Bella scooped up Carrie.

"Do you have food, Alexis?"

"Yes, I only have R-E-C-I-P-E for B-I-R-D and water."

"We'll eat *anything!*" Jim pleaded.

Carrie waddled up to the girls and ate a little bit of Recipe For Bird.

Her little face exploded with an adorable smile.

She squealed something unintelligible, and more birds waddled up to eat.

Finally, Thurston cautiously took a chomp of the leftovers. They ate until the box was empty, and they all splashed, satisfied, back in the water.

"Wow! Thank you guys so much! If you need the 'elp of one pack o' penguins, just ask! We're in your debt!" Carrie waved goodbye, and they dove underwater. The group walked Vanilla with her reins, and they kept going.

"Carrie was *soooo* cute!" Bella said.

Alexis pulled the twins' cell phone out of her pocket and handed it to Bella.

"I got a pic of you holding her," Alexis said.

Bella stared at the picture and cooed over how cute Carrie was.

Finally, they arrived at the entrance to Marina.

"Finally!" Everyone was there, waiting for them. "We were getting worried!" Charlotte looked genuinely concerned.

Alexis felt a pang of guilt. She hadn't been very decent to Charlotte.

All the feelings dissolved, however, when Chidi hugged her sister. "Why are you all wet? And you're *freezing!*"

"I'll b-be ok-kay," Alexis said, her teeth chattering.

Grimwood scratched his chin. "Maybe we shouldn't go on with this adventure."

Alexis jumped up. "N-n-no way! You think I'm some k-kind of snowflake? I'm good to go!"

"What happened, dear?" Charlotte asked, and took a small wool blanket from a bag strapped to her bear. Alexis gratefully took the blanket and told them the story.

"So, yeah, they were just hungry!" she finished, almost dry after telling the tale.

"Quite remarkable!" Grimwood said, admiring Alexis' bravery.

"Yeah, but not the weirdest thing that has happened," Bella said with a chuckle.

"Well, since we are all here, why not tell us what we are doing?" Raggy asked excitedly.

"Well, we talked with Jenny," the Duke and Duchess locked eyes. "And she told us that you both wanted to go scuba diving for your birthday that has passed. So, we would like to fulfill your birthday wish!" Grimwood smiled as the twins stood there dumbstruck.

"YES! Thank you, thank you, thank you!" they screamed.

Alexis examined the cell phone. "It's waterproof! We can take pics of us snorkeling!"

"Hey, what's this?" Chidi said, coming to the picture of Carrie.

"We didn't tell you about Carrie?" Dalia and Bella said.

"She's *adorable!*" Chidi exclaimed.

"Okay, I gotta admit that's pretty cute," Raggy said.

"I know! I *love* her! I wish she were my pet!" Bella whimpered.

Chidi hugged her friend. "Sorry."

"So, are we going snorkeling or what?" Alexis interrupted.

Grimwood chuckled. "She doesn't waste time, eh?" he asked Chidi.

"Nope!" Dalia answered.

....

In the ocean

"Hurry up, get in the water!" Alexis demanded, standing shoulder-deep in the shimmering, crystal-blue water.

"I'm scared of it, okay?" Bella said.

Chidi snorted. "You weren't scared of it at the beach. Remember the bumper boats? Or just now, so come on!"

Dalia defended Bella. "That was a little bit ago. Why don't we help her? Right, gals?"

"Sure."

Alexis climbed out of the ocean with Chidi and Dalia. Then Alexis dove back into the water and pretended to be drowning.

"Seriously?" Bella scoffed. "*That's* just humiliating."

Dalia rolled her eyes. "Well, just *go* in the water!"

The group had asked a nearby peddler if they could buy some of his underwater gear. He gladly accepted, and they put on various colored swimsuits. The boys had swam to the surface, and they had signaled to the others once at the surface. Bella, however, had scrambled out of the water as quickly as she could once she made it to the surface, which was a long swim away.

"B-but what if there is like, a sea dragon or something?" Bella complained, obviously scared. Little did she know, Raggy was sneaking up behind her.

"RAAAAAR!" he shouted, scaring everybody into the water.

"RANKIC! Why did you *DO* that to me?" screamed Bella, who looked like she almost had a heart attack. She shivered in the water, which only came up to her knees.

"Well, I helped you face your fears like any good brother would," he replied solemnly.

"Seriously? Oh, whatever!" Chidi dove down under the calm, clear water.

The adults were waiting on the beach, watching the kids.

Bella and Raggy were having a wrestling match in the water, trying not to kick anybody.

Chidi and Alexis, on the other hand, were having some of those hold-your-breath-contests and talking.

Dalia was the referee with Raggy and Bella, to make sure nobody got hurt.

"Time to scuba!" Alexis called.

Grimwood adjusted everyone's equipment and then allowed them to dunk themselves under.

"Cool, we can breathe!" Raggy said when he emerged.

"We can talk underwater," Alexis pointed out.

"I wonder how the pets and dragons are doing," Chidi said.

"*Ahem*," Charlotte cleared her throat. "What do you mean, *dragons?*"

"We already told you! They helped us escape from the clutches of the evil dragon Malcora! They are *nice!*" Dalia explained.

The Duke sniffed unapprovingly.

"Well, anyway," Charlotte said. "We are going to scuba and then Chidi, Alexis, we will talk to you."

Alexis opened her mouth to argue or fight, but Chidi held her index finger up.

Alexis bit her bottom lip.

The Grahams swam up to Alexis.

"Well?" Bella said. "Tell her what you told me!"

Raggy rolled his eyes at his sister. "Well, we saw this dude coming, and he looks really creepy . . ."

Grimwood and Charlotte had already swam out quite a distance from the shore, though none of the children had noticed.

Bella felt an icy grip on her shoulder and slowly turned around. Then she screamed.

"What are you talking about?" a mysterious figure shouted.

Chapter Twenty Seven

REVEALED

"AAHH!" screamed Bella again.

A slightly chubby man barged up to them and started talking like he had complete authority over the kids. He had come from seemingly nowhere and just started babbling on and on about the twins.

Dalia joined Bella's scream-fest. Chidi racked her brain for what to do in case a TOTAL STRANGER started yelling at you, demanding to know what you are talking about.

Alexis and Raggy got in fighting poses.

"You lay a single finger on any of us and I'll knock you into next Taco Tuesday!" Alexis warned.

The man wrinkled his brow. "What's a taco?" He was obviously mocking them.

Raggy had prepared to drop the guy on the sandy shore and interrogate him, but the thought of someone not knowing what a taco is made him stop. Of course, he didn't know the man was joking.

"A taco is a crunchy tortilla with beef or chicken in it, with cheese and lettuce."

The man, while Raggy was pondering his own taco explanation, grabbed Alexis' backpack, which held all their survival gear.

"Help! Grimwood! Charlotte!" Bella cried.

"Grimwood and Charlotte are gone!" Dalia shouted.

Chidi found a bunch of kelp floating in the ocean. Tying it in a big knot, she used her volleyball skills and launched it and smacked the man in the face, knocking him down because of the force.

Alexis felt like a duck wearing the flippers from the scuba equipment, but she charged out of the water and planted her foot on the man's chest. Raggy scooped up the backpack.

"Make one move and I'll flatten you," Alexis said, glowering with all her might.

"Like an enchilada," Raggy added. "Or a quesadilla. Wait, a burrito—better yet, tortilla chip. Hang on—TORTILLA—no—"

"Will you drop the Mexican food?" Bella snapped.

Alexis held out her hand for the cell phone. She snapped a pic of the man.

"What's your name?" she snarled. "Or else."

"B-Bob," he sputtered. "Bob Brisket."

Bella gasped. "You're Dad's boss!"

Bob smirked. "Yes, little missy."

"Can't we be done with the 'whoa, you're one of the people trying to kill us and we didn't even know it!' things?" Chidi asked.

Alexis dug through her pack again. "I got the hacked tracker he had Dexter plant!"

She attached it to her phone and accessed some files. She then, from Dexter's account, logged into Bob's. "Perfect!"

"What're you talking about?" Bob asked.

Alexis ignored him. "Chidi, look at this!"

"Oh. My. Goodness!" Chidi exclaimed.

Dalia's eyes flashed with anger and scanned the screen. "You've contacted *Malcora*?"

"WHAAAAA?" Bob said. "Of course, I haven't contacted Malcora, the dragon! Why would I?"

"Of course you *have*," Alexis said. "Look, in your *completed tasks*."

"You can't see the completed ones, little missy."

Alexis smirked. "I am not a sassy unicorn, *Bob*. But listen to this: *Contact Malcora and check Dexter's progress*. Right there!" She shoved the phone screen in his face.

"Plus, you shouldn't know that Malcora is a dragon," Dalia added.

"Back to the real problem," Chidi said. "Charlotte and Grimwood have already swum out too far. And what are we going to do with Bobby?"

"It's Bob, you annoying child."

"Potato, patato, tomato, tamoto." Alexis did a *blah-blah-blah* thing with her hand. "Bobby, Billy, Bill, Bob."

"What?" Bob mused.

"Potato, patato, tomato, tamoto, Billy, Bob, same thing," Alexis repeated.

"What *are* you talking about?" he exclaimed.

She repeated the same thing again, obviously getting on his nerves.

"You nonsense child!" he huffed.

Alexis smiled at her sister. They had made it up a long time ago. It was an inside joke.

....

August 7, four years earlier, 3:30 P.M.

The twins had just said goodbye to their mother, who was going on a trip to see a "friend", whom the twins had never heard of.

"*Oh well, looks like she's gone. I can't see her car anymore," Alexis said sadly.*

"*I wonder where this 'friend' lives?" Chidi said, once back in their room.*

"*I don't know, but we are eight years old now!" Alexis exclaimed.*

"*I know, you don't have to say it a million times . . . ," Chidi said, bored.*

Chidi was sick and tired of being stuck in the house twenty-four-seven with her twin sister.

"Dad, can we do something?" Chidi shouted down.

"Chidi, I'm busy!" their father's reply came.

"Potato, patato, tomato, tamato, Bobby, Billy, Bill, Bob," Alexis laughed.

"Why can't we do anything fun?" Chidi asked.

"You mean besides being stuck at home all the time?" Alexis said. "Potato, patato, tomato, tamato, Bobby, Billy, Bill, Bob."

Chidi got very angry when their parents wouldn't tell them or include them in important decisions, meaning she lost her temper easily.

Chidi was so bored she was willing to try Alexis' annoying chant. "Potato, patato, tomato tamato, Bobby, Billy, Bill, Bob."

"It's fun, isn't it?" Alexis teased.

Chidi had to smile. "I guess it is."

Together the twins chanted the silly rhymn and enjoyed themselves, until it was time for dinner. They had forgotten all about their mother's mysterious friend. Until later . . .

....

In the present day . . .

"Uh, were we supposed to see something?" Raggy asked as Alexis and Chidi finished the memory.

"Oh! Sorry." Quickly, the twins re-told the story.

"Potato, pa—" Bella began. "Okay, it's old now."

Dalia grinned. "Let's keep the potato chants to a minimum."

"Done. It's our private joke."

Only when Bob coughed violently did Alexis realize she was still standing on him.

"Rope, vines, or—er—sea kelp, anyone?" she asked, removing her foot from Bob and taking her scuba gear off.

"I'm going to watch this criminal," Raggy said.

"Whoa, whoa, whoa," Bob said. "I'm not a criminal! Leave me alone!"

"Sure. You COME UP TO US and DEMAND TO KNOW what we're talking about, TEAM UP WITH A CRAZY DRAGON, and then SAY YOU'RE NOT A CRIMINAL!" Chidi hollered.

Raggy went to find some kind of binding, and Dalia and the rest kept an eye on Bob.

. . . .

In the castle hallways . . .

Autumn was wandering through the halls of the castle, lost.

"Guys? Hey, guys?" She peeked around corner after corner, still looking for the kids. She sighed and took a rest on the edge of a chocolate vase. "I'll never find them in this gigantic palace!" she said to herself.

A lone knight walked down the hall, almost knocking over the vase.

"Hey! Watch it, bucko!" she cried, dodging out of the way.

"Oh! Er—sorry, madam. Can I help you?" He looked quite embarrassed and gave her a formal bow.

"Actually, mister, you *can!* I am looking for a group of ragamuffins and their pets. Also, their aunt, Jennifer. Have you seen them?" Autumn flitted up to eye level.

"O-oh! Yes, I have seen *that* group of ruffians. They were walking to the royal balcony to meet up with the Duchess and Duke. Jennifer is actually in the throne room right now, as she has taken over for them in their absence."

"Where's the throne room? Take me there at once!" she demanded. "And what's your name, mister?"

"I'm, uh, Sir Chocolate."

Autumn burst out laughing. "What are the names of your troops?"

"Sir Taffy, Sir Candy Corn, Sir Cocoa Powder, Sir Sweets, Sir Caramel, Sir Nougat, Sir Wafer, Sir Sourhead, Sir PB, Sir Malt Ball, Musketeer number one, Musketeer number two, and Musketeer number three."

"That's too good!" Autumn wiped tears of laughter from her eyes. "That's too funny!"

He just stared blankly at her, wondering what the fuss was about.

"That *really surprises you?*" asked Chocolate. "My daughter's name is Cris."

"Okay, that's not as funny. But *what's your last name*?"

"My full name is Chocolate Bartholomew McAlbertson Chocolate."

Autumn straightened her face. "Please, take me to Duchess Jennifer."

"Sir Chocolate!" Jenny exclaimed when they entered the room. "Who is this?"

"I am Autumn," she said with a quirky grin on her face. "I am here to ask where your nieces, parents, and their friends are."

"Are you a personal friend of theirs?" Jennifer asked.

Autumn chewed on her lip. "Yes. And I need to find them."

"Sir Chocolate?"

"Don't look at me! She just showed up and demanded I take her to you!"

Suddenly, a yip was heard from behind a door. It burst open, and Tumbles came bounding out.

"Autumn! I knew it! Where *were* you?"

Autumn smiled and explained how she had met the twins and their pets.

"Oh! *Right!* I am so sorry, I must have not seen you come in the gates with everyone else! Well, I am sorry to say it, but the kids and my parents have already left for Marina." Jenny explained once she was told about Autumn.

"Thank you, Your Grace," Autumn said with a tiny curtsy.

"Of course. And Tumbles, why are you here?"

Because Jenny could understand animals, Tumbles began, "Hiya, pal. If you're wondering why I'm here, it's really quite simple. You see, there was once a brave, true, adventurous dog. He and his noble companions, a kitten named Ginger, a dog named Orco, and a robin named Redd. They—"

Ginger burst in. "Okay, so, what are ya doing?"

"Come on, pets!" Autumn said. "We've wasted enough of Jennifer's time, let's get the dragons, Oreo, and Redd, and go find the kids!"

....

Above Candyopolis, with the adults.

"So, do you have any idea where our kids and that crazy maniac Bill went?" Abigail asked, once they stopped searching—and eating—the general area for Bob.

"His name is Bob. And no, but I might have to stop by the palace to talk to my parents . . . ," Laura responded.

"So, you said a minute ago that this was *above* Candi-o-pol-e? How do we get down to where all the people are?" asked Ben.

"Yeah. It doesn't look like anyone is around," agreed Dexter.

"Well, since no one has shovels, we will need to find the passage, and dig by hand," Laura pointed out.

"*Whoa, whoa!* Slow down! We're new to this! What '*passage*'? And if we are digging, then is Candi-o-pol-e underground?"

Dexter shook his head. "You're acting like we should know this!" he said.

Laura sighed. "I'm sorry. So we just, well, go down. The thing is, Candyopolis is a huge ditch—but it's easiest to dig and slide down, otherwise we need to walk at least three miles to reach it. This is the simplest course. And it is pronounced *Can-dee-op-oh-lis!*"

"And you're *sure* that the kids are in Candlopyious?" Ben asked.

"No. And for crying out loud, it's *Can-dee-op-oh-lis!*" explained an exasperated Laura. "Now, can we go now? We need to find them! They are all alone! And if *anyone* gets in our way, you boys can send them straight into next Taco Tuesday!"

Ben snickered, and muttered, *"And we wonder where Alexis gets it from."*

"I heard that!" Laura snapped.

Ben grinned. "But it's true, isn't it?"

....

The Planning Room

Princess Esmerelda stood in the doorway, pondering the mysterious speech that Malcora had just given.

What is that supposed to mean? It's like she only talks in riddles. Couldn't she just be straightforward?

The princess sighed. "Ugh. Might as well work on something."

"Esmeralda!" Malcora hissed.

The princess jumped. "What? And I'm *Princess, soon to be Queen* Esmerelda."

"Uh, yeah. You must return to the palace with McKenna. And not a word of the ambush to anyone!"

"Yeah, yeah," Esmerelda grumbled.

"Excuse me?"

Esmerelda glared, then said, "Of course. You are excused. You may leave."

"GET BACK TO YOUR PALACE!" Malcora roared.

Esmerelda snatched McKenna and hurried to the palace. She was greeted by her sister when she landed.

"Esmerelda?" Isa asked softly. "Where were you?"

"I was just—uh, exploring around the volcano with McKenna."

Isa frowned. "I thought you knew better than to go exploring before the celebration. But that doesn't matter now! I am so glad you are here!" The diamond-blue dragon hugged her. "Now, why don't you go and get your nice velvet attire on and meet me at the garden balcony when you are done?"

Isa shooed her off and went to go join their mother.

"Ugh! *I'm so high and mighty! Do what I say right now!*" Esmerelda mimicked when she got to her room. "Isa is so—" She stopped, as one of the maids was peeking into the room.

"Excuse my rude interruption, Esmi. Do you need anything?" she asked.

"No, but tell Isa that I will be there shortly," the princess replied.

"Yes, right away." The maid left, and Esmerelda put on her velvet gown. Walking out into the hallway, she saw a giant flood of dragons walking into the garden courtyard.

"Sheesh . . . what a crowd!"

As Esmerelda squeezed through the mass of dragons, she tried to imagine herself as a queen.

"Esmi! Hello? Hey!" The sound of prince Noon snapped her out of her daydream.

"Oh. Hello," she replied haughtily. Prince Noon was an orange-and-light-blue dragon, his colors fading into each other.

"H-hey . . . it's great to have a new queen, right?" Noon blushed as he walked next to her.

Esmerelda said nothing, practically ignoring him. They reached the garden courtyard, and they went their separate ways. Esmerelda took her place beneath the balcony with her brother, Prince Jet.

Esmi had always despised Noon, ever since her betrothal to him had been announced. She thought that he was a dim-witted, reckless, foolish, and creepy fanboy. Seeing everyone lined up in front of the balcony reminded her of the day that she would have to marry him. Snapping out of her thoughts, she reminded herself to look as regal and beautiful as possible.

"The coronation will now begin!" announced the crown-bearer.

Queen Viola started her speech, and the courtyard fell into silence. Esmerelda looked at the sky frantically, wondering if Malcora had called off the attack.

"And so, with great gladness, I pronounce Isa Queen of the Dragon—"

Suddenly, and without any warning, dragons of all shapes and sizes started to descend from the sky. The attack had begun.

Chapter Twenty Eight
THE BEST WORST REUNION

"Really? I don't think that *kelp* will hold him!" Raggy commented, once Alexis had come back with something to tie up Bob with.

"Well, do *you* see anything else to use?" asked Chidi. Raggy sighed and proceeded to yank Bob to his feet.

"You kids are really just gonna leave me here?" he grumbled.

"Well, unless you volunteer to swim out to the Duke and Duchess with your hands tied, then yes," Dalia said, bringing over a coconut that had fallen nearby.

"Well, I have always liked volleyball!" Using Chidi's technique, Dalia spiked the rock-hard fruit at his head to knock him unconscious.

She high-fived Chidi and said, "Man, your technique is great!"

"So, does anyone want to go and get the adults?" Raggy said.

A series of "Not it!" came from everybody except Chidi.

"Oh, fine. But you guys make sure to not let *him* out of your sight!" She splashed into the water and started swimming out to Charlotte and Grimwood.

....

The Dragon Palace

"HELP!" Isa screamed.

"Protect the queen!" "Who is responsible for this?" "SAVE US!" and "Is that *Malcora?*" were some of the cries that came from the random villagers and guards.

"Esmerelda!" Isa cried. "Get to safety!"

"No need," Esmerelda said, snatching the crown from Viola's hands. "I *planned* this attack! It was to get *everything that is rightfully mine!*"

Just as she began to place the glittering crown on her head, Malcora plummeted to the ground.

"Give me that!" she demanded, grabbing the crown and placing it squarely on her head. "I am *Queen Malcora once again!*"

"Hey! I thought we were going to be co-queens or something!" Esmi yelled, yanking the crown.

"It's *mine!*" Malcora yelled back, pulling hard.

"Be careful!" Isa cried. "That crown is—"

It was too late. The crown flew up in the air and disappeared on a solid cloud.

"—Delicate," Isa finished.

"*I'll* retrieve it," Esmi said.

"No, I will," Malcora argued.

"CornFlakes!" Laven hissed. "What should we do?"

While Autumn and the pets were searching the castle, the kids and their grandparents were scuba diving, and Jenny was ruling, Laven and CornFlakes had flown off to attend Isa's coronation.

"I'll fly up and grab the crown," CornFlakes whispered.

"I'll keep them distracted," Laven promised.

CornFlakes kept herself carefully hidden by the clouds. She slowly reached over and took the crown in her hands.

"Whoa," she breathed. "It's beautiful!"

The crown was made of a glittery, sparkly golden metal, encrusted with every kind of gemstone imaginable. When she peeked down through the clouds, she saw that Malcora and Esmi were still arguing. She silently flew down beside Isa.

"Your Majesty?" CornFlakes whispered.

"Yes?" Isa spun around.

"I think this belongs to you," CornFlakes said with a smile.

Isa set the crown on her head and turned to Esmerelda.

"Guards!" she yelled. "Get the intruders! *Including* Esmerelda!"

"Yes, your Majesty," they replied simultaneously before they charged at Malcora.

"Oh, please." Malcora waved her hand, and a thick sheet of ice covered all of the palace guards.

Laven shouted, "Everyone! Evacuate!" as he began to create a lake of lava, leaving Malcora and Esmerelda hovering over the steaming pool.

"Hah!" Malcora roared. "I can *freeze* your lava!"

Then Malcora stilled. "Wait! Weren't you with that Chidi girl? And her sister and friends? I know you! Dragons, get him!"

Laven quickly surrounded himself with lava to block them from grabbing him.

"YOU." Malcora snarled.

"Heh, looks like we meet *again*," Laven replied.

Malcora shoved Esmerelda out of the air, and Esmi landed on the balcony, where the Queen's guards detained her.

"Again?" CornFlakes asked herself, as she watched the two dragons flying in the air.

"Let's settle this. Once and for *ALL!*"

Malcora launched herself off the roof of the palace and rammed into Laven, sending him crashing through a window.

"Kind citizen, please, you need to go! This is far too dangerous, you have no idea what Malcora is capable of," Viola begged.

"No!" CornFlakes stated. "I am *fully aware of what she can do, and I intend to help.*" She pulled a spatula out of her apron, and stood in a battle stance.

Viola sighed. "Then take the Blessing Staff. Please, keep it safe." She thrust a large rigid staff with a blue crystal at one end into CornFlakes' hands.

Viola tugged Isa away, leaving CornFlakes alone on the balcony. Meanwhile, Malcora and Laven were battling on the terrace.

"You ruined my chances!" Malcora roared, slashing with her claws at his face.

Nimbly dodging, he hit her with his tail. "I was protecting the kingdom! The Igneous-Clan Chief is gone now, because of you!"

"I did what was NECESSARY!" She pounced upon him with such force that he fell onto his back. Malcora stood above him, glowering down. "I will not be defeated by you once again." She touched the broken spike on the back of her neck. "You will have to suffer the same humiliation as I did!"

She forced his face to the side and smashed the horn on his head.

"AAH!" she yelled, as she picked him up. "You. Need. To. GO!" She threw him so hard that he smashed through yet *another* window.

"Urg . . ." He tried to get up, but fell to the cold, hard stone floor of the brewing room and blacked out. But not before he sent a smoke signal.

··

In the ocean

"Ugh, this is *so* rough!" Chidi complained when a hard wave hit her. The sandy ground rubbed her elbows.

She heard a little squeal. She turned and saw a tiny, adorable penguin.

"Are you Carrie?" she asked.

"Yes!" another penguin, this one red, said, popping out of the ocean.

"Who are *you*?" Chidi asked.

"I am Thurston!" he announced. "Meet my raft. This is Jim, John, Andy, Matt, Stella, Sophia, and you already know Carrie."

"She's *so* cute!" Chidi said, patting the baby penguin on the head.

"DIVE!" Thurston suddenly exclaimed.

"Huh? What are you—" Chidi stopped when she saw the colossal wave coming, with a *killer whale* coming beside it.

Oh NO! she thought and dove under the water. Her goggles let her see the colossal whale dive right over her head. Under the water, she saw Carrie and Thurston get whipped forward from a riptide. She was struggling herself, as the wave was larger than it looked.

Let's hope that the orca doesn't come back! thought Chidi as the wave subsided. She popped her head above the water, calling out to Thurston.

She saw them under the water. Thurston was getting pulled farther away from his raft.

"Oh, I hope I don't regret this!" Chidi plunged under again and grabbed him.

"What *are* you doing?" he snapped.

"Uh, saving your *life!*" she snapped back.

"Fair enough." He allowed Chidi to drag him to the raft, which had now gathered on a sandbar.

She dragged herself up onto it and spit out a mouthful of seawater.

"Well, looks like we—made—it . . . ," she panted.

A few of the penguins waddled around uneasily.

"Carrie? Carrie? Where are you?" Matt called. "Hey? Carrrriiiie?"

The other penguins called for her as well. A sudden thought struck Chidi.

I forgot Carrie! She looked rapidly around for the little penguin and saw her swimming as fast as she could away from something large underwater. *Think fast!* she thought and started to summon Crystal.

"Oh, I hope you can be helpful!" Crystal appeared, and Chidi instructed her to stay with the raft and she would get Carrie.

"Carrie!" Chidi cried, forcing her head out of the waves. "Carrie!"

The little penguin squealed, terrified.

Chidi finally broke through the waves and reached for the penguin.

Oh, great, Chidi thought. *I just made it to Carrie and have no way back to the sandbar!*

She found a large piece of driftwood and set Carrie on it. She gripped it, careful not to tip the wood. Chidi kicked hard and finally ran aground.

"Carrie!" the raft called, surrounding the little penguin.

Thurston broke away from the group and waddled up to Chidi.

"Now, see here young lady," he said. "You can't ever do that again, do you understand?"

Chidi tried hard not to laugh, but a little giggle escaped. The penguin, which only reached Chidi's thigh, was ordering her around!

"Uh . . . okay," Chidi said, then burst out in laughter.

Thurston frowned. "Now, go wherever you are going! An' thanks I guess."

"Uh, okay."

Chidi began to swim to the adults again.

"Man. This ocean is *rough!*" she said to herself.

Finally, the waves stopped coming. She relaxed a little bit and swam more steadily towards Charlotte and Grimwood.

She finally reached them.

"*Grandmère!*" Chidi exclaimed.

"Chidi? What are you doing?" Charlotte paled when she realized Chidi was alone. "Where are the others?"

"We thought you were going to swim a bit on your own, and we didn't want to get in your way," Grimwood told her.

"We caught a bad guy, named Bob. He came up to us and demanded to know what we were doing. Alexis and Raggy held him off and tied him up. And then I started to swim to tell you all this, but then I met this raft of penguins, and there was this really cute one named Carrie, and anyways, I saved two of them, and then I came here to tell you and ask you what we should do." Chidi looked at her grandparents as if she had just told them she was named Chidi.

"Um . . ." Grimwood doggy-paddled to stay afloat.

"Chidi," Charlotte said, a hint of worry in her voice. "Could you have *possibly, accidentally, maybe, slightly* hit your head?"

"NO!" Chidi cried. "It's true, it is. Come with me!"

Grimwood shrugged. The adults followed Chidi as she swam back to the shore.

"Finally!" Alexis exclaimed.

"Who's *this?*" Charlotte asked.

"His name is Bob," a cloaked figure said. "I guess our leads were right!"

"Dad?" Bella asked, starting to run towards him. Then she stopped. "Wait, you're not going to lock us in the basement, are you?"

"Of doom," Raggy interjected.

"Yes, of doom." Bella looked at her father. "So, are you?"

"No, Bella."

"In that case . . ." Bella enveloped her dad in a hug and was joined by Raggy and Mrs. Graham.

"Mom? Dad?" Chidi asked.

"Chidi! Alexis! You had me worried sick!" Mrs. Parris yelled.

"Sorry, Mom," Alexis said. "But—"

"We feel like we need to be here," Dalia finished for her.

"Yep! We need to find our friends and the pets before *we go home.* We made a deal with one of them," Raggy agreed.

Bella nodded.

"Well, kids," Ben sighed. "You've come *this* far. There is no turning back now."

The adults agreed to stay with Clan Aqua while the kids defeated Malcora. Clan Aqua was the best because it was located in Marina, instead of the Dragon Realm.

"We'll see you soon," Chidi promised.

They set off.

"Hey, what's that?" Raggy asked, pointing in the distance.

"That's . . . ," Alexis trailed off. "That's a distress smoke signal! Laven must be in danger!"

....

About 2 hours later . . .

"Laven! Laven, wake up! Oh, please! Wake up!" a voice came, seeming to warm the cold room.

"Who . . . hey—Chidi?" He opened his eyes, and standing in the doorway were the Parris twins, each holding a lantern, with a scarf and hood covering their faces.

Alexis threw off her hood and rushed over to his side.

Kneeling down, she asked quietly, "What happened to you?"

Without waiting for an answer, she unwrapped her scarf and tied it around his side, where he was injured. He tried to tell her, but he did not have enough strength to explain.

"Oh my word . . ." Chidi examined him and pulled Alexis over to the side. "He could pass out from blood loss," Chidi explained. "Lexi, get me those." Chidi pointed to Alexis' satchel, which had several items sticking out.

She brought them over, and Chidi applied an antibiotic cream to his wound, some fresh bandages, and handed him a long, forked stick to use as a crutch—IF he could walk.

"How are we going to get him to the woods? The Sprout-Clan dragons have healing magic, I think." Alexis gently tightened Laven's bandages, which were already turning red from the blood. "If we can just get him there, maybe they would be able to help him."

"Hmmm . . . maybe we can just try to sneak him out?" The twins sat beside Laven.

"How can we sneak out?" Alexis asked.

"We could try to—uh—carry him?"

"H-heh," Laven wheezed. "You r-really think you can carry m-me?"

"Yeah, we might have to rethink that plan," Chidi stated.

"Boom! We're here!" Raggy, Dalia, and Bella burst through the door.

"SSH!" Alexis shushed them.

"Oh, sorry. Boom, we're here!" he whispered.

"What can we do to help?" Dalia asked, closing the door.

"Hm . . . I got it!" Alexis snapped her fingers. "Guys, we are going to work together. Chidi, summon Crystal to scout ahead. Raggy, you will raise the rocks underneath Laven; Bella, you will help push us with your wind magic, and Dalia, you will be in charge of our disguise."

"Uh, hate to be the bearer of bad news, but I don't have any costumes on me."

"No, Dalia!" Alexis exclaimed. "You need to turn us invisible!"

"OH!" Dalia exclaimed. "*That* makes more sense."

After they each completed their assignments, they were ready to go. Chidi opened the door as quietly, as inconspicuously, as she could.

"Okay, ready, everyone? Go!" Chidi whispered. They moved forward, barely making a sound and turning corners swiftly.

Finally, after a stressful five minutes, they made it into the woods outside.

"'Kay, you can release the invisibility shield," Alexis told Dalia, who had a pained expression on her face.

"*Thank* you," Dalia said, dropping her outstretched arms. "That was painful."

"Tell me about it!" Raggy let the rock down on the ground. Bella agreed and took a rest on a rock.

"Oh no . . . it looks like Laven blacked out again," Chidi noted, letting Crystal dissolve, her work done.

"Where have you kids been? You had us worried sick!" Laura rushed over to Chidi and Alexis.

"Mom, we're okay… We've been through a lot since we got here. Why did you leave and come here? We were trying to keep you safe." asked Alexis.

"So, how're you doin'?" Chidi asked in a carefree voice. "Don't mind her. She's been under stress. *Anyway*, we need to get Laven to the inner forest where the refugees are. He needs medical help!"

They all worked together to make a large stretcher, capable of holding Laven's weight.

"Alright! One, two, three, lift!" Everybody worked together to lift the dragon and successfully carried him into the forest.

....

The Throne Room . . .

A large sea of murmurs arose, as they saw Malcora seated on the throne, minus a crown. She had already assigned new chiefs to her new followers.

Isa and her siblings, Amethyst, Sapphire, Amber, Ruby, Jet, Diamond, and her mother, Viola, had escaped being thrown into a royal dungeon. Even Esmerelda had somehow escaped.

"Clans! If you could, please divide into lines, and new chiefs, you may come and talk to me about whatever, *ahem, problems* you have."

All of the dragons divided into seven lines.

Clan Aqua, Clan Igneous, Clan Sprout, Clan Frostbite, Clan Earthquake, Clan Whirlwind, and Clan Thunder.

"Alright! Clan Sprout's new chief, you may speak."

A green-looking dragon with brown spots and leaf-shaped wings stepped forward.

"Queen, we have some *unexpected* problems," he said.

"Ah, Vine. What might these problems be?" Malcora asked him, her eyebrow raised.

"We are finding this—new position you have acquired, well, er—uh—" Vine stammered, "W-we see fit that you should—uh—*shall* have a p-proper coronation, and a new c-crown."

Malcora sighed. "Yes, of course. We will make it happen, my best metalsmiths are on it right at this moment. Next!"

The Clan Thunder dragon stepped up next. His clan was a neon yellow color, with purple zig-zag frills running down their backs. He was adorned with a large yellow earring and gray fluffy gauntlets.

"Malcora. Hey, I agree with Vine. This whole barging in, throwing a dragon through a window, and kicking out the royal family-thing is really sudden, don't you think?" he stated sassily.

"Strike, you know *better* than to question my judgment. So, my coronation will be held tomorrow morning at sunrise, does *that* make you happy?"

He nodded and strutted out of the room, his Clan close behind.

"Alright," Malcora said, rubbing her claws together, "Clan Frostbite!"

"Dun-dun-dun!" One of her sound effects dragons popped out from behind the throne. "MUAHAHAHAHA!" The other one popped up as well but received a hard look from Malcora.

After that, a dragon of her own icy-white color walked daintily up to her.

"I am Icicle, if you had forgotten," she said coldly. Breathing an icy plume, she continued. "My Clan needs more space. The Ice-Spike Mountains are no longer large enough to house my whole clan. *And* as a new leader, I cannot have my people running out of food."

Shooting a glare at Malcora, she strutted away without waiting for an answer.

The new queen sniffed and continued on, addressing each one of the Clan's needs.

Gem of Clan Earthquake requested a fresh underground river.

Cloud of Clan Whirlwind needed space for mineral deposits.

Tsunami of Clan Aqua asked for private fishing grounds.

There was no representative of the Igneous Clan, she recalled, because she had disposed of him.

After she finished addressing everyone's needs, she took her leave and walked the halls of her newly conquered empire.

"It is *so* much work to run a kingdom," she said to herself.

"Then why not hand it over to me?" Esmerelda snarled, her voice coming from out of nowhere.

"Guards!" Malcora screeched.

"Sorry," Esmi said. "I have the blessing of Mesmerizing. I can make up to six people do what I say."

"Why, you!" Malcora whipped around, searching for the princess.

"Well, if you are so worried about me, why didn't you just throw me in a cell yourself? Well," she laughed sinisterly, "When you had the chance!"

Esmerelda jumped out from nowhere and landed on Malcora's back.

"Get off of me!" Mal tried to shake her off, but she clung on tight.

"You won't win this time!" Esmerelda flipped off over Malcora's head and used her cloak to blind her.

"You'll be sorry you *ever* even came out of your stinking hole in the ground!" Esmerelda roared, flying above Malcora, then dropping out of the sky with such force that she knocked the large blinded dragon over.

"Urg!" Malcora grunted, stumbling over and ripping off her cloak. But when she got back up and looked around, the little emerald-colored dragon was gone. "ESMERELDA!"

Chapter Twenty Nine

FIGURES OF SPEECH

"It's so cool how everything is edible here!" Dalia exclaimed, chomping hard on a candy cane.

"Stop it!" Alexis ordered her friend.

"Who, me?" Dexter asked, accidentally swallowing some bubble gum, which had been the sap of a tree.

"Both of you, please!" Mrs. Graham said. "This is supposed to be beautiful and whole, not filled with bite marks!"

"Sorry," Dalia said, hiding a handful of jelly bean flowers in her pocket.

"I saw that," Chidi whispered to Dalia. "How are you not sick already?"

Dalia shrugged.

"All right, let's find the Sprout Clan dragons!" Alexis said.

"Yeah, we should be coming across the camp soon . . . here!" They all stumbled into a small clearing that was filled full of tents.

"Alright, let's get Laven to the medical tent," Chidi ordered.

"Come on, put your back into it!" Ben called.

"I have to sacrifice my back?" Raggy joked. "Oh, boy."

Ben grinned. "And your left ear."

Everyone worked to haul Laven into the tent. A brown-spotted dragon came to the entrance. "Is that Laven of the Igneous Clan?" he whispered.

"Uh . . . yes?" Laura said, glancing at her daughters to double-check.

Chidi nodded. "Why?"

"Queen Malcora *hates* the Igneous Clan. She says someone from that Clan threw her off her rightful throne," the dragon said. "By the way, my name is Vine."

"Nice to meet you, Vine," Alexis said. "I'm Alexis, this is Chidi, Dalia, Bella, Mrs. Graham, and Mrs. Parris who is also my mother."

"Duchess Laura?" Vine exclaimed, his eyes scanning Laura up and down. "Where did you disappear to?"

"It's . . . not important," Laura said. "We need you to heal Laven, please."

"Yes, your Grace." Vine eyed the girls. "Are you all related to her?"

"Us? No," Dalia said. "I'm Dalia Monroe, this is Bella Graham, and—"

"I'm Abigail Graham," Abby interrupted.

"We're the Parris family," Alexis said, at the same time Chidi said, "I'm Chidi Parris."

"So . . . ," Vine said. "Let's take a look at your friend."

....

The Private Tent

"Isa, this has been so hard, I know . . ."

Viola and Isa were camping out with the dragons that had been thrown out when Malcora took over.

"I-it's just so—*shocking* that Esmi would betray me like this!" Isa sighed.

"Dear, we must remember that we could not have faced her as we are now. You have still yet to get your blessing!" said Viola, trying to comfort her daughter.

"More like a *curse!* I do not have my blessing only because of that failed ceremony! I could've beaten Malcora if she was just a second later!" Isa cried, and buried her face in her talons.

Viola sighed. Taking a long look at Isa, she strutted out of the tent. She watched the terrified-looking citizens and felt a deep sorrow in her heart.

She pulled a blue bandana around her horns, just so that nobody would recognize their distinct shape. Just then, she saw the mustard-yellow dragon walking into the ration tent, holding the Blessing Staff.

Narrowing her eyes, she inconspicuously followed her in.

"*Ahem.*" Viola tapped the yellow dragon on the shoulder as she went to step into the kitchen.

"Oh! How can I help . . . you?" She whipped around, then recognized the queen.

"Ah! Zere you are! I was meaning to give zis to you!" Smiling, the chef handed over the staff.

Expecting that she would have to take the staff from CornFlakes, Viola had her expression fixed in her fiercest scowl.

"Is—something wrong, my—"

Viola burst out laughing. "Ha!"

CornFlakes looked at her strangely. "Is something wrong?"

"Oh—oh my! So sorry, humble chef! I had no intention to scare you! Hehe! I thought you had tried to st-steal it! Ahehehe!" she giggled.

The refugees in the dining tent all stared at her.

"Let's take zis somewhere more *private,*" CornFlakes suggested. They walked out of the tent together, then they flew into one of the insanely large sycamores that were surrounding the camp.

"Much better," Viola stated, seating herself on one of the gigantic branches.

"Why are you hiding your beautiful horns, my queen?" asked the chef.

"Ah, this," Viola untied the bandana. "I hoped no one would recognize me, and in turn, throw rotten fruit!" Viola laughed then sighed. "Please, my dear, remind me what your name, clan, and Blessing is?" asked the former queen.

"CornFlakes. I am—a hybrid, my queen. Clans Thunder and Whirlwind. I was never gifted a Blessing, Queen. My parents worked for Malcora, and so did I, until I ran away with ze Parris twins," she finished and stretched out her unusually large wings to show Viola.

"My wings are from Whirlwind," she said, then tapped her horns, "And these are from my Thunder clan side."

Viola nodded solemnly, seeming to understand. "Hm, twins? As in. . . humans? A group of humans walked into the medical tent a few minutes ago . . ." The queen tapped her chin, indicating that she was thinking. "Hmmm, yes, four of them were young girls."

CornFlakes' eyes lit up. "Oh! Queen, I must go! So sorry to cut zis short. I will see you zoon!" She leaped off the tree branch and glided down to the med tent. Viola stared after her, amused by how abruptly she left. Feeling the rough wood staff in her talons, she remembered Isa's coronation.

"Oh! Maybe . . . yes!" she exclaimed to herself and also dived down from the tree. Landing in front of the private/ secretly royal tent, she strutted in regally with a large grin on her face. Isa was sitting at a desk in the back, her brow furrowed from staring at a book that was labeled, *Guide to Battle Planning Volume 37, Info About the Black Orb, Dark Magic, Local Legend About Clan Frostbite, Grape Growing Techniques, Anatomy of a Catchalope, and so Much More!*

"Isa! I have something to tell you," Viola said cheerily.

"*What?*" Isa snapped.

"Dear, I have—*found* the Blessing staff!" Viola tapped it on the ground, and it made a soft sound.

"Really?" Isa gasped. "Mom, if you bless me, we can overthrow Malcora!"

"Exactly!" Viola cheered. "A kind dragon named CornFlakes gave it to me. Come on, let us do this at once!"

They walked out into the forest, and Isa knelt down in front of Queen Viola. Clearing her voice, the queen started, "In the name of the founding Queen Vindictive, I hereby Bless you, Princess Isa, and for all of time you shall have the Blessing of this Divine Power bestowed upon you." Viola touched the blue crystal to Isa's forehead, and a bright radiant light shone into the woods.

A whisper of a voice said, "*You have now received the Blessing of The Walker. You can now walk on water and on air . . .*" The voice that seemed to come from the staff disappeared, and Isa stood up, a small white scale was visible on the edge of her eye.

"Wow! This feels . . . crazy!" Isa jumped up into the air and landed on solid nothing. Viola nodded.

"I have never heard of the Blessing of The Walker before, it sounds very nice!"

Viola thought back to her own coronation, and her Blessing, Morphing. She could transform an object into another of the same size.

"But—well, how can I use this to my advantage against Malcora? My fight?" asked Isa.

Viola froze. "*Excuse* me? *Your* advantage? We are fighting *together!* This is not only about you, Princess."

Isa was used to getting her way, and she shot back a steely glare. "*Princess?* I'm not a weakling anymore, Mother! I am the new queen! I have my Blessing, and I have my crown!"

"Isa . . ." Viola knew what power could do to shape one's perspective. Isa walked paces in the air, somewhat taunting Viola.

"Don't '*Isa . . .*' me! You are *below* me now! I'll make a better queen than you ever did! I can *actually* be me! I'll get all my revenge against Malcora, and that little pipsqueak, Esmerelda!" Her eyes shone with an angry fire in them.

"You don't know what you're saying!" Viola cried. "You were always my sweet, quiet daughter, and now you want to go around, exacting revenge! This isn't you!"

Isa stopped, and her eyes narrowed. "This *is* me. Just the side you never cared to see. We're done here. I hope you get to see my glorious reign!" Isa took off, flying out of sight.

After looking after her, Viola glared at the Blessing Staff.

"This. Is. All. My. FAULT!" She grabbed the staff and threw it at the nearest tree. It snapped in two, and the blue crystal stopped glowing. She hung her head and turned away from the broken staff.

"Why?" Viola whispered.

Walking back to the camp, she gathered the things that she managed to save when they fled the castle. She wrapped them up in cloth and set out into the forest to look for her daughter.

....

In the castle

Oreo, Ginger, Tumbles, Redd, and Autumn rushed out the front gates of Candyopolis Castle. They had tied themselves together with licorice to make sure they didn't separate.

"Let's go—WHOA!"

Unfortunately, they had not made a plan. All running in separate directions is definitely *not* what you want to do when tied to each other.

"Ow," Ginger whined, licking her paws. Once they all regained their composure, they all decided to go towards Marina, the place where the kids were, or so they had been told.

"Hey, what way is Marina?" Tumbles asked after a second. Autumn pulled out a map that had the same design as Chidi's and Alexis' compass drawn on it.

"Come on, follow me!" Autumn cried.

"No, follow me!" Tumbles yelped as Ginger pulled them towards Marina.

"Guys! Let's go this way!" Oreo barked, pulling them all towards Ginger.

"Guys! I'm a *bird!* I can see farther than any of you! And I see that Marina is *this* way!" Redd lied, as he pulled them all towards Tumbles. "Stop fighting like cats and dogs!"

"But we *are* cats and dogs!" Oreo, Tumbles, and Ginger cried together.

"It's a *figure of speech!*" Redd squawked. "Oh, forget it! Just follow my instructions, go *this way.*" All the pets looked at each other, and Autumn shrugged.

"Sure, Mr. Smarty-Pants," Ginger grumbled.

"I thought that was *my* name," Tumbles said. "And I will lead us to fame and glory!"

"No, *I* will!" Ginger hissed.

"Nope, it's going to be me," Oreo told them.

"Come *on!*" Redd yelled. "You guys are acting like animals!"

"But we *are* animals!" they all chorused.

"Autumn, be a people person, okay?" Redd said. "And stop this arguing!"

"I'm a pixie, not a person, and they're pets, not people!"

"IT'S ANOTHER FIGURE OF SPEECH!" Redd shouted.

"Some animals have issues," Tumbles whispered. "They don't understand what figuring speechly is."

"ARGH!" Redd lost it. "Autumn, be a pet pixie, or whatever! I need a break!"

"I don't want to be a pet!" Autumn called.

"AHHH!" Redd screamed.

All the animals fell silent. Oreo looked up at Redd and nodded, gesturing for Redd to land on his back. They all walked in the direction that Redd was telling them to go.

"Yiiiiiikes," Ginger purred softly. "It's scarier than being scolded by Chidi."

"That's pretty scary," Redd agreed. "Chidi can get mad."

"Scary isn't *pretty!*" Tumbles argued.

"It's a—" Redd began. "What's the use? You guys can't understand a figure of speech or even use it in a sentence!"

"Figure of speech," Oreo said. "There. I used it in a sentence, leave me alone."

"I quit!" Redd squawked. He cowered under his wing as little raindrops started to fall from the covering trees.

"Is *that* a figure of speech?"

"No," Autumn said. "Now come *on*, you're going to kill Redd!"

"I can kill Redd?" Ginger unsheathed her claws.

"It's too late," Redd told them. "I'm fading fast."

"*That's* a figure of speech, right?" Oreo muttered, his coat getting soaked.

"I don't know what a figure of speech *is* anymore," Redd said dramatically. "I tried. And I failed. I hope you can find it in your heart to forgive me someday." His voice squeaked. "When I'm not here to teach you some modern impressions."

"Is that Shaky-smear?" Tumbles asked.

"It's *Shakespeare!*" Autumn corrected, shielding her eyes from the rain. "And no, it's not."

No one noticed, after about thirty minutes of walking, that they were walking uphill.

"Hey, why is this ground so cold?" Ginger asked as she looked down. They were walking up the secret tunnel to the surface.

"Huh. What a co-wink-ee-dink," Oreo said.

"Uh, Marina *is* up, right? Speechy figuratively, uh—Shaky-spoon? Right?" They all shrugged.

"I'm gone." Redd pretended to collapse on Tumbles' shoulders and stuck his tongue out for effect.

"Redd!" Tumbles and Oreo cried.

"I wanted to hear another figure of figuratively Shaky-smear!" Ginger whined.

"He's not actually *DEAD! He might be mentally scarred though,*" Autumn trailed off and told Tumbles to carry him the rest of the way.

They walked for about forty-five more minutes and finally reached the top of the sloped slide.

"That takes a lot longer going up," Ginger complained, "My *feet hurt.*"

"All right, hurry up!" Oreo yelled, racing forward, and tugging everyone behind him.

"'Kay, so, um . . ." Autumn pulled out her map, but she didn't notice that it was upside down and sideways.

"We need to go . . ." She studied the map. "Uh . . . left!" she announced with fake confidence.

"Okay!"

They all started walking left, not knowing that they were walking directly towards a battlefield.

Chapter Thirty

DOWNFALL

"Rescue team is here!" Malcora thundered, landing beside Bob on the sandy beach of Marina.

"OWW! What *took* you so long?" Bob yelled as the dragon ripped through the kelp binding him and accidentally scratched his arm.

"Sorry. Come on, we have another kingdom to conquer!" She picked him up by the shirt and flung him onto her back. "You were lucky that I'm good at my job and that you could get a hold of the goblet and contact me."

"I'm just glad that we can finally meet in person. *And* that we can get busy taking over this crazy world!" Bob smirked, holding onto Malcora's horns as they took off.

They soared through the clouds, and Bob asked lots and *lots* of questions, such as, "Who is Esmerelda?" "What is the food like?" "How much longer?" and "What are all of the Clans?", all of which Malcora gladly answered. After a while of flying, they finally landed on the landing pad.

"That was a *long* flight," Bob complained, trotting into the castle.

"Please, that could only be used sarcastically," Malcora said, stretching her wings. "Like I said, it's only seventeen miles."

"Ugh! Just *thinking* about that hurts my feet!"

"Malcora," a blue dragon suddenly said behind her. "I believe you have my throne."

"I have *my* throne," Malcora corrected, not bothering to turn around. Bob's face turned white, and he ran inside.

"No," the dragon said slyly, "It's my throne, and you'll give it back to me before I make you!"

"Puh-leeze, where did you even come from?" Malcora said, still not turning around.

"I think you know me as *Queen* Isa," Isa stated, walking on air above Malcora.

"What is wrong with you? *No one* questions my authority."

"Until now!" Isa cried as she leaped on top of Malcora and snatched the new crown off her head, placing it squarely on hers.

"That belongs to *me!*" Esmerelda snarled, flying up from nowhere and grabbing it from her sister.

"Esmeralda!" Isa shouted.

"Hey!" A little dog yelped as he zoomed out of the forest and skidded to a stop in front of Malcora. "H-hey?"

All the dragon "queens" stared at the puppies, kitten, bird, and pixie tied together with licorice. The crown clattered to the floor.

"You know," Redd said. "I think we'll let you guys work this out among yourselves."

"Was that a figurely of speech?" Ginger asked.

"Argh!" Redd squawked. "Come on, let's scoot."

They all zoomed off, back into the forest as quickly as they had come.

"Right . . ." All the dragons looked back at Esmeralda, who had scooped up the crown.

"GIVE ME THAT!" all of them leapt at the little princess.

She made a squeaking noise and ducked under Isa's pouncing claws.

"IT'S MINE!" Isa tackled her to the ground and pinned her to the rough dirt. "Now then." She had a vicious gleam in her eye. "Give it to me like a good girl. You know, a little princess," she mocked. Esmerelda struggled, but Isa smacked the crown off her horns.

"Oh, no!" She yelled.

"Oh, *yes!*" Isa cackled, as she leaped off of Esmi, leaving a scratch on her face, blinding one eye.

"Now that *she's* dealt with . . ." Isa turned back to Malcora.

"Let's do this thing." Malcora cracked her knuckles.

"Hey, just don't throw me out a window, okay?" Isa asked.

"Sure, hand me the crown and I won't."

"That's . . . not what I meant," Isa said.

"What did you mean?" Malcora asked pointedly.

"Well . . . I wanted you to just *not* push me out a window and to let me have the crown. And the kingdom. And *peace*. You know?" Isa finished.

Malcora planted her foot in Isa's chest and gave her a shove, landing Isa on the floor. She scurried to her feet and lashed her tail at Malcora.

Malcora rushed at the dragon, but Isa dove to the side, leaving Malcora to plunge through a tinted window and into the palace.

"I am *so* sorry," Isa said, waving the crown in the air. "But this belongs to me."

Malcora shot a beam of ice at Isa, knocking it out of her talons.

Malcora flew through the window frame and snatched the crown from where it landed on the floor. That's when the twins arrived. The whole posse had come to join them, all healed, armored, and ready for battle.

"Malcora!" Alexis snapped. "Dalia, Bella, Mom, Mrs. Graham, and CornFlakes, get Queen Isa to safety, then join us."

"Raggy, Dad, Mr. Graham, and Laven," Chidi added. "Get the crown, please!"

"We'll take Malcora," the twins said together.

Alexis created a huge fireball and Chidi summoned Crystal, but she appeared five times larger than usual. Crystal pounced on Malcora, but the dragon escaped her clutches. Crystal growled, swatting at her like a housefly.

Alexis threw the flame at Malcora, but the dragon froze it and made it disappear.

"Crystal!" Chidi shouted. The two raced at Malcora, who was distracted by Alexis' fire and lava outbursts.

"We're *ba-ack!*" Ginger sang out.

She then saw Chidi and Alexis holding Malcora off.

"We'll . . . see you later?" Oreo offered weakly.

"Bye!" Ginger yelled, pulling the pod of pets away.

"That was weird," Malcora, Chidi, and Alexis said together. Then they resumed fighting. Everybody else had finished their assigned tasks, and each grabbed an item from CornFlakes' stash of weaponized kitchen utensils. Ben grabbed a pot to use as a shield, the mothers grabbed hot butter knives, Raggy and Bella grabbed oversized tongs, and Dalia and Laven decided to brandish large forks. Dexter snatched up what was left, a spatula.

"I have the worst weapon of all," CornFlakes warned Malcora.

"Yeah?" Malcora taunted and blew a fireball back at Alexis. "What is it, kitchen lady?"

"Zis!" CornFlakes thrust a wooden spoon at Malora. "Zis is ze wooden spoon of destiny!"

"Please," Malcora said. CornFlakes thrust the spoon at Malcora.

"Hah!" Malcora jeered. "You couldn't win if you tried!"

CornFlakes chucked the wooden spoon of destiny at Malcora, hitting her foot.

"OWW!" Malcora grabbed her foot and flapped around. "Ow ow ow! Ah! That *hurt!*"

"Betcha you forgot about me!" Bob yelled from the doorway to the castle.

"I got this one," Dexter stated. He barged up to Bob, and promptly hit him over the head with the spatula.

"HEY!" He yelled as he barely dodged the blow and sprinted to Malcora's side for safety.

"Not *now, pipsqueak!*" Malcora was triple-battling an angry lion, giant blasts of fire and lava, *and* a horde of angry parents and dragons.

"Just let me help!" Bob yelled over the commotion.

"How?" she yelled back, getting hit squarely in the face with a lion's paw.

"HYA!" Bob had found a lance from the armory and sent it flying at Crystal. With a cry of agony, Crystal dissipated into tiny white specks. Chidi stood aghast, and everyone stopped fighting.

"Oh *no,* it looks like whittle Miss Wion is *gwon,*" Malcora jeered, as she high-taloned Bob.

"You'll *pay for that!*" Chidi snapped, oblivious to somebody sneaking up behind her.

"See ya!" Esmerelda had recovered and snuck up behind Chidi. She grabbed her by the shirt and sent her flying into the forest.

"AAAAAAaaaah!" Her yell died away, as she landed somewhere in the forest.

"Chidi!" the Parris family yelled, and Laura sprinted into the forest after her.

Ben looked at Alexis. She nodded. Ben tossed her a taser.

"For Chidi!"

Ben used his pot to defend himself from Malcora and Bob's bombardment, and Alexis opened her father's taser. While everyone else was distracting Malcora, Alexis had devised a plan.

"Let's hope this works!" She aimed, and fired the taser, shooting the prongs directly into Malcora's neck, sending a large shock into her body. She let out a tiny gasp and fell to the ground.

"Oooooh no . . ." Bob tried to run, but he was blocked by Dexter, who promptly hit him over the head again, knocking him out. The battlefield was quiet, as all heads turned towards Esmerelda. She sighed.

"I'll go. I'm sorry, but I haven't given up yet. Tell my mother that—that— I'm very truly sorry. To *her, not* Isa." She walked away, with a final glare at nobody in particular. They all watched in silence until the crunching of leaves underfoot died away. Looking at one another, they all tried to figure out what just happened in the last fifteen-minute battle.

"We really *should* write an autobiography. People would think it was a fairytale," Dexter said blankly as he rubbed his eyes.

"I said that in the beginning!" Dalia said. "Right, Alexis? When you first told me all your secrets?"

"Mhm," Bella agreed.

"Guys!" Mrs. Parris was back, a limping Chidi beside her.

"H-hey," she whimpered, having a black eye, two broken fingers, a fractured ankle, and thankfully nothing worse.

"What did I miss?"

"Nothing," Bella, Dalia, and Raggy chorused. Mr. Parris and the adults were talking worriedly.

"Everything," Alexis said. "And, boy, do we have a story to tell you!"

Epilogue

THE FIRST DAY OF THE REST OF YOUR LIFE

Alexis Blaze Parris

Dear Journal,

THIS IS INSANE!

Our family and the Grahams both moved to the magical world. We told everybody that we were moving out of state, but Aunt Jennifer teleported us here.

We still call Dalia, using the magic goblets that used to belong to Malcora and Bob (we confiscated them. Ha. And they call us the good guys), but she stayed with her parents. Dalia told them none of what happened, and said that she had snuck off to a summer camp with her friends. She was in BIG trouble . . . I feel partially responsible. Not enough to take up a lifetime of servitude, but still.

Oh, what about the fairy, Autumn? She went with Dalia. She went to the actual world, and lives in Dalia's closet, where she made a shoebox into a house for her. And the pets? Well, they stayed with us, their owners. Tumbles is my new buddy on all my adventures. (I've climbed to the top of Mount Certain Doom! It's 19, 986 feet tall, I kid you not.)

The dragons also decided to stay at their castle and protect Queen Isa. She is a lot kinder now, and she rules with great love to her kingdom. Blah, when did I get all fairytale-y?

I've been thinking about my middle name. Did Mom know that I would have fire magic? It's probably nothing. But I have so many unanswered questions! I want answers . . . but I can't find any, YET.

Esmerelda disappeared, never seen again. Or so we think, but she might appear in the future. Malcora, her awesome sound effect dragons (they're the best!), and Bob Brisket are in prison, under the watchful eyes of Laven and his royal guard.

Duh-duh-duh!

Mwah-ha-ha-ha-ha!

CornFlakes also made Recipe for Bird at our victory dinner party, and everybody thought it was delicious. Obviously, I didn't say a thing. Everyone thought it was some sort of cake dish. I wasn't about to open my big mouth, because we had a couple of Redd's bird friends there (some of which consisted of woodpeckers? He's weird). At least Redd lost his "This just got personal" thing. He's going on and on about some figure of speech. I don't get it, but I know better than to ask him. If I did, we could be hearing it for weeks.

We now live in Candyopolis, and have an enormous bedroom and are literally ROYAL. The thing I miss most about Earth is the Attic (of fun!) and the Basement (of doom!) Cue the sound dragons! No? Anyway, those places changed our lives forever! They're OUR places. I don't want our parents to sell them. Dad's talking about keeping them . . . I hope so!

Laven has been promoted to the chief of the guard, and still helps me with my fire powers. And of course Tree is still ready to charge at me—oof! I can feel the pain already.

He may deal with a bit of fire tomorrow. He's asking for it, with the way I get shoved. The last time he was here, I literally had several bruises on my midsection. OUCH!

But still . . . we're a lot better than how we started. Can you believe it, Journal, that in the beginning, we were freaking out because we were moving to California? Now we're duchesses in a different dimension! All in all, it's been pretty cool.

Chidi Ann Parris

Bella, Alexis and I are always really busy, working with Aunt Jenny and Mom and Mrs. Graham (who tells us to call her Abigail, but Mom says to call her Mrs. Graham, so I'm kind of torn).

I've never really thought about things as they were before. I don't miss it one bit! Bella, Raggy and their family live in the palace with us. I share a room with Alexis and Bella, just like sisters! Although, of course, they are separated by some small walls, and open doorways.

I've helped around with a couple new hobbies as well! Oh, I also was able to summon Crystal back, even though it took a little more effort.

Sure, cooking and baking is nice, and volleyball is awesome, but I think that being in charge of the royal animals is great! I get to brush them, feed them and sometimes ride them!

I really miss CornFlakes, but she is busy all the time, creating food masterpieces for Queen Isa, former queen Viola, Prince Jet, and Princess Amethyst, Princess Sapphire, Princess Amber, Princess Ruby, and Princess Diamond. Whew, they have a big family! But at least they're all super nice, and they say the Dragon Realm is always in service to Candyopolis. Cool, right?

Redd has his own birdhouse in the garden, and he helps Lexi with her garden (which she's, like, obsessed with. She's weird!).

Ginger and Tumbles are getting along better now that they have gotten over being 'Smarty-pants' and 'Cat'. Plus, they talk about some sort of 'figure of speech'. No idea what they're talking about.

I've talked to Dalia, and we are working on writing our own autobiography! We plan to publish it on Earth, some day. Anyway, that's our story! (So far . . . duh-duh-duh! Cue Malcora's sound dragons again, hurry!)

I can't believe how far we've come in a little over a week. My life is like a snow globe. It has turned upside down a billion times, and then again. But I'm glad with the way it ended up. I've never regretted it.

Bella Cassidy Graham

Whoa! I am in TOTAL SHOCK! In a couple of days, I made, like, twelve friends! Alexis and Chidi are practically my sisters now. And—get this—we live in a CASTLE! (The twins' grandma says it's not a palace because it is made of candy? I don't understand the Candyopolin customs.)

I never thought I'd say/write this, but I somehow actually miss Dalia. We have literally the best life ever, but she has to stay on Earth and live as a totally normal human, and hide her invisibility powers from her parents. Talk about ROUGH!

Oh! And Tree (that deer-thing that gave us magic) is going to help me to understand animals! Carrie and her raft live in the moat now, and she can visit me anytime! It is so fun. She's practically my pet now! But she seems different now . . . whatever!

All in all, we have the absolute *best* life ever. We are soooooo lucky! I am so excited! Chidi, Alexis and I have a royal lesson. They're literally going to let us become second-in-command to the Parris family! I mean, honestly. That's crazy! I am a DUCHESS (maybe?)!

It turns out that Candyopolis (unlike the dragon realm) doesn't have kings, queens, princesses, or princes, but is governed or ruled by the Duke and/or Duchess. Weird, huh?

Lexi is attempting to teach me how technology works. I've never been so bad at anything in my life! She says I'll get better . . . I'm not sure I believe her. Seriously, I don't know the difference from a keypad to a keyboard (but I don't think Chidi does either, so that's my only consultation).

She and Chidi are always filling out paperwork, writing in journals (that's totally just Lexi, though), or whatever. Lady Charlotte makes me, Chidi, and Alexis practice our table etiquette several times a day. I can't believe how many kinds of forks there are! Fruit fork, salad fork, dinner fork, dessert fork, table fork, spaghetti fork, oyster fork (I hope I never use that one! Ugh!).

There are actually more than thirty-five kinds! I'm going to make a fool of myself sometime, in front of some royal, important person. Help!

I am the luckiest girl ever, in the entire universe! I am still in shock! THIS IS THE BEST DAY OF MY LIFE!

Dalia Ember Monroe

Oh. My. Goodness! I feel like any day now I will wake up and realize this is all a dream. But Autumn will flutter out and say good morning, and I know this is real.

Mom and Dad asked me if I had anything I wanted to do after school, and I pretend to take an after-school art class once a week, but I really sneak away to Candyopolis or one of the twins meets me somewhere here on Earth.

Chidi and I are working to write an autobiography, and Bella, Alexis, and Raggy are very interested in adding details. Raggy needs to make sure we add his 'heroics' in. Like THAT happened! (it kinda did though. Weird!).

I miss Alexis, Chidi, Bella (how did I just write that truthfully?), and Raggy, plus the pets and dragons. Anytime I feel alone (whoa, so emotional), I think back to the epic battles we fought.

I can't wait until the next one, and I'll ALWAYS be ready to fight the enemy. Esmerelda hasn't caused problems . . . yet. It's best to always be prepared.

I think one day I can tell my parents about Candyopolis and my magic, but until I KNOW they won't send me to a psychiatrist, I'm keeping my mouth closed. I wish I could live in Candyopolis, but I know I can't abandon my parents.

Sometimes I'm tempted to turn myself and my stuff invisible and run away, but of course I can't do that to them. Looks like I'm gonna need to stay prepared though, for our next adventure.

Raggy Danger Graham

I can't believe I let Chidi convince me to write this to catalog our adventure. Why did I give in? I already have a cramp in my hand!

I guess I owe it to them . . . they moved us into a candy house, where I can eat my room! I'm not kidding. And I've eaten Bella's things without her permission. HAHA! (Seriously, though; her pen toppers are history.)

I have to say, I'm disappointed that Laven is the chief of Queen Isa's royal guard, but I know he deserves it. And there are no more 'THIS JUST GOT PERSONAL' showdowns between Redd and Chidi. BOO!

I gotta admit, I am glad we don't live on Tidy Avenue anymore. The name really cramped my style. But I cannot believe the twins don't hate us, after Dad giving them the creeps for like a year. (Bella's reading over my shoulder and told me it's only about a month. Did you hear that?! You're not as sneaky as you think you are!)

Our magic is getting stronger, but Bella and I still have some issues. We're not limited to a certain amount of magic a day, but using it too much will strain us.

I still can't believe it! This is the coolest thing that has ever happened to me!

I just kinda miss the old life, you know, when we were home and Dad was out chasing Alexis and Chidi and trying to kidnap them—those were the good old days, you know what I mean?

But oh well. At least we have a pretty cool life . . . even if Laven is too busy running the entire Dragon Realm. (Wait, Isa's in charge? WHAT?!)

So that's it. Not writing ANY MORE. PEACE OUT, THIS WAS RAGGY GRAHAM!

Acknowledgements

Writing this book made us feel like we really had been DITCHED. We went insane, and couldn't have made it back to reality without:

Chase Jones, Creature Design & Feedback Crew
Brady Leavell, Illustrator
Abigail Erselius, Feedback Crew
Noah Erselius, Feedback Crew
Nathan Erselius, Feedback Crew
Grace White, Feedback Crew
Cathy Jones, Editor
Sarah & Steve Jones, Editor, Feedback & Ideas
Jason & Kristy Erselius, Feedback & Ideas

And there are so many others, starting with . . .

Anna, my twin cousin.

Grace, my cousin and writing partner.

Henry, Mary, Eleanor, Thomas, and Stephen, The Cool Cousins.

My parents—Jason and Kristy Erselius!

The aunts and uncles, who rock in every way possible.

The grandparents, who were unimaginably awesome.

The siblings, who drove me crazy—a LOT.

My friends! You guys know who you are!

My not-so-small small group! Ice Ice Isai, Kristin, Sarah, and Mia! You guys rock. Oh, and I know you would kill me if I didn't mention you, so Reid and B-Zack! (Okay, girls in my small group, I love you too—I just can't name you all, otherwise this would be another hundred pages, okay? -(;)

The people I love but can't fit in the acknowledgments: YOU ARE UNBELIEVABLE, and I am *so* lucky to have you.

Cassidy! Thanks for sticking with me and this book from the idea of *Mystery Story* to *The Beginning of Magic* to *The Quest for Magic*. I can't thank you enough for what you've meant to me.

And finally, all my glory and honor to my LORD and Savior, Jesus Christ.

—**Elizabeth J. Erselius**

First of all, to Chase Jones: Thank you for being my amazing brother and teaching me the patience I needed to finish and edit this book! I couldn't have done it without you.

Brielle: We always need somebody with a listening ear! Thanks for being that person, and also being my new church buddy!

Lydia, Thank you for being such a great friend! I'm glad we can talk about stuff we both enjoy, it makes small group just that much more enjoyable.

Julia: Thanks for being there. Just having a like-minded friend always helps through tough times.

Sarah and Steve Jones: You are awesome parents! You told me countless times how cool this is! I love getting to share this adventure with you!

Yaya, Papa, and Abby Shuman: You guys are amazing grandparents and the best aunt ever! Couldn't have done any of this without your hugs and support!

Gram & Papa: Also the best grandparents! You teach me so much! (Shout-out for the awesome edits, Gram!) I love ya!

The Martinez family! You guys are great, and so supportive! I hope Camila will read this book one day. Love you guys!

Thanks most of all to Ellie! She's the best friend anyone could ever ask for. I'm so glad we stuck through this until the end. Thank you Elizabeth!

—**Cassidy Jones**

We could not have done this without all of them! They're incredible, special people.

And last, but (duh!) not least, YOU! The readers . . . we love you guys so much! We hope you were captivated by the book, so drawn in that you couldn't put it down, and that you liked it!

You are incredible! Our books are absolutely *nothing* without you.

Yes, a book is where an author (or two) writes with all they have and works just as hard to get it published, but it's up to all the incredible readers to take it off a shelf, to take the time from your day to read our books and make our dream a reality, otherwise it's absolutely nothing, just a lot of paper and ink.

Thank! You! So! Much! Every! Single! One! Of! You!

And without every single member of our families, we would never have the *Never Did I Ever* series! Yes, series. We seriously hope you liked it enough for book two, Frozen Waves!

We are so blessed to be surrounded by all these amazing people who love and care for us. When we finished this book, they were just as excited as we were. Really excited!

They didn't want us to give up, and nurtured, inspired, and created this book by their sheer enthusiasm. They also led us on our OWN Quest for Magic.

Honestly, this is one of the best parts to write. (Aside from Figurally Speeching and Shaky-spoon, of course.) We get to give credit to all the incredible, magnificent, astonishingly talented people who helped us with this.

And, of course, thank you to Eden Tuckman with Gatekeeper Press who walked us through this book publishing process and did her best to make it as painless as possible. Thank you for your patience as we took time getting through each step while we worked around school and activities.

And we know that most of you are going to skip this and go straight to the excerpt from *Frozen Waves*, so I don't know why we're taking the time and effort to write this part, but every book I've ever read has one of these, so I guess that's why.

Before writing this, we didn't understand how important the acknowledgments really are. (Skip it if you want, you'll understand someday. That's a GUARANTEE!)

With such incredible, remarkable, (are there any other words we can use?) and brilliant people, always ready to spend a couple of hours working with us, you have to thank them again, again, again, and twenty thousand more times! You all rock!

NEVER DID WE EVER.

—**Cassidy Jones& Elizabeth J. Erselius**

By the way, guys, there is a secret message hidden on page 112! Can you figure it out?

NEVER
DID I EVER
FROZEN WAVES

A Tale of Two Girls and Their Rambunctious pets

Cassidy Jones

Elizabeth J. Erselius

Illustrated by Brady Leavelle

HIDING OUT

"Ugh, this place is so *rotten.*" A small dragon wrinkled her nose.

"But this is the only place humans cannot go," her fairy companion peeped up.

"What do you think I am, a *goblin?* Of course I know that!" The dragon kept on squelching through the mud in the deep dark tangle of overgrowth.

"Hey, be useful for once, and see if this fruit is edible." The dragon ripped a large, juicy-looking purple fruit off of a warty willow tree and thrust it towards the pixie.

"B-b-b-but what if it's—it's—poisonous?" the fairy shrieked, fluttering away. The emerald dragon gave her a fiery glare and shoved it towards her.

"O-o-o-okay . . ." The pixie took a little bite of it while it was still clutched in the dragon's talons, then another, then another. "Mmm!" She licked her lips, and took another bite. "It's very good!"

The dragon smiled and gave the fruit to the fairy.

"Well, thank you, Mac. That was very helpful."

She ripped off another juicy fruit and chomped into it. Nodding, she finished it off, throwing the seed in the middle onto the slimy ground.

"We'll call it purple wartfruit," she stated.

"B-but, we already found green wartfruit, and black wartfruit, and—and . . ."

The fairy was silenced again with another glare.

"Hmph." Without another peep, the dragon continued on through the dripping, muddy, foggy jungle.

They continued on until the already dark jungle got even darker. They settled down on a gigantic tree limb, large enough to hold a small dragon. McKenna wiggled onto a small limb and put a leaf over herself as a blanket.

"Stay here and get comfy. I'll be right back, okay?" the dragon asked.

"Y-yes, I will," stuttered the fairy.

Lifting off into the sky, the emerald green dragon soared up and above the mist barrier that was blocking the fresh air from reaching the ground below. She soared up so high that she could see all of the many winding rivers that ran through the Mist Lands. She landed on a cloud and took in the view.

"I am the rightful heir to the dragon throne," she repeated to herself. "Nobody will get in my way again. Not even my family."

She opened the little satchel that she had 'bought' by terrorizing some humans and pulled out a tiny knife that was barely sharp and had an emerald hilt.

Running it alongside the edge of her talon, she admired its great craftsmanship. Sliding the dagger back into her satchel, she flew back down into the mist barrier and back into her miserable life. She let herself just *fall* most of the way down.

Catching herself with her wings, she landed on a thick branch of the tree. She found a safe spot among the folds of the leaves and drifted into cold, restless sleep.

Before she slept, she had one thought echoing in her mind. *Someday, I'll be Queen Esmerelda.*

Chapter One

HOME SWEET HOME

"Can you believe it?" Dalia told her friends. They were using magical goblets to talk. Dalia lived on Earth, while the Parris family and the Grahams lived in Candyopolis, a magical world that was underground.

"My publisher said, and I quote, 'This is a new fairytale.' Remember when *I* said that? I told you, if we were to write our autobiography, everyone would think it was a fairytale!" Dalia grinned.

"Ooh!" Autumn, a fairy who had come to Earth to live with Dalia, fluttered up. "Are you talking to Chidi, Alexis, Bella, and Rankic? Let me talk!"

"Hi, Autumn!" Alexis cheered. "How are you?"

"I'm *good*," she said. "But can you believe it? Humans have cupcakes too!"

Chidi beamed. Autumn had been the jailer when Alexis, Dalia, Raggy, and Bella had been stuck in jail, and helped them escape. She had a special desire for every kind of cupcake.

"We miss you!" Bella called.

"Same here," Oreo, Dalia's dalmatian dog, added.

Chidi and Alexis were twins who had grown up on Earth and moved at least twice a year.

Moving from Texas to California, they moved to their aunt Jennifer's house because a man named Bob Brisket was after them.

When they went to their newfound friend Bella's house for dinner, they were trapped by Bella's former villainous father, Dexter.

They escaped but fell into a portal to a magical realm.

Then, in Candyopolis, where they were secretly royalty, they found their grandparents and wound up defeating a former dragon queen Malcora and her betrayed partner, Princess Esmerelda. It's been about a year since everybody saw each other at the same time.

"Wait, *your* publisher?" Chidi asked. "Are you . . ."

"No, I just found a guy. He's going to publish it as soon as he gets an editor!" exclaimed Dalia.

"That's so—"

"Dalia!" Her mom was calling her downstairs.

"Daaaalia!"

"Oops. I have to go, my mom is coming upstairs! Bye!" She slid the lid onto the golden goblet and hid it under her pillow. Autumn rushed into the closet and hid in her shoebox. Oreo flopped onto Dalia's bean bag chair.

"I'll see you soon!" Chidi exclaimed as Dalia closed the cup.

"Uh-oh."

Then Dalia picked up her phone, and pretended to text. Her mother opened the door.

"What did I say about screen restrictions? Don't forget that you're still grounded for half a month."

Her eyes scanned the room.

"Who were you talking to? Oreo fell asleep, and Nat is downstairs playing 'Guns vs. Zombies.'"

Dalia sighed. Nat was her older brother, and they used to be best friends until Nat turned fourteen. Then all he wanted to do was make fun of her, and play with his friends online. Now that he was fifteen, he was worse.

"I—I was FaceTimeing Madeline," she lied.

"Well, that's okay, but no more phones or computers today, okay?" Her mom took it, and put it on top of her tall wardrobe.

"I'll get it down for you tomorrow. Don't forget to get in the car at five-thirty to go to the rescue center for Nat's birthday!"

She strode off, out of Dalia's room. They were going to get Nat a cat for his birthday, and Dalia was less than excited.

"Oreo, why couldn't our adventures in Candyopolis *never end?*" she asked and flopped down on her bed.

"Rrruff!" Oreo woofed.

"That's not helpful," Dalia sighed. "Hm?" She looked at her clock, and it was three-o-five, just enough time for her 'Afternoon Classes'.

Dalia's eyes brightened, and she called down to her mom, "I'm gonna go, I'm late for my classes!"

She ran down the stairs, and out the front door.

"Bye!"

Before her mother could object, she had already sped onto the sidewalk. Taking her usual route, she whipped around corner after corner, and stopped at an apartment building.

"Here we go!" She concentrated, and soon, she was completely invisible. She climbed up the ladder to the top of the building, and watched as the cars zoomed across the road below. Sometimes, Alexis, Chidi, Bella, or Raggy would be up here too, as this was their usual meeting spot. She looked around, but nobody was here.

"Seriously? Chidi said she would meet me here today!" she said to herself. Sitting down on the edge of the roof, she watched the cars beneath her.

"What a rip-off," she complained to the sky.

"I have to get a *kitten* for my brother as a surprise, but last year, he gave me a *pickle jar,* and told me happy birthday!" She stood up, and danced around the rooftop, because why not? Nobody could see her.

"OW!" she yelled when her foot hit something hard. She knelt down and fingered a small purple crystal. "Ooh, a note from the girls!"

Dear Dalia,

This is called a portal crystal. If you squeeze it tight and say, "Candyopolis", it will take you there. We have some things to tell you.

Your Friend,

Chidi

P.S. Tumbles, Ginger and Redd hope you'll bring Oreo with you!

Dalia grinned ear to ear. She raced to her house, clutching the crystal.

"C'mon, Oreo!" she whispered. "We're going to see Tumbles!"

"Ruff!" Oreo barked.

"Shh!" She opened the window and he jumped into her arms. Dalia stuffed the note in her pocket and wrapped her arms around the dog and crystal and said, "Candyopolis."

"Dalia!" Alexis cried, jumping out of her seat. "What are you doing in my room?" She had appeared smack-dab in the middle of Alexis' room.

"I just said, 'Candyopolis', and I ended up here!" Dalia patted Oreo on the head quickly and then set him down.

"Tumbles is in the royal gardens," Alexis told him. "I'll call Chidi and Bella to come over!"

Alexis pressed a pink and purple button on her crazily high-tech desk. Everything had wires and some electronic device or screen. "Dalia is here. Repeat, Dalia Ember Monroe is here, report to the bedroom!"

"So," Dalia said. "What were you doing?"

"Uh, just some boring paperwork," Alexis said. "*Grandmère* said I need to fill in everything because Chidi and I are the twin heirs. Chidi decided to do it later, because she's working with the royal animals."

"What was the news?" Dalia asked.

"Oh!" Chidi exclaimed as she skidded into the room, Bella at her heels. "Dalia! We missed you!"

She and Bella squished her into a hug.

"Let the poor girl breathe!" Alexis called out.

Dalia smiled. "So, what was the news?"

Alexis tossed a glare in Chidi's direction. "We—um—"

"Come on," Chidi said gently. "Let's go say hi to Raggy and everybody else! They miss you!"

Dalia wrung her hands. "What is it? I can take it! It's not some evil guy though, right?"

"Hey, we're kids, we don't have to worry about archenemies or diabolical plans!" Alexis joked.

"Seriously, just *tell me!*" Dalia exclaimed. "It can't be *that* bad!"

"It . . . is," Bella said. "I'll get the adults to let them know."

"Wait, your *parents* don't know?" Dalia asked.

"We just found out this morning," Alexis said. "Bella, I'll come with you."

Bella nodded, and they walked out of the room.

"Uh . . . well, Chidi, can I see the animals?" Dalia asked casually.

Chidi said, "Yeah, sure."

And they started downstairs to the barn.

. . . .

In the throne room

"Alexis, what is it?" Dexter or Mr. Graham asked the second she flung herself into the room. "Did you get a papercut from this *paperwork?*" He pointed at the three inch stack of paper and groaned. "How am I supposed to do all this?"

"Hush," Abigail, otherwise known as Mrs. Graham, told him as Bella skidded into the room.

"We need to tell you something," Bella panted.

"What?" Aunt Jenny asked, dropping her papers like hot potatoes.

"Is something wrong?"

Bella and Alexis nodded.

"*Very* wrong. I received a report from my *spy—I mean* friend, and—

....

To Be Continued!

Cues Sound Dragons!

"Duh-duh-duh!"

"Mwah-ha-ha-ha!"

About the Authors

Cassidy Jones is a friend, co-writer, and sister-in-God to Elizabeth. She and Ellie began *The Quest for Magic* in 2020, but she has come far since then! Cassidy is twelve years old and lives in Texas with her parents and older brother. In her free time, she writes, takes care of her thirteen pets, writes some fan-fiction, reads, and obsesses over *Never Did I Ever*.

Elizabeth Erselius, or Ellie, co-writes the *Never Did I Ever* series with Cassidy Jones. She lives in California. Elizabeth is thirteen and adores writing. When she isn't writing, she bakes, uses tech, reads books, and is at church with her small group, planning a preposterous way to win the lip-sync or winter camp!

Made in the USA
Columbia, SC
02 November 2023

25385028R00176